Also by **NANCY GARDEN**

Annie on My Mind
Prisoner of Vampires
Peace, O River
What Happened in Marston
Berlin: City Split in Two
The Loners
Vampires
Werewolves
Witches
Devils and Demons
The Kids' Code and Cipher Book
Lark in the Morning
Meeting Melanie
My Sister, the Vampire
My Brother, the Werewolf
Dove and Sword
Good Moon Rising
The Year They Burned the Books
Holly's Secret
The Case of the Stolen Scarab
Endgame

The Fours Crossing Books
Fours Crossing
Watersmeet
The Door Between

The Monster Hunters Series
Mystery of the Night Raiders
Mystery of the Midnight Menace
Mystery of the Secret Marks
Mystery of the Kidnapped Kidnapper
Mystery of the Watchful Witches

Molly's Family
(Pictures by Sharon Wooding)

HEAR US OUT!

HEAR US OUT!

LESBIAN AND GAY STORIES OF STRUGGLE, PROGRESS, AND HOPE, 1950 TO THE PRESENT

NANCY GARDEN

FARRAR STRAUS GIROUX · NEW YORK

"Loving Megan" originally appeared, in slightly different form, in *One Hot Second: Stories About Desire*, edited by Cathy Young (New York: Knopf Books for Young Readers, 2002).
"Parents' Night" originally appeared, in slightly different form, in *Am I Blue?: Coming Out from the Silence*, edited by Marion Dane Bauer (New York: HarperCollins Children's Books, 1994).

Distributed in Canada by Douglas & McIntyre Ltd.
Printed in the United States of America
Designed by Barbara Grzeslo
First edition, 2007
1   3   5   7   9   10   8   6   4   2

www.fsgkidsbooks.com

Library of Congress Cataloging-in-Publication Data
Garden, Nancy.
    Hear us out!: lesbian and gay stories of struggle, progress, and hope, 1950 to the present / Nancy Garden.— 1st ed.
        p.   cm.
    Includes bibliographical references.
    ISBN-13: 978-0-374-31759-1
    ISBN-10: 0-374-31759-3
    1. Gay liberation movement—United States—History—Juvenile literature.   2. Gay rights—United States—Juvenile literature.   I. Title.

HQ76.8.U5 G357 2007
306.76/6—dc22

                                        2006040080

In memory of Craig Rodwell,
founder of the Oscar Wilde Memorial Bookshop,
activist, youth advocate, and dear friend

Also to Jean Mayberry and in memory of her partner, Aleta Fenceroy
(1948–2006), who together formed the amazing "Fenceberry" team
that from 1996 to 2004 collected and distributed national and
international LGBT news over the Internet when such news was
impossible to get in any organized way—and who encouraged us all
to participate in the struggle for LGBT rights by reacting to the news
in letters to the editors of our local newspapers

And with thanks as always to the talented, skillful, dedicated,
patient, and ever-cheerful folks at FSG, especially Margaret Ferguson,
Beth Potter, and Elaine Chubb. Talk about grace under pressure—
you're the best!

CONTENTS

HEAR US OUT!

INTRODUCTION

Many years ago, I began writing a series of stories about gay life that I called *Aspects*. I was so committed to it that I took it with me when I traveled in Europe for five months, continued working on it while I lived in various parts of New York City, and finally, still many years ago, moved it with me to Massachusetts, where I live now. I'd written most of the stories by hand on lightweight airmail paper because of carrying them around Europe—scrawled them, really, since I worked on them at odd moments and in odd places.

By the time my partner and I moved to Massachusetts, I had been concentrating on writing books instead of stories for some time. Eventually, though, prompted by a request for gay stories for Marion Dane Bauer's marvelous anthology, *Am I Blue?: Coming Out from the Silence*, I began writing stories again, and that gradually led to this collection. While I was working on it, I hunted for my old *Aspects* manuscript, thinking there might be something there that I could use, or at least material there that would remind me of the old days. But alas, I wasn't able to find it.

Story collections need some kind of glue to hold them together, but it wasn't until I'd written most of the ones in this book that I decided to arrange them in a time sequence starting with the 1950s (which is when, at around age sixteen, I began to realize I was gay) and ending with the present. And that led quickly to my thinking it would probably be helpful to include essays that described each era in terms of what was going on during it among gay people and in the battle for gay rights, a battle in which I've participated in a small way, especially in the sixties. I also wanted, when applicable and possible, to indicate how those events affected (or didn't affect) the lives of GLBT (gay, lesbian, bisexual, transgender) youth.

For reminders, corrections, and expansions of my own memories, and for details of which I wasn't aware, I am indebted to a number of sources, especially but by no means exclusively to *Making History: The Struggle for Gay and Lesbian Equal Rights, 1945–1990* by Eric Marcus, and *Becoming Visible* by Molly McGarry and Fred Wasserman. I've listed them along with other works, almost all of which I've also used, at the back of this book. For recent developments, especially in gay marriage, I have also relied greatly on Ron Buckmire's Marriage Digest Listserv (principal contributor, John Wilkinson).

If you're interested in gay history and in other material about being GLBT and about GLBT life, by all means seek out the sources I've listed, in addition to reading the historical essays here. But please don't feel obligated to read the essays; if you prefer, just concentrate on the stories, keeping in mind that each one reflects events that could have happened in the era in question.

Terminology in the gay community can be awkward; we've called ourselves many things over the years, and have been called many things by others. Many gay people feel that *queer*, which once had the same cruel force as *faggot* used as an epithet, is acceptable now and is more inclusive than *gay*. *Gay* remains the easiest and least controversial word when it's awkward to say "gay and lesbian" or when it wouldn't be accurate, given the era or the situation, to include bisexual and transgender/transsexual people by using the very handy initials *GLBT*. That term is changing, too; as *Hear Us Out* nears completion, *LGBT* seems to be emerging as the preferred term within the community. By the time you read this, though, that may have changed again—or another term entirely may have taken its place.

In any case, you'll see all these terms at various places in this book, plus *Q* (for questioning) added to *GLBT*. That term is used to describe people who aren't yet sure of their sexual orientation. Please understand, though, that often when I say *gay* I'm referring to all of us, not solely to gay males. And know that when I use *GLBT* I'm in no way suggesting that my lesbian sisters are in a secondary position. Please also understand that I sympathize with those of you who'd like to get rid of labels altogether—but I couldn't figure out how to write a book like this without using them!

I was an active member of the Mattachine Society and the Daughters of Bilitis (DOB) in New York, mostly in the sixties, and, with my then-partner, Renée Cafiero, I participated in many early demonstrations for gay rights, including the very first one. Back in those exciting days, I was privileged to get to know some of our movement's heroes, pioneers such as Frank Kameny, one of the founders of the Washington, D.C., chapter of Mattachine, who worked tirelessly to combat the federal government's anti-gay policies; and Barbara Gittings, an early editor of the lesbian magazine *The Ladder* and a principal founder of DOB's New York chapter. Both of them, like California activists Del Martin and Phyllis Lyon, continued their work for decades, and it is on their shoulders and those of countless other early activists that the progress of the fifty years I've tried to document here has been built.

Nancy Garden
Carlisle, Massachusetts
West Tremont, Maine

1950s

THE DECADE

IF YOU'D BEEN A TEENAGER IN THE 1950S, AS I WAS, AND YOU'D LOOKED UP
"Homosexuality" in the 1952 edition of *Collier's Encyclopedia*, as I
did, you'd have found yourself directed to "Sexual Pathology." And under that, you'd have read the following:

> Homosexuality is commonly found in regressive mental disorders,
> psychopathic personalities, some alcoholics and drug addicts, and
> in residents of segregated institutions. Freud [one of the most fa-
> mous and widely respected psychiatrists of all time] associated ho-
> mosexuality with paranoia and with alcoholism . . .

Pretty discouraging and not very helpful, right? And other encyclopedias of the same era gave similar "definitions."

It's no wonder, then, that gay life in the fifties was lived largely un-
derground! In fact, just about the only people who knew then that the
word *gay* means "homosexual" as well as "happy" were gay themselves,
or were in the arts, where I was glad to discover that we'd found a
measure of acceptance. As far as I can remember, *queer, lezzie, pansy*,
and *fairy* were the words most often used by straights, *queer* for both
males and females, *lezzie* for girls and women, and *pansy* and *fairy* for
boys and men. I don't remember hearing the word *faggot* in the fifties,
although since it had been around for many years, it was probably in
use. The words used within the gay community, like *butch, femme,
queen, dyke*, and others, weren't used much by straights. Masculine-
seeming women were often described as *mannish* by straights to imply

they were or might be gay. In earlier times, lesbians had sometimes been described as *lady lovers*.

In the fifties, gay and lesbian adults could lose their jobs, could be dishonorably discharged from the military, or could even be arrested for being openly gay. Gay and lesbian young people risked expulsion from school or college if they were found out. Many were disowned by their parents. Others were forced to see psychiatrists, or were committed to mental institutions, for, in addition to supposedly being morally evil, homosexuality was widely believed to be an illness. To "cure" them, gays and lesbians were sometimes subjected to painful electroshock treatments or to aversion therapy (for example, being made to vomit when shown pictures of naked people of their own gender). You may have heard of the modern-day version of "curing" homosexuality —"reparative therapy," which is practiced by "ex-gay" groups like Exodus International and Love in Action International. These programs are usually religion-based, and they claim success in getting gays and lesbians—including gay and lesbian teens, sometimes at away-from-home camps—to change. But their critics, a number of whom have been enrolled in such programs, dispute that, and say reparative therapy does more harm than good, sometimes even driving enrollees to suicide.

Back in the fifties, and later as well, many gay and lesbian young people dated straights and even married them in the hope that they, too, would learn to be straight. Others stayed deep in the closet; playing straight was far less risky than coming out.

There was little support for GLBTQ people in those days—no gay-straight alliances, no gay pride marches, no openly gay celebrities— and only a handful of (mostly dead) artists and writers were known publicly to be gay. The fifties did see a very few panel discussions of homosexuality on TV, and there were a few more or less positive portrayals of homosexuals in contemporary literature, but sometimes, as had also been true earlier, the sexual orientation of those characters was more hinted at than overtly revealed. For the most part, though, the handful of gay and lesbian characters that appeared in books, in movies, or on TV were negative stereotypes. Often those portrayals ended grimly, with the homosexual characters dying, committing suicide, being sent to mental hospitals, or turning straight. But even so, some cheap paperback lesbian novels published in the fifties primarily for straight men actually paved the way for the more hopeful, serious, and realistic portrayals that followed in later years. They were also read avidly by many lesbians who were grateful to find any acknowledgment of their existence, if only in books.

The fifties saw the height of the cold war, the nonfighting "war" against Communism. During it, homosexuals fell victim to the federal government's frantic attempts to find and get rid of Communists in high places. Gay people were considered security risks; it was thought that, since gays were afraid of being discovered and exposed, they could easily be blackmailed into revealing government secrets to, especially, Communist agents. As of 1953, no one who was known to be gay was allowed to work for the federal government, and despite the efforts of one of our pioneers, Frank Kameny, who was himself a target of the government, and others, that policy wasn't changed till the late 1980s. Gays and lesbians, even those who didn't have terribly important positions, were fired from government jobs—and, primarily because of their assumed immorality and instability, they were fired from jobs in the private sector as well.

Again, it's no wonder that most gay people remained invisible in the fifties!

Even so—and even when the FBI infiltrated them—there were starting to be gay organizations and publications, especially in San Francisco and Los Angeles. Some gay and lesbian adults were beginning to fight actively for their rights, despite the fact that, as they became more visible, they were subject to increasing harassment from the police and the public at large. A magazine called *ONE*, first published in Los Angeles in 1953, was devoted to information and news about homosexuality. It contained articles exposing gay bashing and arrests of people for being gay or for being suspected of being gay, along with articles about the nature of homosexuality. Since just about anything to do with homosexuality was legally considered obscene and therefore not fit to be written about, published, and mailed, *ONE* was soon accused of obscenity by the post office. There followed a court battle lasting around four years till finally, in 1958, the U.S. Supreme Court ruled that *ONE* was not obscene.

For lesbians, starting in 1956, there was a monthly magazine called *The Ladder*, originating in San Francisco. Its first editor was Phyllis Lyon, followed by Del Martin, followed by Barbara Gittings; all three women were lesbian pioneers whose work for our community spans the fifty-plus years covered by this book. The magazine's purpose, as symbolized by the cover drawing of women in front of a tall ladder, was primarily to educate and to encourage lesbians to accept themselves and grow in confidence. Although it started as a mimeographed edition of about 170 copies, it soon became a national magazine that gave hope and solace to hundreds of isolated and closeted lesbians as well as to their more activist sisters, and by the late sixties it was a professional-looking bimonthly with a more generally feminist viewpoint.

Most people in the fifties, gay and straight alike, were unaware that the gay revolution was beginning and that it would gradually change our lives forever. But for most gays and lesbians, especially gay and lesbian teens, the fifties were bleak and lonely. It took enormous courage and optimism for them to sustain hope for a bright future.

DEAR ANGIE, SWEET ELIZABETH

Sunday, June 29, 1952

1 a.m.

Dear Angie,

Surprise!

I'll stuff this in your suitcase tomorrow. Maybe while you're in the ladies' room at the bus station, so PLEASE have to go there like you always do!

You've just left here. God, I already miss you! Mom and Dad are finally in bed. Casey got up for a drink of water a few minutes ago, but he's back in his room now. (Probably asleep.) (It's great the way little kids fall asleep so fast.) Carole used to, too. Did I? I'm not sure.

Remember the first time I put two sets of parentheses together the way I just did a couple of sentences ago? We were taking algebra and you said you tried to multiply them. I really cracked up. Remember?

Oh, Angie, I miss you! I know you're still only six blocks away. And yes, I know I'll see you tomorrow before you leave. Not for long, though. I won't be able to kiss you or hold you the way I did tonight. Bless Carole for playing Monopoly with Casey! She's an okay kid for thirteen. She said she knew we wanted to talk in private. (Not that that's all we did.) And thank God Mom and Dad wanted to watch that movie on TV.

Angie, I didn't even think it was wrong tonight. Not for a minute. The more we're together, the less I think it's wrong. You're part of me, my friend, as much as my hands or my eyes or my brain or my soul. It's almost as if you were born with me and we were somehow split apart at birth. So of course we want to hold hands sometimes and kiss each other hello and goodbye. Right? It's still pure. Platonic.

Hey, thank you for saying you wouldn't go away to summer stock if I said not to. But I couldn't say that. How could I? Theater and being an actress means so much to you! And I don't think you're "too intense" about it the way Mom does. It would be awful if you gave up your apprentice scholarship! Green Hill Players, that sounds really professional. Well, I guess it is, from what you said about the actors and actresses being in the union you told me about—Actors' Equity, isn't it? But I have to admit I'll count the days till August 16 when I can come up to New Hampshire and see you in the show you and the other apprentices will be in. And then I'll count the days till Labor Day, when you'll be back home and we'll be seniors together. But ask you not to go? Not on your life!

I wish I cared about something the way you care about theater. But I'll be busy at the bookstore, I guess. And I'll read a lot when I'm not working. Maybe I'll finally try to teach myself real botany, how about that? And surprise Miss Jaconsi when we get back to school. I know it won't bore me, like she said. But I don't think I'll ever care as much about anything as you care about theater.

You, though. I care about you that much.

Maybe I shouldn't have said that.

Short pause. Carole saw my light and came in. It's hot and her fan's broken, so she asked if she could sleep in here. She's getting her stuff now. So I guess I'd better stop this letter. (It's just as well. I'd probably go on talking to you all night otherwise.)

I wish you were still here.

Angie, my friend, my dear, dear friend with the fading freckles and the curly red hair I love, have a wonderful summer! I'll try to understand if you don't have time to write. Just remember what we said to each other tonight. Love can't be wrong, no matter who it's between. Hold on to that, okay? And so will I!

Love,
Elizabeth

॰

Monday, June 30, 1952

Sweet Elizabeth,

So I walk into my room at the inn, biggish, with a small window but not very many street noises, and this blond bombshell named Darla walks in and says she's my roommate, and I start missing you even more than I did during the bus ride up here, and I decide to unpack so she won't see that I'm trying not to cry—and I open my suitcase and there's your wonderful letter! And suddenly I'm laughing instead of crying even though I know I can't read your letter for hours, because I'm sure not going to read it while Darla's around (she thinks she's God's gift to the theater and to boys, at least she keeps telling me about all the community theater stuff she's done and about all her boyfriends), and I want to savor it.

I'm still savoring it, sweet Elizabeth, every word.

It can't be wrong—us; you're right. If only we'd had more time together to—I don't know—understand it more! We'll have all next year, though, so I'm not worried—except I miss you so much I want to forget acting school and go to a real college instead. Maybe I could apply to the colleges you're applying to, and if we got into the same one, we could be together after we graduate from high school. But your parents would probably die, since I know they think I'm a bad influence for being "intense" about theater.

Damn! Here's Darla again, popping in, popping out—no, wait; she's leaving. Wait—

What happened was some boy apprentices who live out at the theater came by—Darla got all twittery—and wanted us to go someplace with them. Darla's going. I'm not. I'd rather be with you, even if it's only on paper. There are three boy apprentices and seven girls. We had a meeting out at the theater earlier tonight, and tomorrow classes start. We'll have classes in the morning—acting and movement—and in the afternoon we'll work in the scene shop or the box office, or we'll be gofers at rehearsals, or help actors with their lines. You should see the theater—it's great—an old barn. You'd love it, I think. Well, maybe not.

One guy—he's the set designer—said they had to clear the bats out last week when the resident company—that's the professional actors—arrived! I guess you wouldn't love the bats, right? But you'd love the rest of it!

Hanging from the ceiling is a big wagon wheel with the houselights on it, and the seats are just folding chairs, so they can be moved around easily. We'll stack them up every morning and have classes in the theater—but never on the stage—while the company rehearses in the rehearsal hall, which is a separate building.

I get excited just writing about it!

But God, I miss you! My "fading freckles" miss your lopsided smile. I wish you were here. Yes, I'm counting the days till August 16, too. And then to Labor Day. Please God I'll get a good part in the apprentice show and do it well on August 16 so you'll be proud.

Love,
Angie

P.S. I'm wrapping up a tiny present for you, in soft tissue paper, and tying it with that fancy gold string they sell at Christmastime. Guess what the present is? A kiss!

⌁

Thursday

Dear Angie,

Your letter is the best thing that's happened all week. It's done nothing but rain, for one thing. My boss at the bookstore has been rotten, making us unpack books till our fingers are almost bleeding. Mom and Dad have been out almost every night because all their shallow friends are giving parties before going off to the shore. Why couldn't they have done that while you were still here? Tonight Mom and Dad'll be back late. I'm sure Mom wouldn't let you sleep over, but if you were here, you could stay really late.

But you're not here. So I better not think about what if you were.

I just got your letter today and I wanted to answer it fast. This has got to be short because Carole's going to a party and I promised Casey I'd take him to the movies. I've been writing to you all week, but I tore everything up. (Too morbid!) Mom's been at me about Will again. Lots. I guess I'm going to have to go out with him. (I don't know why she thinks that just because he's her best friend's son we're made for each other!) Please don't mind too much. I mean, I know you won't mind because you know Mom's making me see him, but you might mind because of us—you and me—whatever us is. (We are.)

Oh, Angie, I wish I knew! I wish I knew what we really are to each other. I know I love you. I know I want to be with you. I loved your little present in its tissue paper with the gold string. It made me smile and feel tingly inside, almost as if you were really here. (For a minute anyway.)

Here's Casey. I've got to go. Maybe I'll finish this later.

Later

Hi!

The movie was awful. Even the acting was bad. I kept thinking how good you'd have been in it. And Casey was awful, too. He wanted popcorn and peanuts and candy and soda and he insisted on having this obnoxious friend of his sit with us. You don't want to know about that, especially the part where Casey's obnoxious friend spilled his lemon and lime soda all over the front of my shirt. Was I embarrassed! And Mom was mad when she got home because I'd left the shirt on the bathroom floor so I'd remember to wash it in the morning. What a rotten night!

Love,
Elizabeth

Sunday, 7/6/52

Sweet Elizabeth,

You poor kid! Oh, I can just see you, with lemon and lime dripping all over you, having to cope with two obnoxious little boys! Not a great evening; no lopsided smile that night, I bet.

My first day: I was working in the scene shop scrubbing flats; you wash the paint off one show's flats and then repaint them so they can be used to make the set for the next show. It's not a very exciting job, but it's part of theater so I love it. And the people are really nice. Anyway, after a while, the designer said we could have a break and I went out to this back stoop off the shop and looked at the flats drying in the sun, and back at the shop where a couple of people were sitting around having Cokes, and there were tools on the floor and others neatly hanging on the wall, and someone was mixing paint and it smelled almost as good as greasepaint, and I could hear the actors rehearsing in the rehearsal hall—and, Elizabeth, the most wonderful, special feeling came over me, and I knew—I KNEW—that this is what I was born to do! Now I know, I really <u>know</u> that there are two reasons why I was born: theater and you. And besides just BEING half the reason, you've helped me find out the theater half—yes, you—because you've been so sweet to watch me rehearse and hear my lines and take notes about what I'm doing wrong and make suggestions and—oh, and everything! Thank you, Elizabeth!

Elizabeth, maybe I shouldn't say this, but—well, you said you wished you knew what we really are to each other. Maybe I'm not sure either, not sure enough to label it, to put it in a neat little box and tie it up with string—but I know I love you. I really love you. I'm glad you liked the kiss present, because I wasn't sure if you liked the real kisses on our last night. Yes, sure, you seemed to, but I think you've always been worried about our feeling too much for each other—yes? <u>Can</u> there be too much feeling between people if they both feel it? I don't think so. If you DON'T feel the way I do, please, PLEASE tell me, Elizabeth, and I'll try—I'll really try—to just be friends. I mean it—I promise—I'll really try, because I hope we can be friends, always, no matter what. But if you DO feel the same way I do, more than friendship, I mean, please tell me, too.

Oh, God, I hope you do!

I think—I know—I should cross that sentence out, but I want to be honest with both of us, so I won't.

Sweet, sweet Elizabeth, I want to feel your arms around me, and mine around you, and I want to hold you very, very close and I want to look into your lovely blue eyes and see you looking back at me with your funny smile and the special look you gave me the night before I left. That look, that wonderful, loving look—the memory of it—has given me the courage to write this—to send it. I've been writing it all week, throwing it away, writing it again—along with things about the people I've met. Example: One of the boy apprentices is really nice; we've become friends. Example: We had to pretend to be ice cream—melting ice cream—in acting class the other day. Example: There was a power failure last night in the middle of the third act, and we lit the actors with flashlights—the emergency houselights don't really hit the stage. But none of that—NOTHING—is as important as what I'm trying to say here: that I love you, Elizabeth, and I miss you terribly.

> All my love,
> Angie

↢

> July 18, 1952

Dear Angela,

It seems only fair for me to write directly to you, although I have written your parents as well.

Adolescence is a time of strong emotions and confused passions. I remember that from my own girlhood, and I know how strong feelings can be at your age, and how intense. Your enthusiasm about the theater is a case in point. You are a sophisticated enough young woman to understand that hormones play a big part in one's growing up at your age, but what you may not know is that they sometimes send confused signals. Friendship is special, but it should not be confused with love between men and women. You are, I suspect, a somewhat late bloomer, perhaps because of your intense feeling for theater and your love of acting, of pretending. That, plus your strong imagination, has perhaps colored your friendship with Elizabeth, who is, of course, like her sister, a perfectly normal person. I feel that you are also, I pray that you are. In any case, I cannot let the intensity of your feelings for Elizabeth confuse Elizabeth, especially now that she is starting to go out with boys at last, for she, too, has been a late bloomer as you are no doubt aware. I trust that when you are older, you will laugh over this melodramatic interval in your lives.

For this summer, my husband and I feel it would be best if you and Elizabeth no longer communicated with each other. Naturally, you will not be able to keep from seeing each other in school in the fall, but perhaps by then your feelings will have assumed more normal proportions. It would be best, though, if you did not plan on seeing each other outside of school when this summer is over and you are back home.

Elizabeth will not be going to New Hampshire in August, as originally planned. I have forbidden her to write you, and there is no need for you to answer this letter.

I hope you have a successful and pleasant summer.

Best wishes,
Mrs. Taberd

⸙

Tuesday

Dearest Angie,

Oh, sweetie, Daddy and I know how you must feel! Your tears on the phone last night nearly broke my heart, and Daddy and I both still wish you'd agreed to let us drive up to see you right away. We <u>will</u> come this weekend, though, whether you want us to or not. So there.

I don't think I'd better tell you the words Daddy and I used to each other about Mrs. Taberd when her letter came, but I think you can imagine them. What an insufferable prig she is!

Sweetie, she <u>is</u> right that your friendship with Elizabeth is pretty intense, but that's how friendships are at your age. You are <u>not</u> abnormal! Daddy and I do <u>not</u> agree with Mrs. Taberd, and we are behind you in everything you do. And we are also here if you want to talk to us about anything. We love you and trust you and believe in you.

See you this weekend.

Love,
Mom

⌾

Wednesday

Dear Angie,

All hell has broken loose. I bet she's already gotten to you. I hope you get this letter first, but you probably won't.

Oh, Angie, it's my fault! I could kill myself. (I don't think I'm serious about that, but I'm not sure.) I left your letter under the blotter on my desk because I wanted to answer it later, and Mom found it when she was dusting. I guess a corner of it was sticking out. I should've put it in the drawer. God, I'm sorry!

You can't imagine the scene. She screamed and yelled a lot, she wanted to know what I'd said to you and how I felt and everything. At first I didn't say anything, I just stared at her. But then I couldn't stand it anymore and I got real angry and I yelled something like "Yes, I love her, and yes, I've kissed her and she's kissed me and I don't see anything wrong in that."

When I said that, she screeched something like "Homosexuality is what is wrong with that!" Then she got all cold and controlled like she was some kind of judge or something and she accused you (YOU, not me, as if I wasn't involved) of being abnormal. Then she said, "A lesbian. You know, female homosexual. A woman who sleeps with women. Abnormal and disgusting." (She didn't have to explain. I guess I should tell you I've looked it up. You know, wondering.) Anyway, I kept saying that if you were, I was, too, but she said I wasn't, that you were just influencing me. So I got mad, out-loud mad, I mean. I finally got really, truly mad at her, Angie! I was so mad I looked her right in the eye and said, "I love Angie Greening. I am in love with her. I miss her terribly and I want to be with her all the time. I like it when we kiss. I don't think that makes me a lesbian, but if it does, then that's what I am." I walked out of my room then and into Carole's room (Carole wasn't there) and lay down on her bed and cried.

It was awful. The worst fight we've ever had. I wanted to die. I still do. That wasn't even the worst part, as maybe you know by now.

After I'd been in Carole's room for a while, Mom stormed in and said (icily) that for my own good she wasn't going to let me see you or call you or write you anymore. I didn't say anything. She got all red in the face. She yelled, "Elizabeth Taberd, did you hear me?" I just nodded. She made a sort of exasperated grunt. And stormed out again.

Angie, I'm still shaking inside. I'm so mad and upset and sorry I can't think. Listen, she can't stop me from writing you or from calling you when I have the money for toll calls. But she can stop me from getting your letters (if you still want to write to me). So today I went downtown and rented a post office box. It's Post Office Box 1139. I hope you'll use it. Oh, please, please use it, at least once, at least to tell me how you are!

Angie, I don't know how I'll get to see you in August. Please understand, please! Maybe I can fix something up with Will. I wish I could drive up by myself or with him to see the show, but I guess it's too far, especially if the show's at night, which I bet it is. I don't know where I could tell Mom we were going. Besides, she'd be suspicious about the date, I guess; she knows when the show is. I'm sorry; I wish I could come!

I've already had to go out with Will twice. He isn't too bad, thank God. He hasn't tried anything yet, but if he does, well, don't worry. I don't want anything like that with him. Just with you. (But only if you want it, too. Who cares what that means we are? It's just an ugly label. Lesbian. Homosexual.)

I probably should tear this letter up and start again.

Angie, I'm so sorry! The one good thing about this is that it's forced me to face what I really do feel. I'm not sure of much else, but to answer your question (it seems like years ago!), yes, I want us to be friends always, no matter what. But more important than that, I love you. I don't think I'm scared of that anymore! I love you, friend. Whatever that means. All I care about is that I love you. I love you. I love you. I LOVE YOU! Please be all right. We'll figure something out.

All my love,
Elizabeth

⊕

Saturday

Dearest, sweetest Elizabeth,

Okay, well, I guess I'm not surprised. I think your mother is capable of just about anything—ANYTHING—although maybe I shouldn't say that. Maybe I shouldn't use the word I want to use for her; it begins with B. She's also, I don't know. Sick, maybe?

Mostly, I'm worried about you. Don't YOU worry—I'm all right. I was—well—stunned by it, but it's so much worse for you! To have to live with her—I'm not sure I can quite imagine that, even if I am an actress.

The first thing that came was your mother's letter. It was pretty blunt, about hormones and adolescence and passion and her old song: influence. You're normal, says she, but I'm not—just like you told me. Then my parents called, and I was pretty upset by then, but better than I'd been at first. Then I got a letter from <u>my</u> mother. She's trying to help, and she and Daddy came up and saw the show tonight and took me out afterward and we talked. She and Daddy said they like you a lot, and that it's okay with them if we go on seeing each other. That's worth something, anyway, even if they don't really understand. I guess that's just as well, though.

Back when I got your mother's letter I was with a whole bunch of kids, apprentices, and I thought, Oh, no, Elizabeth's sick, she's had a car accident, so I ripped it open, and first I thought thank God you were okay, and then I saw what it was and I ran out into the woods, crying. Eddie—that's the boy I mentioned becoming friends with—came after me and asked me what was wrong, and I was so upset I blurted everything out. Well, guess what? Eddie's like us! He's a homosexual. I know we haven't used that word about ourselves, and damn your mother for using it in such a rotten way. But, Elizabeth, I think maybe she's right. I think we've been hiding from it—but I feel fine about it now, because I'm pretty sure that's what I am. Eddie says there's a nicer word for it, not so clinical: gay. That's the word gay people use, he says. Elizabeth, sweet Elizabeth, being that way—gay, lesbian—makes such sense to me, not just because of you, but also because of the way I've always felt inside. I know maybe you don't want that, but it's the truth about me, anyway. Maybe it isn't about you. If you don't think it's true about you or if you don't want that kind of relationship, I promise I won't push you about it, but I hope we can still be friends.

But I'm clinging to all those "I love you's" at the end of your letter.

Eddie is—what? Kind, wonderful, a true friend. We talked for hours, and he said if there's anything he can do, like be a go-between or something, he will. So he might call you sometime if that's all right. Since he's male, I bet your mother might not mind!

Anyway, I got your letter after your mother's letter. God, how awful for you! That—damn it, I have to say it—that BITCH! I wish you could talk to Carole. Could you? You need—badly—someone to talk to, and from everything you've said, I guess she doesn't get along with your mother any more than you do.

I'm so lucky I'm in theater and that I've met Eddie. I'd be lost if I didn't have him to talk to. Elizabeth, there are lots of gay people in theater. There are a couple of others here, too, and they're nice. They're not horrible people at all. Eddie even knows two men who live together like a married couple!

The post office box—you're a genius—is a wonderful idea! Of course I'll use it; how could I not use it? Remember—please—that I love you! I'll do anything to stay in touch with you. But I agree it would be too risky for you to come up for the apprentice show (yes, it's at night). Much as I'm aching to see you, I don't want you to get in bad trouble.

I did get a good part in the apprentice show, by the way. A character part. I get to wear pale makeup and eyebrow-pencil wrinkles over those freckles you like so much and I'll have gray hair instead of red. There's thick horrible stuff you can put on.

Please, please, take it easy. How's the botany? I know it sounds strange, out of place, asking that now, but I feel guilty for having theater to drown myself in. Oh, how I wish you had something like that to concentrate on instead of just this awful situation!

Elizabeth, I've read that you should take it seriously when people talk about suicide. It scares me that you mentioned wanting to die. Please, my sweet, sweet Elizabeth, don't even THINK of killing the person I love most in the world, the person I want to spend the rest of my life with! We'll find a way to be together, I know, if we both want to. At least we'll be able to see each other in school next year. And after next year we'll both be away from home. Your parents won't be able to control us then, at least not as much. No matter where we both end up after high school, we should be able to be in touch and maybe even see each other sometimes if we're careful. So please, be patient! And if you ever start thinking seriously about it—about dying—call me, or even drive up here yourself (the risk would be worth it then).

All my love,

Angie

✧

July 30

Dearest Angie,

I've been to the post office three times this week, as if a letter from you had wings or something and could get here before you'd even had time to write it. And thank God today your letter was there. You DO understand! (I should have known you would.) (But I was so scared.) And I guess you're right about it being too risky for me to come up for your show. But I'm aching to see you, too, believe me!

Don't, don't worry. I DO love you, always. Friends, yes, but more, too, I'm pretty sure. Believe me. Please. It's just that it's so hard, with everyone, even the encyclopedia, saying homosexuals are bad. I'm glad you met Eddie and some others and that they're nice. That helps. I know I love you. That's what really counts. In my good moments I know we'll find a way.

No, don't worry, I don't think I really want to die. I'm pretty sure I wouldn't ever kill myself. It's just that the time seems endless till we'll see each other. Even more endless till we can really be together. And my mother's being so awful. I think she's even been searching my room. She makes me come right home from working in the bookstore unless I'm with Will. She hasn't even smiled at me in days. And she's asked Carole all kinds of questions. Carole told me she thinks Mom's rotten for snooping into my life, and for saying we can't see each other except at school.

I keep wondering how we could live together after high school. I could probably find a college to go to in New York, if you go to acting school there. (I know you said you might apply to colleges instead, because of me, but I know you really want to go to acting school, so you should.) But if I applied to places in New York, I'm sure my mother would figure out why. If she knew you were there, I know she'd say I couldn't go. I don't know what to do about that.

I did talk to Carole (except about the gay part), and she was wonderful. She said she'll help, too, if she can. She likes you and she told me that she wishes she had a best friend as close to her as you are to me. She also said maybe she and your friend Eddie could pretend to be friends, if we could figure out some way she might have met him, and maybe we could communicate through them. She's a pretty neat kid. I'm lucky, I guess. Someday I'll tell her the truth. When she's older.

Maybe you're right about botany, drowning myself in it. I haven't done much about it yet, but we're going to visit my aunt this weekend. (No forced date with Will this weekend at least. Yay!) I've decided to go on a big wildflower hunt, press a whole bunch of stuff. Mom'll be ecstatic. (Maybe she'll even smile.) She thinks it's "appropriate" for a woman to be interested in flowers.

See? I'm better. I really am.

Did I say congratulations on getting the part? Congratulations on getting the part! Oh, I wish I could see you! It's hard to picture you with gray hair instead of red, though. It'll be a preview, I guess, of when we're old. (When we're old <u>together</u>—right?)

You know what? Except for not being able to come and see you, I guess things aren't that much different right now in spite of what Mom said. Going to the post office is pretty easy.

Good luck with rehearsals and stuff!

All my love,

Elizabeth

P.S. In the bottom of this envelope is a tiny speck. Put it on your lips and it will grow and turn into a kiss!

⊕

August 2

Sweet Elizabeth,

Wow, that tiny speck really worked! In fact, it turned into many kisses. I've put a bunch of very similar specks in the bottom of this envelope, some big, some little, so I hope you were careful about opening it. Look again if you didn't find them!

I'm glad you don't really want to die. What would I do if you did, my sweet friend?

Yes. We'll be old together. Old sounds awful, but together makes it fine.

I can't write long because I'm on break from rehearsal. It feels so good to be rehearsing! I don't think I told you much about my part. It's even a lead! And I have a long speech, a soliloquy, with no one else on-stage. That's pretty scary, but it's a wonderful speech, about my character's whole life. The play's just a one-act—we're doing three one-acts for the apprentice show, so more people can have leads. Darla has a small part—she can't act at all—and she's FURIOUS. She bitched so much about it that Eddie quoted the great Russian director Stanislavski at her: "There are no small parts, only small actors."

Eddie has a crush on one of the actors. He's had it ever since the first week we were all here, and finally the actor—his name is Milton, of all things—began noticing him. They're not that different in age, really; Eddie's seventeen and Milton just turned twenty and this is his first year in a resident company. He's great onstage and he's very good looking—Darla calls him the Greek god. (Poor Darla! If she only knew!) Milton and Eddie went to a lake near here on our day off. Eddie hasn't talked about it much yet, but he keeps grinning to himself, so I think things must've gone pretty well. I'm glad. They're both such special people. You'd like them, I think—no, I'm sure.

Oh, Elizabeth, when I think of you and what you're going through, I feel guilty, again, for being so far away. If only I could hold you! Do you smile your special smile now? And I keep thinking of your hair, your beautiful soft hair, and sometimes I can almost feel it in my hand.

I want to stroke it, to comfort you, to tell you everything is going to be all right and that someday we'll be happy and together. Oh, please believe that, Elizabeth, because I think if we both believe it, hard, it will have to come true. How can it fail? Your parents can't control us forever!

All my love,
Angie

❧

August 6

Dear Angela,

I have always thought of you as an honest person, if nothing else. But now it has come to my attention that you have not obeyed my restriction on communicating with my daughter. This only proves that I am right about the nature of your relationship. I have told Elizabeth that if there is any further contact between you, we will, after she graduates from high school, send her to secretarial school instead of college and that she will live at home, with us, until she is twenty-one or married. If there is communication between you outside of school next year, we will send Elizabeth to her aunt's, where she will be able to finish high school out of state.

Sincerely,
Mrs. Taberd

❧

August 6

Angie,

She's writing you, the bitch. (See? I don't mind the word!) She told me she would. She's sending me to a headshrinker. My first appointment is this afternoon. I'm scared, Angie. I'm even scared about us writing. It's not that I don't love you, but it would be awful if I had to be a secretary and live at home till I'm twenty-one. That's what's going to happen if we "communicate" again. Oh, yeah, I can leave before then if I get married, but that's not going to happen. (I sure wish I could marry you! We could elope. Would you elope with me?) (But I bet not even those two gay guys your friend Eddie knows could get away with doing that. It seems so unfair!) (But at least they can live together. That would be enough.)

Look, if you want to write to me, how about having Eddie write to Carole and have that really be you writing to me? It was sweet of him to say he'd help. Maybe he could put what you want to say to me in code or something. I know that sounds really juvenile, but it might be safest. Could you call me, to work it out? My parents are going to a party Sunday night. I'm sticking a money order in here. It should cover at least part of a call. (I know you don't have much money up there.) I'm sorry this is so incoherent. I wish I could decide what to do. I feel kind of lost. I can't seem to concentrate on botany. I did press those flowers, but I can't do anything more with them till they dry.

What happened this time was that she lost her damn car keys and took mine, and the P.O. box one was on the ring. Another stupid mistake of mine. I'm too miserable to even apologize.

All my love,
Elizabeth

⊷

Sunday—no, Monday!

Dearest Angie,

It was so wonderful to talk to you! I can't believe we talked for two hours. It was funny hearing all the clanks from the money dropping in. And that guy who wanted to use the phone was so nice when he thought you were talking to your boyfriend. (Wonder how he'd have acted if he'd known, though.)

Angie, Angie, Angie. (I just want to say your name. Yes, I said it out loud each time I wrote it.)

I'm glad you (and Eddie) understood about using code. Substitution code, I think Eddie called it? You just use the next letter of the alphabet for the letter you want, "B" for "A," "C" for "B," right? It's a great idea pretending that he and Carole got together through some kids' magazine and that he's her age instead of older. That'll help explain playing around with codes, too. Mom'll probably be glad Carole has a pen pal. I just hope Mom doesn't decide to crack the code. I hope it's not going to be too hard for Eddie to go across the border to Massachusetts to mail the letters so Mom won't get suspicious. You're right that she would if Carole got letters from New Hampshire where you are. And yeah, I know we can't use the code for long letters (or even very often). Please thank Eddie from me!

I'm going to miss your long letters, though!

Don't be surprised if I write you a lot. I know you won't be able to answer much, but I'd still like to write you. It's the only thing that keeps me sane.

Damn. She's lurking in the hall. It's 3 a.m., so you'd think she could leave me in peace!

All my love,
Elizabeth

⊷

August 11

Dear Carole,

Hey, it's great you're interested in codes, too. That's a neat magazine, isn't it, to have thought up the idea of code pen pals. But I thought I'd write in "plain text" first. Okay? Just to get acquainted.

My name is Eddie and I'm thirteen, the same as you, and I have a big sister, the same as you, but instead of a little brother, I have another sister. She's a pain. I bet your brother is, too. I like movies and racing cars and I'm good at math but not at sports. And I hope high school is going to be a lot better than junior high, but I'm not counting on it.

BOHJF TBZT UP UFMM FMJABCFUI FWFSZUIJOH JT GJOF BOE TIF MPWFT ZPV

Bye for now.

Eddie

[*Angie says to tell Elizabeth everything is fine and she loves you.*]

↬

August 13

Dear Angie,

This is a quick good-luck letter. (Should I say "break a leg" instead, like you told me actors say to each other?) I hate it that I'm not going to be there for the apprentice show. But you know I'll be there in spirit. Please, please know that! And I know you're going to be terrific.

I got your code message! Thank you. Mom was only mildly curious about the letter. Carole told her the stuff about the magazine, and Mom believed her.

I'm having to go out more with Will. Last night I told him more about the situation. I didn't say we're gay ("homosexual" is the word I used to him), just that my mother thinks we are. I was really scared, though! But he was okay about it!!!!!!!! He thinks my mother's wrong to "mess up our friendship" and that it's "awful to accuse someone of being homosexual." Also he said he's been going out with Sarah Whiting this summer, and he said he likes me more as a friend than as a girlfriend anyway. He said he hoped that was okay with me!

I'm not sure what the psychiatrist thinks. She doesn't say much.

(Thank God she's a woman, though! I don't think I could talk to a man.) I hope you don't mind, but I was so upset when I went to her and so mad that when she asked me about you and said that what I told her would be "in confidence," even from Mom, I blurted out that we're gay and that we're not going to change and that we love each other. Her eyebrows (she has heavy fuzzy ones. Black) went up. She asked me if we'd slept together. I told her we hadn't but that I wished we had. Up went the eyebrows again.

Do you mind that I told her?

Do you wish we had?

All my love,

Elizabeth

P.S. See? I'm really gay! I must be to have said that, and to have felt it, too. It just came out. I didn't plan it. But I do feel it. And it's okay with me. Especially if it is with you.

P.P.S. Is it okay with you?

P.P.P.S. Oh, Angie, do you wish we had?

↬

August 15

Dear Carole,

J EPOU NJOE ZPV UPME

ZFT JU JT PL

ZFT J EP

CVU JU TDBSFT NF

UIBOLT GPS UIF HPPE MVDL MFUUFS

Eddie

[*I don't mind you told. Yes it is OK. Yes I do. But it scares me. Thanks for the good luck letter.*]

↬

August 19

Dear Angie,

It scares me, too. But I'm glad we both wish we had.

HOW DID THE SHOW GO? I bet you were great. I bet your gray hair was great. I was thinking of you that night, hard. Fingers and toes crossed. (Eyes, too, only it was tough reading the left side of the page with my right eye, and the right side with my left eye!)

Angie, it's awful here. Mom is still watching me like I'm a criminal. I think she was a little suspicious of that last coded letter. The shrink doesn't say much, but I can tell she thinks I shouldn't be gay.

Last week after I saw her, I kept thinking about running away. I've got some money in the bank from my grandmother. I figured I could take it out. I talked to Miss Jaconsi (I called her up) and she said I could get a science scholarship easily, so I wouldn't have to worry about college. But then I realized I'd still have to finish high school someplace. I'd have to pay living expenses there and then in college, too. I guess I could pull it off, but I'd have to get a job, and that might mean it would take a pretty long time before I even got to college. And that's something I'm very sure of, that I want to go. How else am I going to figure out what I might want to do with my life? So I decided not to run away. I've just got to wait it out.

But, God, I want to see you! Look, what if I take a day off from the bookstore on your day off next week and ask Will to drive me up since of course I can't take Mom's car? That'd be using him, I know, but maybe he could take Sarah. (Sarah Whiting; remember? The other girl he's going out with.) She could keep him company while we're together. I've got to see you, really see you, before school starts!

What do you think?

All my love,
Elizabeth

August 23

Dear Carole,

JMM DBMM ZPV

JMM IBOH VQ JG JUT OPU ZPV

ZPV IBOH VQ JG JUT OPU TBGF

Eddie

[I'll call you. I'll hang up if it's not you. You hang up if it's not safe.]

⊕

August 26

Dearest Angie,

I still can't get over hearing your voice again. Oh, Angie, you sounded wonderful! I'm glad the show went so well. Someday your name's going to be up in lights.

Thank you for understanding about college. And running away. And please don't worry so much about me having to deal with my parents and the shrink. (I've complained too much.) It's really not all that bad. Okay, yes, it's bad, but I guess I'm getting used to it. It'll be worth it, if it means you and I can be together someday. And you're right. That's the most important thing, the thing we've got to work for, and we shouldn't take too many risks now. It would be awful if Mom called the bookstore and found out I'd taken a day off. She'd probably suspect right away that I'd gone to see you.

I still wish we could see each other before school, though.

But at least we <u>can</u> see each other in school. Mom can't take that away from us, not yet, anyway. Maybe there'll be some times this year when we can really be together.

Anyway, you've only got a little longer there in New Hampshire and then you'll be HOME! It's going to be almost impossible not to run over to your house the day you get back. But I won't. Unless Mom and Dad are out. I'll be careful, I promise. We both will, won't we?

I believe. I do believe in us. We WILL do it, we will be together someday, I know we will!

All my love, forever,
Elizabeth

✧

SILENT SONG

JINX STRETCHED AND THEN GROANED, SIMULTANEOUSLY OPENING HER EYES and pushing off the covers. The ancient air conditioner still hummed, but it was obviously doing little to cut through the heavy, thick air that had infiltrated her hotel room.

Staggering with sleepiness, Jinx padded to the window and, lifting the blinds, looked out onto the silent gray Miami Beach street. Nothing much was moving: a lone taxi, a couple of street people, a cop. None of her father's fellow conventioneers, certainly, were up and about at— she glanced at the hands of the clock that squatted on her night table— 5:30 a.m.

As she woke more fully, pain flooded her again, with an almost physical ache in her throat, her chest, her eyes. Why wake up, she thought, but she *was* awake, so she stripped off her damp pajamas, then pulled on her shorts and one of the T-shirts she wore for gym at school and for running to keep in condition for basketball and field hockey.

Maybe I'll just walk into the sea.

It wasn't a new thought; it had haunted her ever since she and her parents, who ran a small office supply company, had arrived in Miami Beach the day before. Her parents were there for a convention; Jinx was there because they'd said they couldn't let her stay home alone and there was no other place for her to go.

The hotel backed up on the beach; she'd had a quick run along it yesterday while her parents were arguing in their room about where to go for dinner.

If I walk into the sea, she thought, I will be at peace and there will be no more pain. I will not have to hide anymore, or argue with my parents, or lie, or miss Kathy . . .

Thinking of Kathy made her throat ache again—Kathy, who was the only person who had ever understood her; Kathy, whose laughing eyes had pulled Jinx into their almost constant joy; Kathy, who had held her, kissed her, taught her how to love, who had looked up at her trustingly with the tenderest of smiles—Kathy, whose parents had walked in one afternoon when she and Jinx were lying in each other's arms. They'd called Jinx's parents and then agreed with them to order Jinx and Kathy never to see each other again.

That was really why Jinx's parents had taken her to Miami Beach. They knew she'd try to see Kathy if she stayed home alone or with some other friend.

But there were no other friends anyway—none I'd want to stay with, Jinx thought, thrusting her feet into her sneakers and pulling violently on the laces. No other friends who knew, who cared, no other friends with whom she could be honest about herself and Kathy.

Jinx scrawled the words "On beach" on a piece of hotel stationery, slipped silently out of her room, and was hit immediately with air heavier and damper than the air she'd just left, proving that perhaps the air conditioner did help after all. She slid the note under her parents' door and walked to the elevator, in her mind writing a letter to Kathy that she wouldn't be able to send: *I couldn't sleep last night, missing you, wanting you with me. Every time I closed my eyes, my hands felt your softness and I ached all over for you. Kathy, Kathy, Kathy— So now I'm going to go out to the beach and run till I drop and then maybe I'll just walk into the sea and drown, dreaming of you, my sweet darling Kathy . . .*

My English teacher, Jinx thought as the reluctant elevator creaked and bucked its way to the lobby, would call that melodramatic.

But it's how I feel.

She nodded politely in the direction of the sleepy desk clerk and, without really looking at him, hurried toward the door that opened onto the alley leading to the beach. He gave her an indifferent nod back. "Need a towel?" he whispered as she passed, as if the lobby were full of sleeping guests.

"No thanks," she murmured, and let herself out into even heavier air.

God, I can't breathe in this, she thought—but this is how my lungs will feel as they fill with salt water.

There was no point to life without Kathy, none. The things Jinx had once loved—her posters, her records, her books—they were meaningless now, like fake store window dressing. Houses looked movie-set flat, and people seemed like automatons; even the people on the plane to Florida had looked that way, even her parents. Maybe especially her parents.

The alley was bounded on one side by the pale yellow brick of the hotel's windowless side wall and on the other side by a sagging board fence, puny protection from the construction that was going on in the next lot. Another faded hotel had been razed there, and yesterday, staring through holes cut in the fence, Jinx had seen workmen digging rubble out of what was left of its foundation. NEW SITE OF MIAMI TOWERS LUXURY HOTEL proclaimed a large green and white sign, stained with flying dust.

Luxury, ha! How could anything be luxurious in such a setting? The street outside was lined with scruffy shops, the most prosperous of which was the drugstore where she'd indifferently bought toothpaste and, at her mother's urging ("So you'll have something to do while Daddy and I are at meetings"), a bus pass. The least prosperous was the coffee shop at which she'd had a mayonnaise-soaked tuna sandwich, after insisting on being alone instead of going with her parents twenty blocks away to where the sidewalk was smoother and lined with real luxury hotels and cafés where beautiful people sat under bright umbrellas and watched other beautiful people pass by. They'd come through that section on their way from the airport, and her father had grumbled that, had he known, he'd have insisted on taking his family to one of those hotels.

Jinx and Kathy had decided never to care about that kind of thing, never to bother with it. "Pretentious," Kathy would call it. "Not for us. We'll live in a tiny gray cottage, with flowers outside and a well for our water, and a fireplace for cold winter nights."

The beach was almost deserted, a narrow strip sandwiched between hotels and the sea. A few couples and individuals were sprawled out asleep despite the notice that ordered NO OVERNIGHT CAMPING. Near an empty sleeping bag beside one of the couples, a small boy was playing tug-of-war with a black dog. Wire trash baskets bulged with the detritus of tourists and locals, and a man and a woman strolled hand in hand along the water's edge, where the sand was hard-packed and cool. A sudden gusty breeze tumbled a red-and-white popcorn box toward the black dog, who gave it a perfunctory sniff and abandoned it. Gulls mewed overhead.

The seascape wasn't much better. The water was flat and gray, with seaweed and sticks floating in it, plus sodden bits of cardboard, a waterlogged movie magazine, unidentifiable bottles, and an abandoned grayish tennis ball. Jinx stooped, picked it up, and lobbed it to the dog.

"Thanks," the little boy called, and Jinx, calling "You're welcome," waved. For a moment she smiled; for a moment the ache actually lessened—but only to return with renewed force. Kathy would have hugged the dog.

Blinking back sudden tears, Jinx started her run, jogging for a few minutes till her muscles stretched, and then picking up the pace. Her head cleared and the ache eased again a little as she felt her own wind plus the breeze's push back her hair and dry her sweat, cooling her skin. The heavy air was still hard to breathe, but she found she could do it, and soon the motion, the freedom, soothed her. If only I could run forever, she thought as a gull swooped down and stabbed the water's surface with its beak; how far could I run into the water? Turning, she tried it, but gave up when she was only thigh-deep. The warm water pushed against her, stopping her. Of course it would, stupid, she scolded herself. But she felt disappointed anyway; she would have to walk into it after all, to drown—and it was disgusting, too, warm as a bathtub, and full of trash.

I have to run more, first.

The sand near the water wasn't as hard-packed as it had looked, but there was a boardwalk on the upper part of the beach with several workmen hurrying along it to the construction site. Jinx ran to it, climbed its steps, and joined her pounding footsteps to their heavier, slower ones, ignoring the odd looks the workmen gave her. The hotels she passed grew steadily fancier, and more people emerged from them as the sun burned through the haze, raising the temperature. The air thickened still more, and Jinx no longer felt the sweat drying as quickly as it formed, despite the soft breeze that had risen with the sun.

The boardwalk was built out of some reddish brown wood, cedar, maybe, and smelled like the place in Maine she and Kathy had visited once, before their parents knew what was between them. They'd lain on the forest floor, on beds of moss and spruce needles under star-topped trees, holding hands and talking. Later, quietly and with gentleness and awe, they'd made love for the first time.

Waist-high railings separated the boardwalk from both the hotels and the beach, and the boardwalk itself curved and bent, following the contours of the land. Benches ran along some of the curved sections; approaching one, Jinx heard what sounded like soft bells, and then, rounding the corner, she saw a girl close to her own age sitting on a bench facing the sea, head bent and light brown hair shielding her face from passersby. Her hands supported a small harp, and at first Jinx thought she was strumming it, but then realized she was simply holding the harp to the wind, letting the wind stroke its strings.

Jinx ran past, then turned, wanting to see the girl's face, sure it would be as beautiful as Kathy's.

But it wasn't. Her mouth was a little too large; her eyes, half-closed, a little too wide apart; the planes of her face too flat. Still, there was a sweetness and a serenity about her that mesmerized Jinx, made her stop and watch.

The girl hardly moved at all. Her graceful hands held the harp lightly, and her head was bent as if listening to its almost silent music; her long paisley skirt draped down to her bare and none-too-clean feet.

A man lying on a bench diagonally opposite the girl, with a sleeping brown dog connected to him by a worn leather leash, grunted and unwrapped himself from the tattered raincoat that covered him. He was young, Jinx could see behind the blond beard that curled across his face, perhaps only a little older than she was.

Wary of exciting his interest, Jinx turned, about to run again, but by then he'd seen her and smiled, saying, "Good morning. Cora's harp's good today, isn't it?"

"Um, yes," Jinx said. "It—it's lovely."

"Sure beats an alarm clock." The man stood, and his dog stood also, shaking itself, then stretching and yawning. The man went over to the girl, put his hand lightly on her shoulder, and said something quietly to her. The girl gave him a sorrowful smile and turned back to the harp.

"She doesn't speak," the man said, gathering up his raincoat. "Something bad happened to her a while back. But the harp speaks for her. And someday, in time, she'll talk again, I think. Meanwhile, Rex and I here, we keep an eye on her. We've gotta go do number one. Tinkle, maybe you call it," he added.

"I—I can keep an eye on her while you're gone, if you want." Jinx's own words surprised her, and she realized her mouth had suddenly gone dry.

The man studied Jinx for a moment, as if weighing the possibility that she might harm Cora, or maybe, like the workmen, thinking it odd for a girl to be out running. "Well, that would be nice," he said at last. "I think she'll be okay now that it's morning, but it'd still be nice of you. Okay, Cora?" he said to the girl. "This lady says she'll keep an eye on you while Rex and I go see a man about a horse. Maybe we'll find some breakfast, too, you never know."

Quickly, Jinx reached into her pocket and brought out the sweat-dampened and crumpled five-dollar bill she always carried just in case. "Here," she said boldly, surprising herself again. But Kathy would do it, she knew. "Get us all some breakfast, okay?"

The man looked at it, and then at her, gravely. "You sure?" he said. "Five bucks is a lot of money."

"I'm sure," Jinx said, and then added, grinning, "I'm hungry. Running's hungry work. I play basketball," she explained in case he did think it odd. "Hockey, too. That's why I run."

"Okay." The man slid the five into a grubby pocket. "Okay. Come on, Rex." He held out a grimy hand. "I'm Tommer," he said. "It's not much of a name, but it's the only one I've got anymore."

"Jinx," Jinx answered, shaking his hand, trying not to mind the grime.

"Be back in a jiffy," Tommer said. "Rex, let's go, buddy."

When Tommer and Rex had left, Jinx sat tentatively down on Cora's bench, a little distance from her. "I love your music," she said cautiously.

Cora smiled, less sadly this time, and moved the harp a little as the breeze shifted. For a few minutes they both sat silently, listening.

The sea, Jinx decided, can wait.

1960s

THE DECADE

IN THE 1960S, THERE WERE STILL FEW OPPORTUNITIES FOR GAY PEOPLE TO meet or even recognize one another. Straight people had odd ideas about that. For years, even back in the fifties and much to my amusement (my school uniform was green), a rumor had circulated that gays wore green on Thursday, which was supposedly "fairy day." Rumor also had it that we all had a secret handshake by which we recognized one another. There were, though, some real clues. For example, some closeted gays mentioned being "on the committee" or "a friend of Dorothy" in order to identify themselves safely to other gays. (The latter was a reference to Dorothy in *The Wizard of Oz*; the movie, starring Judy Garland, was especially popular among gay men.) And membership on a women's softball team was more than a clue, for many such teams were exclusively lesbian.

Gay organizations and gay bars, two places where gay and lesbian people could meet in relative safety, were primarily limited to big cities. The bars had been around for a long time, and many were dingy, smoky places where straights sometimes went to gawk at gays as they might at animals in a zoo. Even so, gays and lesbians could meet there, dance and talk, listen to music, watch gay and lesbian performers, and hope to meet someone with whom to share the night—or even begin a lasting relationship.

But the bars could be dangerous, too. Homosexual relationships were in effect illegal, and many bars had to be licensed by state liquor authorities that could in turn revoke a bar's license for allowing homosexuals to meet there. Therefore, owners of gay bars, many or most of whom belonged to the Mafia or other mob outfits, paid police to pretend they weren't catering to homosexuals. Despite that, gay bars were often raided by the police, many of whom had few scruples about beating up the people they arrested or about calling their employers to notify them that they were gay. The usual employer reaction? Fire the gay person!

Even when the courts in some states said that it was okay for gays and lesbians to patronize bars, police frequently interpreted general rules against "indecent behavior" and the like very loosely. For example, they rounded up gays and lesbians simply for dancing with each other, or harassed, arrested, or beat them just for being on streets near gay bars. Frequently, vice squad officers went into the bars pretending to be gay and tried to "entrap" gay men by flirting with them. When a gay man responded, the police officer identified himself and arrested him. Gays, lesbians, and transgender people sometimes, especially in the bars, dressed in clothes traditionally worn by the opposite sex; in New York City they were subject to arrest if they were seen without at least three articles of clothing considered appropriate for their biological gender. (Most women's pants, usually called "slacks" in those days, were cut very differently from men's and didn't have fly fronts. But one popular exception was "Mister Pants," which were almost exactly like men's except for being designed to fit women's bodies.)

Some gay and lesbian organizations that had been founded earlier really took off in the sixties. Most prominent were the primarily male Mattachine Society, founded in 1950 in Los Angeles, and the exclusively female Daughters of Bilitis (DOB), founded in 1955 in San Francisco. By the end of the decade, there were more than forty such organizations. But they were off-limits to teens, for gays were always vulnerable to trumped-up charges of child molesting and of contributing to the delinquency of minors. Still, gay, lesbian, and questioning teens sometimes phoned Mattachine or DOB looking for advice, reassurance, and help. Sympathetic adult members of those organizations did their best to at least answer the teens' questions and assure them that there were many other people like themselves.

The Daughters of Bilitis concentrated on providing social occasions like dances, "Gab 'n' Java" coffee sessions, and "covered dish" suppers. DOB also held discussions, sometimes with invited speakers, about such issues as the place of religion in gay people's lives and the problems of coming out to parents and friends. Mattachine sponsored speakers and discussions, too, especially in its early days, but it quickly became an activist organization, dedicated to protesting against and changing anti-gay laws, and helping gays who ran afoul of them.

The first pro-gay protest demonstration was held in front of the Whitehall Military Induction Center in lower Manhattan one Saturday in 1964, when a handful of us, terrified, marched and held signs in the pouring rain. Why the army? Homosexual soldiers were viewed as being disruptive to "normal" troops. They were also still seen as security risks; the army, like other government branches, had long reasoned that, because gays were fearful of being revealed as homosexuals, they were subject to blackmail. Gays and lesbians had therefore been officially banned from the military since the 1940s, and they were discharged dishonorably if they managed to serve and were found out—which meant they couldn't collect veteran's benefits, even if they'd had exemplary careers.

The Whitehall demonstration was the first of many. The sixties in general were a time of widespread protest and social change. The black civil rights movement was working in the South to desegregate schools and to end the cruel Jim Crow laws that relegated African-Americans to second-class citizenship. The feminist movement was gathering strength in its battle for women's equality in all spheres of life; college students were organizing for various causes; and people young and old were marching to protest the Vietnam War.

And gradually our voices were also beginning to be heard. The New York branches of Mattachine and DOB, along with several similar groups, joined together to form ECHO (East Coast Homophile Organizations) in 1963. A few years later, NACHO (North American Conference of Homophile Organizations) was formed and soon had more than six thousand members. Membership lists in all these organizations were confidential and closely guarded, for of course people's careers and lives could be ruined if those lists fell into the wrong hands.

There were demonstrations in several cities, for example, Washington, D.C., San Francisco, and New York—and in front of Independence Hall in Philadelphia annually between 1965 and 1969. (In 2005, those Philadelphia demonstrations were commemorated by the installation of an official state historical marker!)

I remember many of us being amused at demonstrations in Washington, D.C., when we easily spotted Secret Service men keeping an eye on us, for they were all dressed in business suits and wore identical lapel pins. I remember, too, when members of the American Nazi Party tried to crash an ECHO conference. A group of us kept them out of the auditorium where a meeting was in session by holding hands in a line in front of the door. That was scary—but it got us onto that night's evening news!

In the sixties, we were still so invisible to the public at large that almost any mention of us in the media was worthwhile, especially, of course, if it was accurate. There were a few panel discussions on television, and articles, some of them more or less positive, in national magazines like *Time* and *Harper's*. Public discussions, along with articles in the mainstream press, gradually made it a little harder for people to think there weren't very many of us. They also helped to challenge the belief that we were exhibitionists, cowards, sick, or immoral.

Some psychiatrists and psychologists soon began considering new theories about the origins and nature of homosexuality, and some religious organizations, after much soul-searching, considered positive views as well. A group called the Council on Religion and the Homosexual was founded in San Francisco in 1964, a project of the Glide Memorial United Methodist Church, which ministered to gay people, the poor, ethnic minorities, and others. A handful of religious leaders tried to open their church or synagogue doors to gays and lesbians, and tried to convince the faithful that we weren't evil monsters. Around this time, too, the Friends Home Service Committee in England issued a pamphlet called "Towards a Quaker View of Sex," in which homosexuality was viewed with understanding and acceptance. Gays and lesbians here in the United States took heart from it when it was made available here.

In 1968 on the West Coast, a gay minister, the Reverend Troy Perry, started the Metropolitan Community Church, a Christian church whose members were primarily gay. In the years that followed, more and more religious groups wrestled with whether homosexuality fit into their belief systems, and many are still wrestling with that question. Gay organizations for Catholics (Dignity) and Episcopalians (Integrity) were formed around the same time. During the early seventies, Jewish groups started in various cities; they and others came together later in the World Congress of Gay, Lesbian, Bisexual, and Transgender Jews: Keshet Ga'avah. All these groups remain active today, as do Jewish synagogues that welcome gays and lesbians, and "open and affirming" or "welcoming" congregations in several faith communities, including congregations of the United Church of Christ and Unitarian Universalist congregations.

Religious groups continue to agonize over whether to accept GLBT worshipers, church officials, and clergy. For example, in 2003 the Episcopal Church in the United States confirmed and consecrated its first openly gay bishop, V. Gene Robinson of New Hampshire. But as of late fall 2006, three years after Robinson was confirmed, the controversy was still raging, both in the United States and in the worldwide Anglican community, to which the American Episcopal Church belongs. Many people were so pessimistic about a resolution that they feared a permanent schism—an official split within the church—between those favoring acceptance of gay clergy and those opposed. Similar controversies have threatened to split the Presbyterian Church (U.S.A.).

Still, progress toward acceptance has continued over the years in other religious groups. In 2006, a group of Protestant congregations joined with a major gay rights organization to encourage more congregations to welcome gays and lesbians, the Black Church Summit resolved to work against discrimination against gays and lesbians in African-American churches, and Conservative Jewish leaders continued to wrestle with whether to allow gay rabbis or to sanction ceremonies celebrating committed relationships of same-sex couples.

Unfortunately, though, despite these and other positive developments, numerous religious gays, including many gay teens, are still excluded from their faith communities and feel as damned by their faiths' beliefs as GLBT people did in the sixties.

The Glide Foundation, which had founded the Glide Memorial Church, was instrumental in the sixties in starting the Central City Poverty Program, whose goal was specifically to encourage self-help among runaways and homeless kids in the tough part of San Francisco known as the Tenderloin. These kids, like runaways everywhere, were easy targets for drug dealers and other criminals; many had no means of supporting themselves except through prostitution—and many of them were gay. In 1966, some of the gay kids involved in the Central City program formed a group called Vanguard, which held consciousness-raising meetings and discussions, spoke out against various forms of what today we call homophobia, informed needy kids of where to turn for help—and issued a magazine called V, in which gay street kids wrote about their lives. Vanguard was probably the first organization for gay youth in the United States.

In 1967, gay activist Craig Rodwell established the first gay bookstore in the world, the Oscar Wilde Memorial Bookshop in Greenwich Village, New York City. (Oscar Wilde was a famous nineteenth-century Irish author and wit who was jailed for homosexuality.) There weren't many gay books and periodicals in 1967, but over subsequent years both the supply and the demand grew. Oscar Wilde Memorial Bookshop, like most of the gay bookstores that followed it, often had to struggle to stay in business, but unlike many of those others, it has survived into the twenty-first century, and is now called simply Oscar Wilde Bookshop.

Also in 1967, *The Advocate*, which today is the major GLBT news and entertainment magazine, began publishing in Los Angeles. Today in addition to news articles about politics, law, religion, health, movies, fashion, and the like, *The Advocate* covers some news of youth, and, since the fall of 2003, it has run a regular feature called "Generation Q," in which kids in their teens and twenties speak out on matters that concern them. In 2005, seventeen-year-old Kerry Pacer, who won a long battle to start a gay-straight alliance (a club for kids of any sexual orientation) at her Georgia high school, appeared on *The Advocate*'s cover as its Person of the Year.

The progress and protests of the fifties and sixties came to a head in New York City early in the morning of Saturday, June 28, 1969, when, fed up with police raids on the bars, gays rioted in front of the Stonewall Inn, a gay bar in Greenwich Village. Up until then, the gay community's protests against mistreatment had been largely verbal and nonviolent. But tensions had been building for years, not only because of raids and arrests in and around gay bars but also because of the many other forms of discrimination and the belief of most straight people that homosexuals were inferior, immoral, or sick—in effect, subhuman. Years of pain and anger, combined with resentment at two weeks of other bar raids in New York City, exploded that hot night in the Village—perhaps, some straight people thought, also sparked by the recent death of the movie star, singer, and gay icon Judy Garland, beloved by many gay men.

Accounts of the Stonewall riots vary, but they began in the small hours of that June morning, when, at a little after 1 a.m., police raided the Stonewall Inn for the second time that week. According to *Stonewall* by David Carter, which is based largely on eyewitness accounts, as patrons who'd been questioned by police left the bar, they stayed nearby, and a crowd gathered. For a while, the crowd was mostly good-humored, but when other patrons, who had been arrested, were taken outside and loaded none too gently into a van, and when a butch lesbian resisting arrest was finally roughly subdued, the crowd exploded, shouting insults at the police and hurling whatever they could find at them. More people—many of them homeless gay street kids—joined in and the battle escalated. As it did, the police barricaded themselves inside the bar, but the crowd succeeded in breaking down the door. People threw burning trash into the inn and sprayed plywood barricades with lighter fluid and ignited them. Finally flames erupted inside the bar; the police drew their guns and managed to send for reinforcements. First more police and then the TPF (Tactical Patrol Force, New York's riot control squad) arrived. The TPF eventually broke up the melee—but not before street kids and drag queens led them a merry chase, singing and dancing defiantly.

The next night a much larger crowd, perhaps as many as two thousand, gathered and clashed again with the police and the TPF. On Sunday, Mattachine Society leaders tried to calm things down, but although the protests were quieter that night, they continued despite rain on Monday and Tuesday. On Wednesday, when the weather cleared, more people, some estimate around one thousand, again rioted violently, but this was the last time.

Nothing like the Stonewall riots had ever happened in our community. Word of them galvanized gays and lesbians all over the country and spawned the formation of less patient and more confrontational gay and lesbian organizations, plunging the gay revolution into modern times and changing its face forever.

But if you were a GLBTQ teen who lived outside major urban areas, none of this, even if you heard about it, seemed to have much to do with you. If you were young and gay in the 1960s, you usually had only yourself to rely on.

COLD COMFORT

GENTLE SHEPHERD UNION CHURCH WAS A HUMBLE STRUCTURE SET AT THE edge of Port Tilden Marsh, little more than a cabin, really, with a steeple stuck onto its roof like a magician's hat. Salt breezes wafted through its open clear-glass windows in summer, keeping it cool, and sharp northeast winds rattled the same windows when they were closed in winter, whistling through the places where the windows fit loosely into their frames.

Port Tilden was a fishing community whose people were helpful to their neighbors and worked hard and long, but those who attended Gentle Shepherd observed strict rules of conduct as well as of religion and were, on the whole, harsh and unbending in their goodness, though they meant well. Theirs was a stern faith, headed by a loving God, yes, but a God who demanded unquestioning obedience and who recognized, as did the congregation, that all people, though sinners, can earn forgiveness and salvation if they repent their evil deeds.

Sternest of all was Charity's father, the Reverend Brown, who ministered to his flock with fearsome tongue and dire words Sunday after Sunday to rid them of the ills of the week before and steel them to face the week ahead. He himself had once fallen, as he reminded them often; several years after his marriage he had kissed a woman-not-his-wife (Charity and her brother, Jonathan, wondered if he'd done more than kiss her), but he had repented and God had forgiven him. He frequently reminded his congregation, especially in spring, when the younger members of his flock felt their blood rise and their limbs stir and their eyes stray to one another—he reminded them in spring of Paul's harsh pronouncements against carnal sins, of the commandment against adultery, and of the fires of hell that awaited them if they gave in to the lust of their bodies. And every fall, when school was about to start again, he renewed his warnings.

Charity tried not to think about her father's sermons, especially the fall after she'd turned sixteen, when her own eyes strayed more than once to the pew in front of her family's pew and to the sweet back of Andrea Carey's neck. Andrea and her family were new in the community and new to the church, not fisherfolk like most others, but merchants. The Careys had bought the small store on Sea Street that sold hardware and magazines and stationery as well as food to the locals, plus, mostly in summer, sandwiches and soft drinks to the few tourists who stopped by on their way to someplace else, and to the even fewer artists who spent a day or so there painting seascapes and "quaint" dockside scenes. Charity had met Andrea in late summer, soon after the Careys had taken over the store—met her, and felt a catch in her throat and a sensation in her body that she didn't immediately understand. Andrea had been standing behind the meat counter, where fat tubes of bologna and salami and pale cubes of American and Swiss lay on greased paper behind the curve of glass that protected them from those flies that were too smart to get stuck on the coil of brownish yellow paper that extended over the counter, waiting to trap the unwary.

Andrea looked terrified.

Her yellow hair was not quite fully restrained by the two braids that fell to just below her shoulders, and the white bibbed apron she wore over her plain light blue blouse was spotlessly clean. Mrs. Tucker's—Mrs. Tucker was the recent widow who had sold the store after her husband's sudden death—Mrs. Tucker's apron had always shown a grayish cast and a streak or two of unidentifiable food.

"Can—can I help you?"

Andrea's voice was thin but courageous, belying the fear in her cornflower blue eyes. Her skin was flawless, and a brave smile slowly turned up the corners of her soft and welcoming mouth—an afterthought, for politeness, perhaps.

Charity tried not to stare at her beauty, but in her heart she knew that she had never, ever, seen any face to rival this one. She straightened her shoulders and flicked an imaginary fly off her old faded blue jacket, wishing she could unzip it surreptitiously to show Andrea that the shirt she wore under it was as clean as Andrea's apron—although, admittedly, it was considerably older, since it was a hand-me-down from Cousin Tilly, who'd outgrown it two years earlier.

"Yes," Charity said firmly. "Quarter of a pound of bologna. Please." Then she smiled. "I'm Charity Brown," she said. "Welcome to Port Tilden."

Andrea's smile grew, and, gratefully, she said, "Thank you. I'm Andrea Carey. We—my folks—bought the store. I—" She laughed self-consciously, halfway between a chuckle and a giggle. "I'll have to get my dad. I don't know how to run the slicer yet."

Charity wasn't sure what possessed her to do it, but she said swiftly, "That's okay; I know how," and she stepped briskly behind the counter.

Andrea moved back, clearly alarmed. "Oh, but I don't know if . . . I—I mean," she sputtered, "I'm not sure Daddy would let anyone—"

"I've worked here," Charity said, smiling in what she thought was a reassuring way. "Miz Tucker, she always used to let me slice my own, 'long's I was careful." She reached for the bologna but then stopped, realization hitting her. "Of course," she said, "if your pa's worried about the amount and the thickness and stuff . . ."

"It's just that we don't really know anyone here yet," Andrea said apologetically. "You know, to—to trust them. I'm sorry, I'm sure you—"

"Andrea?"

An authoritative male voice drifted to the meat counter from the cash register, and a moment later a tall, ginger-haired, and bearded man with a pleasantly open face strode around the glass case and stood beside them. "How do?" he said, extending a hairy, freckled hand to Charity, who took it. "Bill Carey, and you must be the preacher's daughter if your name's Brown. We'll be seeing you Sunday in church, for sure. Now, it was bologna you wanted, right?"

Charity, annoyed without quite realizing why, but liking him anyway, nodded.

Mr. Carey patted her shoulder and grasped the bologna, plopping it down on the slicer. "I'm sure you'd do just fine at slicing," he said, switching the machine on, "seeing as how you've done it before. But even an experienced slicer can slip"—here he displayed a healed but foreshortened middle finger to Charity—"and I sure don't want no customers of mine getting hurt. Quarter of a pound, you said?"

Charity nodded and glanced at Andrea, who shrugged, and as they watched, she felt she and Andrea had become conspirators in allegiance against this friendly, bearlike man who had interrupted them in the interest of safety first.

When school opened a couple of days later, Charity found Andrea standing forlornly outside the main door, again looking terrified, and also much smaller. She was not a big girl, certainly, nowhere near as big as Charity, who at five ten towered above most of her female classmates and whose large bones made her look awkward in anything but the jeans and shirts that she wore as often as she could, even, on most days, to school. Of course, on Sundays and on occasional trips to Gouchville, the county seat, for supplies, the Reverend insisted that she wear dresses, no matter how much she railed against it.

"Andrea!" Charity said, grinning as she hurried up to her. "Hi!"

"Hi." Andrea smiled wanly.

They looked at each other for a painfully silent minute.

"So," said Charity, "want me to show you around? What grade are you in?"

"Tenth, my last school," Andrea said. "I've got my records." She held up a somewhat battered manila envelope. "My folks've been too busy settling the store to take them over. And when I tried before, the school was locked."

"Best we go now then." Out of the corner of her eye, Charity spotted class bullies Jason Smithson and Harvey Ripple loping toward the steps, and she put her hand lightly in the small of Andrea's thin back and turned her to face the door. Charity was confident she could hold her own against Jason and Harvey, who'd called her names since second grade, but she saw no reason to subject Andrea to them and their remarks on the very first day of school.

"I'm a junior," Charity said as she opened the door, "and you must be, too, if you were in tenth last year. So we'll be in the same class, looks like."

"That—that would be nice," Andrea said shyly.

She seemed so timid and so fragile that for a minute Charity resented her own friendliness, not wanting to be saddled with someone so needy she'd never have the gumption to match her own looks. But then Andrea said, "You go on to your homeroom or whatever. I can find the office. You must have friends you want to see, after the summer."

Whereupon Charity melted. "Oh," she said merrily, "that's okay, I'll show you the office. Besides, no one in Port Tilden goes away in the summer. The boys fish with their dads, mostly, or work in garages and body shops and stuff, and the girls pick crab or babysit or work in stores. And every night kids hang around Sea Street." She didn't feel moved to add that she wasn't one of the ones who hung around. As the preacher's daughter, she tended to make other kids feel watchful about their language and their actions, and, anyway, the Reverend restricted her to no farther than the front porch on most summer nights, guarding her as zealously as fairy-tale dragons guarded treasure, guarding her from other kids, i.e., guarding her from boys.

Not, though, from Billy Jack Nickerson—who just now sauntered in through the door and stood, huge hands on slim hips, looking down—yes, down, for Billy Jack stretched higher than six feet—at both girls.

"Well now, Charity," he said, his wide mouth beaming, showing his very white front tooth and the little yellowish pointy one beside it, half of which had fallen out when the boom of the *Molly N* had given it a fatal crack two years earlier, jibing in a fierce storm. "Here you are, big as life!"

"Yeah, and here you are, too, Billy," Charity said, answering his grin with one of her own.

It had been a week since they'd seen each other, for Billy Jack had been out on his father's boat so long and so late every day that there hadn't been time for socializing. It was understood, though, and had been for three or four years, that Charity was the closest thing he had to a girlfriend, and vice versa. The Reverend, who'd grown up with Billy Jack's father, approved.

Charity knew that her relationship with Billy Jack wasn't what her parents hoped, but she liked Billy, and he was a good friend who didn't make demands on her or make fun of the way she dressed, and seemed as content as she to let people think what they wanted.

"This is Andrea Carey," Charity said. "You know—her folks bought Tuckers' Store."

"Ummm." Billy looked Andrea up and down in a way that made Charity mad. "Hi. You going to be in our class?"

Andrea smiled up at him with her cornflower blue eyes sparkling, which made Charity even madder, and she felt annoyed at herself because she wasn't entirely sure who she was mad at.

"Hi," Andrea said. "I think so. But I'd better go check in at the office and see."

"Want company?" Billy said, moving closer.

Charity started to step between them, but there was no need, for, wonder of wonders, Andrea turned her smile and those blue eyes back onto her and said, "No thanks, that's okay. I've already got company."

And Charity, feeling ten feet tall and still not quite understanding why, gave Billy a triumphant look and hurried off with Andrea before the bell rang.

It was in church that Sunday that Charity discovered the back of Andrea's neck, and she stared at it so hard and so long, imagining how the smooth, white skin with its tiny hairs would feel under her fingers if she touched the spot with infinite gentleness—she stared at it for so long that she failed to stand up in a timely fashion for the second hymn, and her mind drifted so far away from her father's sermon that at Sunday dinner, when he asked her opinion of the lesson he'd drawn from the parable of the prodigal son, she wasn't even able to make use of her brother's whispered prompts and had to admit she hadn't been paying attention.

"And what," the Reverend Brown thundered, "was so important that it occupied you more than the Lord's Word?"

Charity sensed that this would not be a good time to tell the absolute truth and was about to make up a convincing lie when Jonathan betrayed her, perhaps innocently, by saying, "She was staring at that new girl from Tuckers' Store the whole time."

Charity gave Jonathan a not-so-gentle kick under the table in an attempt to convey to him that this was henceforth a Forbidden Subject.

"I was admiring her hairstyle," Charity said, whereupon both her parents stared at her and Jonathan laughed.

"My goodness," her mother said, "that might be the first time I've heard you admiring someone's hair! But you can't have seen much of it from the back."

"Well, I've seen the front in school," Charity said. "I wanted to—to study how the back was done."

"Just braids if I remember right," said her mother. "You let your hair grow, honey, and we'll braid it that way if you like. It'll take a while, though, it being so short now." Mama poured herself a little water. "Still, I'd sure like to see you with longer hair."

"May I remind you both," the Reverend said sternly, "that this is the Lord's Day and not a time for vanity? Not a time," he went on— and Charity could tell he was warming up and would probably preach on vanity next Sunday—"not a time for considering vain adornment. We need no more adornment than what the Lord has bestowed upon us; our own God-given faces and hair, and simple clothing to hide our nakedness are all the adornment we need—"

"Yes, that's right, dear." Mrs. Brown stood up and began hastily to clear the table. "Although surely allowances may be made now and then for a young unmarried girl."

"Not a preacher's young unmarried daughter," the Reverend said, "who needs to set an example of purity and modesty. No daughter of mine is going to become a mantrap!"

Jonathan appeared to choke on his milk; Charity thumped him on the back.

"The last thing I want to do, Father," she said with complete honesty, "is to become a mantrap."

"See to it, Daughter, see to it that you don't."

Alone in her room later, Charity studied herself in the mirror. She had brushed her short black hair with unusual vigor that morning before church, wanting it to be especially sleek and shiny, and she had scrubbed her face till it looked polished.

But why?

Not for Billy Jack, certainly, who sat one pew over and two down.

Not for Harvey and Jason.

Not for any of the other boys she knew and had, until sixth grade or so, played with.

For myself? she wondered, looking into her own serious brown eyes and then turning away.

But she knew, deep inside she knew.

She knew it was for Andrea, to impress her, and she knew that the Bible said that what she felt was wrong.

Even so, she couldn't stop. She did try. She tried to be more friendly with Billy Jack, even to the point of sitting with him at a church supper, with her father's permission, of course, and with his own father as a distant chaperone. She tried looking everywhere but at Andrea in church, and she tried ignoring her in school. But that was impossible, for she and Andrea had become friends. Also, Andrea, who was behind in math, needed help with homework, and the Reverend agreed to let her come to the house and sit at the kitchen table surrounded by math books and yellow paper after school twice a week.

Fall slowly froze into winter, and on Christmas it snowed in Port Tilden. On the twenty-sixth, after the endless church services the day before, Charity met Andrea down by the fish pier, and they walked, huddled in dark coats against the wind and the cold, along the shore, shoulders touching and then hands clasped. Charity made sure to put herself between Andrea and the wind, and once, when an especially strong gust blew her body into Andrea's, Andrea threw her arms around her and whispered, "Oh, Charity, I'm so glad we're friends."

Charity's body sang with the remembered contact for days afterward.

And as winter warmed into spring, the math sessions grew longer and longer, and had less and less to do with math than with whispered conversations and notes scrawled at the bottoms of equations; poetry gradually replaced word problems.

"Ruth and Naomi," Charity said stubbornly to herself over and over, thinking of the Bible story about pure love between two women—mother-in-law and daughter-in-law, true, but at least two women—and to Andrea she quoted from the story, "Whither thou goest, I will go. Thy people will be my people."

In answer, Andrea retold the story of David and Jonathan, who were about the same age, and although both were men, they loved each other deeply. She and Charity reminded each other often that theirs was a rare and special fondness, as innocent and pure as those famous biblical friendships.

Still, spring was difficult, and when the Reverend's sermons blustered and blew more strongly than the March winds and his fiery eyes scanned his congregation for signs of lustful straying, his gaze fell more and more on his own daughter. Charity tried to meet that gaze with certainty and defiance. I am innocent, she said to herself, preparing to say it to him; we are innocent.

And they were, for since that one chaste hug on the wintry shore, they had not touched.

It was Jonathan who betrayed them, unknowingly, unintentionally.

Exams were coming, and the twice-a-week sessions again concentrated closely on math. Afternoon after afternoon, the two heads, one close-cropped and black and the other blond and braided, bent over books and papers at the Reverend's kitchen table, and Charity patiently went over the intricacies of angles and sine curves and proofs with an increasingly confused and, it must be admitted, bored, Andrea.

At last they both rebelled. One late May afternoon, when it had been especially hot, Charity and Andrea moved their work outside to a battered picnic table at which the Browns sometimes ate on summer evenings. Math once more gave way to English and equations to poetry; the two made a game of scrawling poems—"Shall I compare thee to a summer's day?" "How do I love thee?" "My love is like a red, red rose"—to each other, each trying to use poets' words to express her own feelings, then explaining and expanding on those feelings in notes written—oh, so neatly!—at the bottoms of the pages: "This is how I felt when I first saw you," "This is how I'll feel forever," "I love you even more than this."

A sudden thunderstorm that afternoon set them to gathering up their papers and books in a hurry and fleeing indoors to wait for Andrea's father to pick her up, as he occasionally did when he had deliveries to make from the store, mostly to the town's sick and elderly.

And a little later, when Andrea had gone and the storm had cleared, Jonathan went outside to shoot baskets at the hoop he had been given for his latest birthday. There, on the ground and plastered against the side of the house, were a few wet papers, which he picked up without examining, took inside, and put on the kitchen table before he returned to the hoop.

Soon after, the Reverend came out of his study, where he had been working on an especially blistering sermon, to get himself a glass of iced tea.

And there they were, a few of Andrea's and Charity's annotated love poems.

Not many, but enough.

The Reverend Brown, even though he had often said "Spare the rod and spoil the child" to those members of his flock who had wayward children, had rarely hit Charity and Jonathan. He had spanked them once in a while when they were small, but he had never beaten them as he beat Charity after he had confronted her with the poems.

"Yes, they're mine, mine and Andrea's," she admitted, actually relieved to say it at last. Though she'd imagined this moment, she'd never quite believed it would come. But now that it had, she felt oddly removed from her father's blazing eyes and the furiously contemptuous set of his mouth. "And yes, it's true, that's how we feel—like Ruth and Naomi, David and Jonathan."

"I do not believe," the Reverend shouted, whipping off his belt and seizing Charity, turning her, bending her over a chair back—"that you are as innocent as they. I have seen you look at her, I have seen her look at you, and I have seen the lust—the unnatural lust—on both your faces. The Devil is in you, and the Devil"—here he raised the belt and brought it down hard across her back, time and time and time again— "the Devil must be cast out."

She did not cry, not then, and not later, when her mother brought cool cloths and a bowl of hot soup to her room. She did not speak either. When her mother left, she sat by her window, silently talking to God, at last admitting to her Heavenly Father what she hadn't dared admit to herself or to her earthly one: that she did indeed love Andrea and Andrea loved her, and that their love was more than Ruth and Naomi's, David and Jonathan's. Their love was all that and more, and, no matter what anyone thought, it could not possibly be all the evil things her father said it was—for weren't they gentle and kind with each other, and didn't she feel in love with God's whole beautiful world because of the love she felt for Andrea?

"It's my father who's evil," she whispered very late that night, when everyone else in the house was asleep. "My father who preaches love. But love is kind and good, love protects and nurtures. God can't be cruel when His own Son was kind and loving and forgiving"—for she had looked carefully through her Bible and had not found anyplace where Jesus himself condemned love, not even the kind of love she now understood she felt for Andrea and Andrea felt for her.

Just before dawn, Charity opened her closet door and removed the small brown suitcase that she had taken to family Bible camp the summer she was ten. Into it she put underwear and socks and a few outer clothes. She slid her poetry books into her knapsack along with her wallet, which held twenty dollars in babysitting money and thirty dollars in crab-picking money left over from the previous summer. And then she wrote a note to her mother:

Mama,

I've gone away. I'm not sure where. When I find work and settle someplace, I'll let you know. I love you and Jonathan, but I can't stay here anymore. I am what Father thinks I am, and I know he wouldn't want for me to stay. I love Andrea and she loves me. I know that our love is good and I am going to try earn enough money to make a life for us someplace, if she'll have me, where someday we can live in peace and not have to be afraid of people like Father.

Love,
Charity

Charity folded the note over, wrote "Mama" on the outside in her best and most elegant script, and put it on her pillow.

She wrote another note also, a letter, really, this one to Andrea, full of love and pain and hope, ending with

So when I call you or write you, please tell me if you don't want to be with me that way, and I'll understand. But if you do want to be with me, please, please say yes, and I'll come back for you and take you to where we can be together.

All my love forever,
either way.
Charity

Then, taking that letter with her to mail, she wiped away the tears that had finally spilled from her eyes and very quietly left her parents' house.

STONEWALL

LISTEN, I WASN'T IN IT. BUT I SAW SOME OF IT. AND I BOTH CHEERED AND cried when I found out what it was about, what it meant. I thought it would be the end of everything bad, the beginning of everything good. In a way it was, but in a way it also wasn't. But it sure as heck made a difference, and even though I didn't know much, I knew that as soon as I saw what it was.

Let me back up a little. My name's Waverly Terras. I know that's a heck of a name for a guy; I agree. At least my friends call me Wave, which is a whole lot better. But I always have to explain Waverly. It's because eighteen years and nine-plus months before the night I'm going to tell you about, I was conceived on Waverly Place in New York City, where my parents lived. They couldn't agree on a normal name, and they were pretty sentimental, so they named me after the street where my mom's apartment was. No, they weren't married then, but they were soon afterward, and they'd meant to get married all along anyway. When I was two, my folks moved north of the city to Scarsdale, which, if you know anything about New York, tells you that my parents are pretty upscale. I went to a private school in the city, commuting every day with my dad, who's a stockbroker (but also a nice guy). Mom's a librarian in Tuckahoe, which is near Scarsdale. I'm an only child, which I've always hated being. I'd tell you more about that except it's beside the point here.

I guess I've always been pretty sheltered. Well educated but sheltered. Most of what I know—okay, knew then, anyway—came from books. That was okay, of course, but there's a lot books can't tell you. For instance, books can't tell you anything but the facts about what happened on June 28, 1969. Facts are good—heck, I'm in premed now and sure need to know them—but facts are no substitute for feelings.

I'm ahead of myself again.

The summer before the one I'm going to tell you about, I had a job as a waiter and kitchen helper at a fancy inn on Cape Cod. Even the dishes smelled of money! The guests' rooms were all done in what I guess one could call New England kitsch, with chintz and fireplaces and flowered wallpaper and little doilies on the dressers and a patchwork quilt neatly folded at the foot of each bed. And that's where I met Larry, who was a waiter, too, but doubled as a sort of bellboy and assistant gardener.

In real life, Larry's a dancer besides being a student like me, only he's studying dance. He says that when he's too old to dance, he wants to be a gardener or a landscaper or something along those lines. In real life I want to be a neurosurgeon, which is why I'm doing premed. That means I'll be studying a heck of a lot for a heck of a lot of years, which adds up to a heck of a lot of tuition money, which was why the summer job on the Cape. I've wanted to be a doctor just about all my life.

All of us hired-help people, those of us who were teenagers anyway, slept in big dormitories on the top floor of the inn, guys on one side, girls on the other. Top floor = attic = hot. We closed the windows at dawn, and one of us always ran upstairs to open them at sunset, but even so, it usually took almost till dawn again for the attic to cool down. Most of us spent a lot of time outside at night, on the beach or on the inn grounds, which were extensive. Larry and I had a favorite spot under this big tree at the edge of the yard where we used to talk and stuff. No, not that kind of stuff; there was always a chance someone else would come by. Sometimes all of us went swimming at night in the ocean, and once in late August, I think it was, our bodies were outlined by phosphorescence from tiny jellyfish. Larry caught some, and it looked for a minute as if he had a handful of sparkling jewels.

Larry's the reason I was in the Village—that's Greenwich Village, New York City—that night in June the summer after we met on the

Cape. Larry lived in the Village then, and I was going to see him before we went off to different summer jobs, me back to the Cape and Larry to a dance study and performance center. His parents and little brother were away visiting some relative or other, and Larry was alone overnight in their apartment; my folks even said how nice it was of me to go down there to keep him company!

It was going to be the first time we'd be completely alone together for a whole night, and, yeah, okay, I was pretty nervous. Okay, pretty terrified. I knew what I wanted to have happen, but I'd never done it before (I'm not counting stuff I did with my best friend when I was around ten), and I was pretty sure Larry hadn't either. We'd fooled around some on the Cape, but no matter where we went, we couldn't trust that we'd be alone, and besides, maybe it sounds weird, but we didn't want to rush it. I guess maybe we already knew it was going to be really important, because we already really mattered to each other. So we'd spent that summer on the Cape getting to know each other and like each other better and better, and then that fall, Larry had to go away to boarding school. We wrote letters at first, but I'm not good at that and neither is he, so they didn't say much. We did talk on the phone a few times. At Christmas, I had to go away with my family, and, both at spring vacation and after graduation, Larry had to go away with his, so we hadn't really been in touch with each other much for almost a whole year.

By that time, I'd gone out with a couple of girls, and Larry had, too. We had a really awkward phone conversation about it when he got back to New York the week before that June night. I finally admitted I'd gone out mostly to please my parents and to get them to stop bugging me about girls, and he said he'd slept with one girl to see if he could do it. "I could," he said—and, wow, instant jealousy on my part! "But I didn't, you know, care about it much," he added really fast. "And I kept thinking of you anyway." Instant relief!

I told him I hadn't stopped thinking about him all winter, and he said the same, and then he invited me down to the Village. He said he lived pretty close to a bar called the Stonewall Inn, which turned out to be pretty close to Waverly Place, where, as I said, I was conceived! He wanted to go to the Stonewall with me, but he said he wasn't sure we should because the cops raided it a lot and hauled guys off to jail and stuff just for being there or dancing with each other or wearing female clothes. So, like a real jerk, I sort of sputtered, "You mean it's a—a homosexual bar?" and he laughed and said, "Yes, Peter Pan, a *gay* bar." He called me that sometimes when I was really naïve.

Then he said he'd gone to that bar once with a guy from his neighborhood who'd been a couple of classes ahead of him in school—just friends, he said. The guy had gotten drafted, but then he was thrown out because he was gay. It was pretty dingy in the bar, Larry told me, but he said it was still kind of nice to be with other gay people. There wasn't a raid when he was there, but there was the next night, he said.

But I wasn't thinking of any of this when I got off the train and on the subway to go to Larry's. I was remembering Larry's rich voice and the funny way he crinkled up his nose when he was surprised or didn't quite understand something. I wondered if he still did that, and if he still practiced dance positions when he was bored and jumps when he had enough space. And I was hoping that the deodorant I'd put on before I'd left the house would be strong enough if I went on sweating as much as I was sweating while the subway roared and clattered through the dank, dark tunnel. I was thinking about the way a certain part of my body was reacting to my anticipating being alone with Larry and hoping it wasn't too obvious, and I was thinking about how fast my heart was beating when the subway pulled into the Christopher Street–Sheridan Square station and I got off.

It was only about eight o'clock, and although the streets were busy, things weren't exactly jumping yet. There were lights on in most of the shops and restaurants, and there were groups of people standing around and talking. Someone was playing guitar in one of the coffee shops, and I could see the performer through the open door in a haze of cigarette smoke—well, mostly cigarette. She was very thin and pale, and dressed all in black. Her long black hair hung over the guitar like a thin, organized waterfall, and I wondered if it ever got caught in the strings.

It was still early enough for young couples to be out with their babies and little kids, and for older kids of around eight or ten or twelve to be chasing each other around or eating ice-cream cones or walking dogs. One huge, hairy black dog, a Newfoundland I think, gave my hand a friendly lick. He seemed to think it was okay that I was probably about to lose my virginity to another guy.

When I went by a bookstore that had prints in the window, my eye was caught by one of a tree that looked like the one we used to sit under, so on an impulse, I guess, I went in and bought it for Larry. I'd never been able to remember what kind of tree ours was, and I still don't, but I knew he'd remind me. Larry still kids me about never knowing the names of things—trees, songs, movie stars. It was one of the many details he knew about me even back then. I wondered how many he still remembered.

I liked that—having him know details about me that no one else knew.

I knew details about him, too. Like that he got the tiny scar-bump on his hand in a wood-carving class when he was seven. He was carving a duck out of balsa wood when his X-Acto knife slipped.

I was thinking of his hand and that scar when I got to his building, and my stomach gave a sudden lurch and I felt something hot and tight in my chest. I didn't think I was having a heart attack or anything, but it was pretty startling. I thought maybe I should walk around some more, but I suddenly had to take a leak really badly, so I took a deep breath and walked up the steps to the front door and pushed the bell marked Ludlow–3B.

The buzzer buzzed immediately, and I felt myself smile; Larry must have been watching out the window.

And then he was standing in the doorway at the head of the second flight of stairs, with a big grin on his face.

We just stood there for a few seconds, grinning, and then I tore up the stairs and we hugged like we hadn't seen each other for years instead of months.

The rolled-up tree print almost got squashed.

"Shit," Larry said, looking at the almost squashed print.

"You're welcome," I said, and we both laughed.

"Come on in." Larry took my hand and pulled me inside.

He was wearing tan chinos and this really wild shirt in all kinds of dark but vibrant earth colors that were terrific with this really gorgeous tan he had, I figured from having been to Bermuda with his parents as a graduation present.

"You look great," I said, handing the print to him, and at the same time he said the same thing, and we laughed again. Larry unrolled the print and grinned. "Thank you," he said. "It's just like our tree—our *copper beech*," he added loudly, obviously knowing I didn't have a clue, but by then I'd spotted the bathroom, so I mumbled something about having to go and headed for it, thinking dubiously about my blue-and-white striped short-sleeved shirt and my new dark blue pants, which I suddenly realized were pretty un-June-like. I'd never been too great about clothes, not like Larry, who always looked terrific—he still does—a little arty but terrific. I wondered if he'd be embarrassed to be seen with me, you know, if we went to a bar or something.

Larry was in the kitchen when I went into the living room, so I sat down on the sofa.

In a couple of minutes Larry came out of the kitchen with a bottle of wine and two glasses.

Okay, listen. Scientist that I am, I know from a couple of English classes that there's a point in lots of old Victorian novels where the author says something like "And now, dear reader, I shall draw a veil." I know you're really interested in what comes next, and I'll tell you some of it, but I warn you right now I'm not going to tell you everything. Some things are private. I hope you'll understand.

We drank some of the wine, and we talked a lot, mostly filling each other in on the time we hadn't really been in touch. We were both very nervous, which is why our conversation, if you can call it that, really isn't worth repeating. We got hungry and went into the kitchen and found some crackers and cheese and a bag of corn chips, but as I was putting the crackers on a plate and Larry was hunting for a knife for the cheese, we suddenly stopped doing what we were doing and put the food down and our arms around each other and had this really long, deep, wonderful kiss. And then Larry smiled his great smile and put his hand on my shoulder and steered me into his bedroom.

I told you I was going to draw a veil, didn't I?

I will say that we were kind of clumsy and a crazy combination of eager and polite. Larry knew more than I (and for a second or two I wondered about that guy he'd been to the Stonewall Inn with, but that didn't last long). I think we made most of it up as we went along, at least I did, and it was pretty fine. We laughed a lot sometimes, which helped.

And then we fell asleep.

Let me tell you, one of the most wonderful things in the world is to fall asleep in the arms of someone you love, or curled up close to him anyway; sometimes hugs have a way of putting one's arms "asleep" after a while and keeping the rest of one awake! Larry and I slept for a few hours, and then when I woke up, he was looking down at me and brushing his hair against my face, tickling me. He bent lower and kissed me and lay for a few minutes on top of me, not moving, and then he whispered, "I'm starving!" and I whispered, "Me, too!" and we both got up. He put on an old bathrobe he said he'd had forever and gave me his regular one to put on, and we went into the kitchen and made bacon and eggs and toast, and then decided to go for a walk. We got dressed, and it was twenty of two or so, I think, on Saturday morning when we crept quietly down the stairs and out into the street.

There were still lots of people out, and we heard sirens, but I knew that one almost always does in New York. For a while we just walked, sometimes daring to hold hands but usually not. There seemed to be a lot of cops around, and we didn't want to take any chances. I think we both felt new, reborn, almost, and as if we shared a special, exciting secret about ourselves and each other. Every once in a while we'd look at each other and grin. "Look at all these people," I whispered at one point. "They don't know what we've just done!"

For some reason that seemed like the funniest thing in the world, and I burst out laughing. Larry laughed, too, and we were still laughing when we turned onto Christopher Street and heard louder sirens and saw a big crowd right near a bar Larry said was the Stonewall Inn. People were yelling and throwing things, coins and bricks and bottles, mostly, and there was a lot of smoke—smoke from fire, not cigarettes or pot. Some made-up guys—drag queens, I guess—were dancing around, throwing stuff, too. We saw cops pushing people, mostly men but a few women, into paddy wagons, but some of the people got right out again. There were lots of scruffy-looking kids there, you know, teenagers and maybe a little older. I didn't see very many women, but one guy said a tough-looking lesbian kept fighting back when the cops tried to arrest her. He said he thought they finally stuffed her into one of their cars.

We stood there at the edge of everything that was happening, staring.

"My God," said Larry. "It's a real riot!"

"You bet it is, honey," this queen said, glancing at us as he—maybe I should say "she"—ran past in heels. "We're gonna show them we're not gonna take it anymore."

"Larry," I said stating the obvious but realizing it for the first time, really. "He—he's gay! They're all gay. The people rioting. They're like us. And they're—they're hitting back at the cops. They're trashing that bar—the Stonewall Inn . . ."

Larry nodded, and we stood there, definitely hand in hand this time, moving out of the way when we had to but not looking away from what was happening, even when we saw real flames inside the inn. It was hard to keep track of what was going on; it was like a million little dramas were happening all around us. A bunch more cops roared up, and someone said they were the riot squad—the TPF, which was known for breaking up peace demonstrations, you know, demonstrations against the Vietnam War. Those guys started grabbing people and beating them up when they could catch them. One came up to us and shoved us farther away, and Larry grabbed my arm when I guess I was about to shove him back—shove the cop, I mean.

Then someone yelled "Gay power!" and I saw a bunch of the scruffy kids dancing in a sort of chorus line and singing what sounded like "We are the Stonewall girls, we wear our hair in curls." I couldn't hear the rest of it, but those kids were taunting the cops and looked like they were having fun doing it, even though some of the cops were chasing them. I was a little scared and a lot excited, and part of me ached to join in, but I didn't want to leave Larry standing there maybe in the path of some cop's nightstick or a flying bottle or something. I think we both tried to shield each other from the worst of the fighting, and I tried to be ready to catch whatever came toward us, so I could throw it back, maybe at the cops.

As we stood there watching, I suddenly felt tears in my eyes—excited, happy tears—and I thought of the race riots I'd heard about that had gone on in New Jersey and other places where black people were so angry at the cops and at how slowly they were getting their civil rights that they were tearing their own neighborhoods down. It hit me then that that was what this was about, and I wondered if gay people—*our* people, I thought, feeling for the first time that I was really one of them—were going to tear down the whole Village.

They didn't, of course, but the Stonewall riots lasted a few more nights, and I was mad I had to go back to uptight Scarsdale and hear about them on the phone from Larry or on the radio. I'd never heard anything about gay people on the radio before, but I sure did then. A lot of it was pretty mean, but some of it was okay, and people were saying that things would never be the same again, never as bad for us.

And they weren't. There are still lots of battles to fight and win, but people are fighting them harder and louder now than ever before. Larry and me? We've had our ups and downs, but we're both still in New York, living together, and, when he can take time from rehearsing and I can take time from studying, we're helping fight some of those battles.

But that's beside the point. The point is that on that June night, bad stuff like those bar raids and the army's rules and other things that I found out later had been simmering for ages and had been protested about softly and politely, finally burst angrily out into the open, giving birth to a whole new movement, louder and stronger than before. And that's made me and Larry realize there's no stopping us now.

1970s

THE DECADE

IT WASN'T JUST STONEWALL THAT MADE 1969 A LANDMARK YEAR IN GAY AND lesbian history. Although as far as I know there was no connection, it was also in 1969 that Harper & Row published the first young adult novel that openly acknowledged homosexual feelings on the part of teens, the late John Donovan's *I'll Get There. It Better Be Worth the Trip.* In Donovan's groundbreaking book, there's a scene in which the main character, thirteen-year-old Davy, and his best friend, Altschuler, are playing on the floor with Davy's dog when suddenly the mood changes and they kiss. This incident and one or two others put a strain on their friendship and for a while fill Davy with guilt. Eventually, though, the boys reestablish their friendship. Are they gay? Maybe, maybe not. That's not clear, probably intentionally. What is clear is that Donovan's book heralded the beginning of a new, gay-friendly era in young adult publishing, just as Stonewall heralded the beginning of a new era in the battle for GLBT rights.

There were many important firsts in the seventies. Stonewall had galvanized gays nationwide, but especially on the East and West coasts, and it has rightly been called the start of the modern gay rights movement. On June 28, 1970, a few hundred members of the gay community marched on the streets of New York in the Christopher Street Liberation Day parade, commemorating Stonewall. Hundreds more—thousands, in fact—celebrated in Central Park after the march, which amounted to the first gay pride parade. Since then, gay pride parades and celebrations have been held in a growing number of cities across the country, most of them in June. And in 1979, an estimated 100,000 people marched in Washington, D.C., in the first national March for

Lesbian and Gay Rights. No one could even have imagined that back in the closeted fifties!

The impulse to marry has long existed among gay and lesbian couples in love, even dating from long before the United States was a country. For example, in some Native American tribes, men who dressed as women and did women's work lived in close relationships with other men, and in modern times, many gay and lesbian couples have lived together and shared their lives "for better or worse" just as closely as straight married couples. Among lesbians, sometimes in order to actually marry, one woman would dress and pass as a man, or pretend to have a man's name, and, using that disguise, the couple would seek and obtain a marriage license. But of course those licenses weren't really legal, since they were obtained fraudulently. In the 1920s in Harlem, a number of black lesbian couples got marriage licenses in this fashion, or by having a gay male friend apply for one of the two women. More often, though, gay or lesbian couples, often holding private ceremonies of their own creation, quietly set up housekeeping and remained together for many years—without the benefit of the legal protections of actual marriage, or, in many cases, without even the knowledge of their friends and families.

But it was in the 1970s that gay and lesbian couples openly began to seek legal marriage.

The first couple to apply openly were from California, Neva Joy Heckman and Judith Ann Belew. In California at that time, two people who had lived together for two years, as these women had, were allowed to have a church wedding, receive a church certificate attesting to that, and be considered married by the state. But although Heckman and Belew were married by the Reverend Troy Perry of the Metropolitan Community Church, they were not granted an official California marriage license.

Also in the early seventies, James Michael McConnell and Richard John Baker, in Minnesota, and Tracy Knight and Marjorie Ruth Jones, in Kentucky, applied for marriage licenses but ultimately were not successful, nor were Manonia Evans and Donna Burkett (also spelled Berkett), in Milwaukee. This lesbian couple, when their application was denied, protested by suing in federal court in 1971, but they eventually dropped their case.

All these courageous couples were among the first gays and lesbians in this country to try to marry legally, but they were certainly not the last. In fact, for around a month in 1975, some same-sex couples actually succeeded in getting marriage licenses in Boulder, Colorado. Six couples got married before the practice was outlawed, and according to the gay newsmagazine *The Advocate*, at least one couple, Anthony Sullivan and Richard Adams, were still living together in the early twenty-first century.

But legally sanctioned same-sex marriage was still a long way off.

New gay organizations, some of them much more confrontational than the old ones—some were even offshoots of the old ones—sprang up on both coasts in the seventies and, as the decade progressed, in other parts of the country as well; as early as 1974, there were more than a thousand! Two of the first new ones, both founded in 1970, were for trans people: Street Transvestite Action Revolutionaries, known as STAR, and the Transsexual Transvestite Action Organization. All-lesbian organizations burgeoned as lesbian feminists broke away from predominantly male groups, joining together in their own organizations, plus founding or participating in lesbian-feminist presses, bookstores, the famous Michigan Womyn's Music Festival, and other new ventures.

In 1972 for the first time, gays tried to get the Democratic Party to add a gay rights plank to the platform that they would present at the Democratic National Convention—that's the one that chooses the party's presidential nominee. They weren't successful, but an openly gay delegate, Jim Foster, was allowed to speak at that convention, and a pro-gay plank was finally accepted in 1980.

In 1973, the American Psychiatric Association voted to remove homosexuality from its list of mental illnesses. Two years later, the Amer-

ican Psychological Association did the same. Also in 1973, the National
Gay Task Force (now the National Gay and Lesbian Task Force) and
the Lambda Legal Defense and Education Fund were both established
and soon were working for the passage of gay civil rights legislation
across the country. A lesbian, Elaine Noble, was elected to the Massachusetts House in 1974—the first openly gay person to be elected as a
state legislator. And in 1975, David Kopay, an NFL running back, became the first professional athlete to come out. It was years before Kopay was followed by other popular athletes, including such stars as
Martina Navratilova, Rudy Galindo, Greg Louganis, and, more recently, Sheryl Swoopes.

Throughout the seventies, resistance mounted to the military's
practice of rooting out gay and lesbian service personnel and giving
them less than honorable discharges if their homosexuality became
known. For decades before that, gays and lesbians who served their
country willingly with dedication and courage had silently borne such
discharges, plus the harassment, investigations, and legal action that
led to them. Robert Martin, Jeffrey Dunbar, Copy Berg, and Leonard
Matlovich were among the first who finally protested the military's in-
stitutionalized homophobia. The servicewoman perhaps best known
for protesting the military's anti-gay policy emerged long after the seventies. She was the much-decorated army nurse Colonel Margarethe
Cammermeyer, who came out in 1989 when she was being questioned
before being given a security clearance—and as a result was discharged. After a lengthy court battle, she was finally reinstated in 1994,
the same year her autobiography, *Serving in Silence*, was published. A
year later, a TV movie with the same title publicized her story further.

Many of the early protesters were reinstated toward the end of the
seventies or had their discharges changed to honorable ones, but despite protests, court battles, and stories like Cammermeyer's, the military's anti-gay policies have continued into the twenty-first century.

In the 1970s, gay and lesbian college students agitated increasingly
for their rights, both on and off campus. But gay adults remained

nervous about reaching out to minors, and many straight adults doubted that teenagers still in high school or younger could be genuinely gay. "It's probably just a stage," the kindest of them said. Other adults still believed homosexuality was a curable illness or morally evil, and still tried to "cure" or "reform" teens.

Even so, in the seventies, attitudes toward gay and lesbian youth were at last—quietly, slowly—beginning to change. In 1972, at the second annual Christopher Street Liberation Day parade, a courageous elementary school teacher named Jeanne Manford marched next to her gay activist son Morty, carrying a sign that read PARENTS OF GAYS: UNITE IN SUPPORT FOR OUR CHILDREN. Soon she was appearing on TV on behalf of gay and lesbian youth, and in 1973 she and other parents of gay kids formed a group that began holding regular meetings. Similar groups formed in a number of states and were the forerunners of PFLAG (Parents, Families and Friends of Lesbians and Gays), a national organization that has helped countless families adjust to and accept their GLBT children. Today PFLAG groups are enthusiastically and gratefully cheered at gay pride parades, and PFLAG parents are considered heroes by most of us.

At the end of the decade, Damien Martin, a speech and audiology professor at New York University, and his partner, psychiatrist Dr. Emery Hetrick, incensed at the gang rape and beating of a fifteen-year-old gay boy and at his being thrown out of a shelter, also realized it was high time more was done to reach out to gay youth. Many gay and lesbian teens, especially those outside big cities, didn't know that other gays even existed, and many still were so despondent and lonely that they were prone to suicide. As in the sixties and earlier, gay teens who ran away from home and had no source of income often supported themselves by prostitution. Hetrick and Martin's Institute for the Protection of Lesbian and Gay Youth, which exists today as the Hetrick-Martin Institute, was one of the first organizations specifically formed for gay and lesbian teens—perhaps the second one after Vanguard in San Francisco.

As the 1970s drew to a close, despite great progress, there was still a long way to go. There had been little mainstream coverage of gay anti-discrimination battles, and there still were very few books, movies, or TV shows that openly and honestly portrayed GLBT characters. Gay, lesbian, bisexual, and transgender people were still harassed and beaten by the police and by ordinary people. Many were denied employment and housing when they were found to be or suspected of being gay. And now a serious backlash against our progress was growing. In 1977, Anita Bryant, a singer who helped the Florida Citrus Commission promote its juice, campaigned against gay rights ordinances in that state's Dade County on the mistaken grounds that we were child molesters and that we "recruited" children to ensure that there would be a steady supply of gay people. She won the support of many straights, and her efforts led to the repeal of gay rights ordinances in several parts of the country.

But to politically aware gays, especially those in San Francisco, one of the worst manifestations of the backlash was the assassination on November 27, 1978, of gay San Francisco supervisor Harvey Milk along with San Francisco's gay-friendly mayor, George Moscone. Both men were fatally shot by Dan White, a disgruntled anti-gay former member of the city's Board of Supervisors. Milk, one of the first openly gay elected officials in the United States, had spoken eloquently about his belief that homosexuals are entitled to the same rights as straight people, and he urged fellow gays to come out of their closets in order to help reach that goal and to show the world that gay people are as diverse as straight people. When after three unsuccessful attempts at running for the San Francisco Board of Supervisors, Milk was finally elected, he introduced a gay rights bill that was passed by the city council and signed by Mayor Moscone. Milk also worked hard to defeat a statewide proposition that would have banned lesbian and gay teachers from public schools and prevented anyone who worked at a school from saying anything positive about homosexuality.

Dan White was the only member of the Board of Supervisors

who'd voted against Milk's gay rights bill, and he had been in favor of the anti-gay school proposition. Not long before he killed Milk and Moscone, he'd left the Board of Supervisors voluntarily—then asked to be put back on it. Milk urged against reinstating him, Moscone agreed—and White crawled through a window with a gun and shot first Moscone and then Milk, killing them both.

Gay San Francisco was devastated by Milk's murder; thousands mourned him in a peaceful candlelight vigil. But later, when White was convicted of manslaughter instead of murder and given a light sentence, gays in San Francisco rioted, causing more than a million dollars' worth of property damage in what came to be known as the White Night Riots.

The intense pain and anger shown by those riots, plus the positive changes of the seventies, showed that, despite serious setbacks, the momentum started by Stonewall and by those who had struggled for many years before Stonewall now could not be stopped.

And thanks to Jeanne Manford and other parents, plus the Glide Foundation, Damien Martin, Emery Hetrick, Harvey Milk, and others, at last that momentum began to be directed toward gay teens as well as adults—although many teens would still be painfully isolated, misunderstood, and victimized for some time to come.

MAYBE SOMEDAY?

"WHAT DO YOU MEAN YOU AREN'T GOING TO CONFESSION?"

Papa's voice thundered down the hall of the Angelinis' railroad apartment, bouncing off the walls and into Teresa's room. Moments later, Papa appeared in her open doorway, a giant silhouette.

Teresa was unmoved. Papa always yelled. He yelled when dinner was late; he yelled when he had to go outside in bad weather; he yelled when the subway stalled in the tunnel; he yelled when any of his three children did something of which he disapproved.

But underneath the yells, he was, as Mama said, gentle as a kitten and sentimental as an old woman. Teresa knew that; Nana, Papa's mother, who lived with them, knew it; Mama knew it better than anyone—but Annemarie, who was ten, still wasn't convinced, and little Joseph, who was seven, had no idea and blocked his ears when Papa yelled if he thought Papa wasn't looking.

"I'm not going to confession because I don't have anything to confess," Teresa explained, outwardly calm.

"Oh, so you're *Saint* Teresa now, even though you run around with that bunch of juvenile delinquent girls and defy the teachings of your church? There's still time; go."

"Papa . . ."

"You heard me, go."

Teresa sighed and reluctantly got up from where she'd been sitting on the edge of her bed. Her unmade bed.

"If nothing else," Papa said, tugging her long, dark hair affectionately as she squeezed past him through the door, "you can tell Father Santini that you didn't make your bed, eh, *carissima*?"

"Yeah, Papa, okay," she called back at him, running down the long hall to the front of the apartment and grabbing her new black leather jacket as she went out.

"And you can tell your mother you'll make your bed when you get home," Papa shouted.

"Supper's at six, Teresa," Mama called from the kitchen as Teresa slammed the door to the hall.

"Yeah, so when isn't it?" Teresa muttered as she ran down the three flights to the building's ground floor, twirling her hair into a lopsided knot at the back of her neck (her parents wouldn't let her cut it), and securing it with pins she took out of her skirt pocket. Moments later she was in a phone booth on the corner, dropping coins into the slot, dialing, tapping her foot and her fingers while it rang—

"Meg," she said softly, urgently, into the receiver, "Meg, it's Terry, he's yelling again, making me go to confession, but I'm not going, so I have to kill time. Meet me on Saint Agnes's front steps, can you?"

She listened for a moment, then slapped her hand down on the phone box, growled "Damn!" and "Bye," and slammed the receiver onto its rack. "Damn parents," she said under her breath, more good-natured, though, than mad, and went to confession after all.

But what she didn't confess and never had confessed sat in her mind like a huge lump of black coal, the kind Papa used to swear Santa brought instead of presents to bad kids, only Santa had never done that at their house, no matter how bad the Angelini kids were. The black lump emerged whenever Teresa walked into church. She could ignore it, some anyway, during the week, when she could block out most reminders of sin and God and the Blessed Mother and priests and confession. "Be glad you don't still go to Catholic school like me," her friend Meg had said to her more than once. Although Meg didn't know about the lump of coal or what prompted it, she did know that church made Teresa feel squirmy. Even her own name made her feel squirmy, despite the fact that when she and Annemarie had gone through *Lives of the Saints* trying to find better names, she'd learned that Saint Teresa of Avila had a father as pious and strict as her own (without the underlying gentleness), and that she herself had been a troublemaker and a runaway. But Saint Teresa had also been a boy-crazy teenager, which Teresa Angelini most certainly was not!

The opposite, maybe.

But that was sick. Mentally. Very, very sick.

And evil. Sinful.

When she was still at Saint Mary's and had preferred playing stickball in the street and FBI in the supposedly dangerous condemned building next door with Tony Faustino—when she'd preferred that to playing dolls and house and bride with prim scaredy-cat Joanie Mirabella, Papa had bemoaned her dirty face and tangled hair, but Mama had just laughed and said, "She's a tomboy, so was I, she'll grow out of it." But by the time Teresa was thirteen, Mama had begun taking her to the beauty parlor and buying her bubble bath and lacy slips and showing her how to shave her legs, and Papa opened doors for her and grabbed heavy things out of her hands, saying she might do harm to her insides if she lifted and carried them. He looked hurt when she exploded with anger and called him old-fashioned, but Teresa couldn't help it, and she felt there was a secret person inside her trying to get out. "They won't let me be me," she'd confided to her favorite nun at Saint Mary's, jolly, round-faced Sister M, who taught art and whose name was too hard for anyone to pronounce and who jokingly called Teresa, Terry Spitfire. "You're fine, Terry, just as God made you," Sister M said, "exuberant and strong. You'll be a fine woman one day, the mother of sons maybe, and a friend and help to your husband."

But the idea of a husband made Teresa squirm.

Secretly, Teresa had thanked God when Papa lost his job the summer she'd graduated from eighth grade. There was no longer enough money for Catholic school tuition, and there was too much pride for Papa to ask for help from anyone, so she and Annemarie had to go to public school that fall. Papa found work that January, but not enough salary to feed six people and pay the tuition comfortably, and Teresa had managed to convince him and Mama and Nana that she'd be better off going to public high school than to Saint Ann's High; she'd made new friends, she said (but she really still preferred the old ones, whom she'd known since they'd all been in first grade at Saint Mary's). "Annemarie," Teresa had told her parents—truthfully—"hasn't made any new friends in public school. But if I go to public high school, there'll be tuition money for Annemarie to go back to Saint Mary's. Maybe there'll even be enough for Joseph when he's old enough."

That had clinched it for Papa, even though he made it very clear he was nervous about Teresa's going to high school with boys, especially non-Catholic ones.

Teresa laughed at that one.

"An angel," Nana had called her, because of her "sacrifice" at giving up a Catholic education so her sister and brother could have one.

"Ummmm," Mama had said, giving Teresa a knowing look, and Teresa had realized that Mama believed Teresa's main reason was the selfish one of wanting to stay with her mythical new friends. Okay, so that wasn't true, but letting Mama believe that it was the reason didn't seem like a really bad lie, unless you delved into what was underneath it. Teresa was sure Mama had no idea how desperately she needed to avoid anything that reminded her of the fear of being crazy and a guilty sinner. She'd even hoped for a while that going to school with those boys Papa was so suspicious of might help change her, but it hadn't. If anything it had made her even surer of her craziness and her sin.

The guilt and fear rose in her throat nearly choking her whenever she thought of the reason she didn't feel about boys the way her old friends Meg and Barbara and Claire and Marie did. She'd looked it up long ago, back when she was still at Saint Mary's and someone had called her a "lezzie," and then had used the real word for it, and although it was a comfort to have an explanation, she knew that if that was what she really was, she could have no future save a life of misery, loneliness, and illness without the comfort of the church. Paranoia, she'd read; schizophrenia (she'd had to look both of them up, too, in the big encyclopedia in the public library)—craziness, they meant— and after that, burning in hell forever; that was to be her fate if she let herself be who she increasingly knew she was.

So at James Dobbs High, she kept her eyes closed in the girls' locker room and shot baskets by herself after school till she dropped with exhaustion, and in classes she did everything she could to ignore the girls. In fact, she'd even pretended to flirt with the boys till they'd gotten interested, but after forcing herself to go out with a couple of them her sophomore year, she'd stopped, and this year she was pre- tending to her classmates that she'd met a boy during the summer and was writing to him. That was another lie, of course, but since she was damned already, it probably didn't matter. And at least, thanks to Sister M, she had enough confidence to go on being as much of her real self as possible, "exuberant and strong," even though she'd vowed never to be anyone's wife or mother. In the back of her mind for years had been the idea that if who she was turned out to be as lonely and miserable as the books said, she could perhaps become a nun; surely that would please her parents and show God she was trying.

But the older she got, the more aware she was of having no real re- ligious vocation. And if she was honest with herself, she knew that put her right back to where she'd started.

At Sunday dinner at the end of the weekend on which she'd ended up at confession after all, relieved after Mass of the coal lump for nearly another week, Teresa, in her dark blue dress with the white collar and the stockings that were itchy on her thin legs and that bagged uncom- fortably around her narrow ankles, dutifully held a platter at the ready in the kitchen while Annemarie stood behind her with the soon-to-be- filled potato dish. All the men and the old ladies Nana's age sat in dif-

ferent corners of the living room, the men drinking the red wine that
Uncle (he was the oldest man, and they always called him just Uncle)
brought every Sunday, smoking and arguing about the chances of
Notre Dame's football team that season, while the old ladies gossiped
about who was in the hospital for what. Mama and her sisters and their
daughters who were old enough to help bustled hotly around the small
and crowded kitchen, talking of babies and sewing and weather, while
they stirred, tasted, added, and peered into saucepans and the oven,
tossing pot holders back and forth and laughing. The youngest children raced around the apartment, getting underfoot and ignoring the
adults who now and then yelled at them halfheartedly. The aromas of
roast veal, potatoes, stuffed escarole, eggplant, caponata, stuffed shells,
tomato sauce, sliced tomatoes and basil and oil and mozzarella, olives,
grated Parmesan, garlic, oregano, rosemary, and hot fresh bread all
mingled like a well-trained choir under Mama's direction—and, finally, Mama announced, "I think we're ready."

Teresa edged closer to the stove with the platter as Mama opened
the oven door and grasped the edge of the center shelf with her oven
mitt, pulling it out—but then she turned, looked, and said, "No, no,
Teresa, honey; you take the—I don't know—the eggplant, something;
get Vincent—*Vincent!* Where is that boy? He'll take the roast; it's too
heavy for you. *Vincent!*"

"No, Mama, it's okay, I'm strong, I'll take it."

"Thinks she's a boy, that one," muttered one of the aunts, Mama's
oldest sister, the one Teresa had never liked and vice versa.

Still stooped over the stove, Mama wiped her perspiring forehead
with the edge of her apron. As the hot air from the oven mingled with
the smell of roast veal, rosemary, and garlic, she pulled the shelf out
farther and, grunting and red-faced with the effort, lifted the huge
roasting pan up and out, sliding it heavily onto the stove top. "Vincent!" she shouted again, her face red and dripping.

"Come on, Ma," Teresa coaxed, making the still-empty platter bob
up and down. "I can do it."

But then in came Vincent, Teresa's cousin, who was nineteen and tall and strong, with biceps that bulged against the sleeves of his close-fitting white knitted shirt. Teresa both admired and hated him. He was the family's hope, the first of them all to go to "real" college as opposed to business or technical college, and he was headed, his proud father boasted at every opportunity, for medical school one day with the help of well-earned scholarships.

"Hey, muscles, I'll get that," Vinny boomed, taking the platter from Teresa and winking at her.

She stuck her tongue out at him, hurt and angry at one more reminder of who she was supposed to be and wasn't. She wanted to shout the truth to them all, and at the same time wanted it to go away and make her like everyone else so her family would truly love her, and so God would, too.

Vincent shook his head, lifting a finger from the edge of the platter and wagging it as Mama and one of her sisters, armed with metal spatulas and giant forks, transferred the roast. Still wagging his finger at Teresa, Vincent marched into the dining room, yelling, "Come and get it!" to the crowd in the living room.

Adults and teenagers squeezed around the big table, and children settled noisily with Joseph and Annemarie at the card table in the corner. Teresa saw that Annemarie, who was grumbling about sitting with the younger children, had spilled gravy on her pale green dress and was trying unsuccessfully to hide it under her napkin.

Quiet fell over the room as Papa asked the blessing and they all crossed themselves. What if they knew? Teresa thought, her eyes filling with tears as she looked around at this, her family, her loud, warm, loving family, who, innocent of the viper in their midst, were eating, drinking, laughing, kidding one another: "So, Tony, that used car you bought? I heard the last owner was a little old lady, only drove it to church." "Vinny, I have this ache in my shoulder, and . . ." "No more morning sickness, eh, Rose?" "Hello, over there, Joseph. You got an A in penmanship, I hear, good boy!" "That new priest over at Saint

Bart's . . ." "Sure, Notre Dame can." "Yeah, out on Long Island, a whole bucket of clams." "Now, look, on the Fourth of July, why don't we all . . ." "Poor old Mrs. Giardina upstairs, she . . ."

Then, above the cheerful Sunday-dinner cacophony came Uncle's voice: "Teresa, keeping the boys at bay, are you? Pretty girl like you, must be hundreds."

And Teresa, her tears threatening to spill over, pushed her chair back and ran from the table.

"Teenagers," she heard softly, apologetically from her mother in the stunned silence that followed. "Moods change like the wind."

Later, her mother came into her room, bearing a tray that held a glass of milk and a plate with a slice of veal and a piece of bread, a single stuffed shell, a generous spoonful of caponata, which Teresa loved, a few olives, and some tomato salad. "You have to eat, honey," she said, setting the tray down on the table between Teresa's bed and Anne-marie's. She herself sat on Annemarie's. "Don't mind Uncle. He means well—no tact, but he means well." She moved to the other bed and brushed Teresa's hair back. "What is it?" she asked softly. "What?"

Teresa shook her head.

"Don't give me 'nothing,' " Mama warned. "Nothing doesn't make people run away from Sunday dinner. You can tell me," she said. "Whatever it is."

"I can't," Teresa moaned, choking back renewed tears. "I can't!"

"Teresa"—and Teresa could see the worry escalating in her mother's eyes, hear it in her mother's voice. "Are you in trouble?"

"Trouble? No, what—"

"You know what I mean, Teresa. In trouble. With a boy. Have you . . ."

Teresa wanted to laugh and cry at the same time. "That way— Oh, no, Mama, no, it's not that, no."

Her mother smiled hesitantly. "You wouldn't lie?"

Teresa shook her head.

"You'd tell me?"

"Yes."

Mama put her hand under Teresa's chin and looked her in the eye. "You promise? You swear on—on the Blessed Mother's name, you swear?"

Teresa closed her eyes; she felt sad, afraid, exhausted, as if she were a hundred years old, maybe.

"I swear, Mama."

"Well, then." Her mother brushed her hair back again and pushed the tray closer to her. "Come on, Teresa, eat, you'll be hungry later if you don't. Uncle brought cannoli, too, for dessert."

Resignedly, Teresa picked at the caponata.

"That's better. Now, what is it? You like a boy and he doesn't like you? Me, too, at your age. Boys are worms then, all they care about is cars and what they can get from girls. Other girls, I mean, fast ones, the wrong kind. You have to watch for that. He doesn't like you, Teresa, he's not good enough for you. Later, you'll see. The boys will get older and smarter, and then, boom, one day you'll fall in love and he'll love you back and it'll be the most wonderful feeling in the world."

Teresa tried to smile. "Is that what happened with you and Papa?" she asked, steering the subject into safe waters.

"Yes and no. But we're not talking about me and Papa. What's his name?"

"Mama, it's not a boy."

"No?"

Her mother's eyes, Teresa saw, looked startled now. If only, she thought fleetingly, Mama could imagine the truth! If only I could talk to her. If only . . .

"What is it then, *carissima*? You can tell me, Teresa, I couldn't talk to my mother, but you can talk to me. Remember when you were a little girl and you took a nickel from my pocketbook and you finally told me? I was so proud, so proud of your honesty and your trust." She eyed Teresa closely again. "Teresa?" she asked significantly.

"Mama, no! No, no, and no. I haven't stolen anything or cheated or been mean to anyone. It's nothing like that, nothing."

"Drugs, smoking those marijuana cigarettes?" Fear flooded her mother's eyes. "You wouldn't, oh, Teresa, no, please no!"

"No, Mama. I wouldn't."

"Your period, maybe? You have cramps? A headache?" Teresa was about to say yes to end the questioning, but then her mother said, "You think something's wrong with you? We could see the doctor . . ."

"No, nothing like that." Quickly, Teresa took her mother's hands. "I'm sorry, Mama. I've just been in a bad mood. You know. Just sad with no reason. I shouldn't have run off like that." She forced a smile and began eating the veal, which by then was stone cold.

Two evenings later, a short while before supper, black-and-white images from the TV set in the Angelinis' living room flickered and flashed their way toward the dining room table, where Teresa, Annemarie, and Joseph were doing homework. The sound, turned down low so it wouldn't disturb them, buzzed across a social studies book, a science workbook, and an early reader. Then—

Teresa's head snapped up when she heard it: "Today homosexuals gathered downtown near City Hall here and in several other municipalities across the country, holding signs announcing and praising this week's vote of the American Psychiatric Association, which removed homosexuality from the list of mental disorders . . ."

"Ha!" Papa boomed as Teresa got up as if pulled by an invisible string and edged toward the living room. "Psychiatrists! What do they know? It's against God, that sickness. They should be curing those pitiful, sinful people, cleansing them, not encouraging them. Look at them, flaunting themselves, it's sick—"

"Marco," Mama said quietly, "shh. The children!"

A small group of normal-looking men and two or three equally normal-looking women, Teresa saw briefly as her father pushed himself out of his chair, the men in suits and the women in dresses, stood silently in front of City Hall, holding signs. As a reporter held a mike up to one, her father arrived at the set and switched channels.

Teresa faded back to the dining room table. But the print on her social studies book swam before her eyes, and in her mind the words "removed homosexuality from the list of mental disorders" echoed all night long.

"God, thank you," she dared to pray once she was safely in bed. "Thank you! They looked so normal. And those doctors say they are. Doctors! They must know."

So, she thought as she drifted toward a restless sleep, so maybe it's really not craziness!

I'm not really crazy.

And if it isn't craziness, maybe it really isn't a sin either.

If it's true that God made me the way I am, how can what I am be sinful?

She sat up, wide awake again.

"I didn't do anything to be who I am, God," she prayed. "I didn't."

Maybe, she thought, her heart beating very fast, maybe Father Santini doesn't understand that. But maybe if priests find out that doctors were wrong about what they thought, the priests will find out they're wrong, too, about what *they* thought, and they'll stop saying it's a sin.

"Please, God, let that happen!"

If it does, then maybe someday I can tell my family.

Maybe someday I can even be me!

DEAR CUZ

Dear Cuz,

Mickey, thank you so much for the talcum powder! You were so nice to remember that I had a birthday coming up! And I really like gardenia—really, truly—even though your mother told you it's "too strong a scent for a young girl." It was so nice of you to pick it out and for you to stick to it in spite of what your mother said, so there.

That family dinner was fun. I love your farmhouse! But I was surprised that it looked smaller this time than it did the last time we visited you all those years ago. I guess that's because I was pretty little then and lots of things looked bigger than they do now.

It was fun seeing all our midwestern relatives again. The only thing I didn't like was the way Aunt Helen and Aunt Frederika and Aunt Sadie and Gramma all sat around and gossiped about people. It was so boring! I didn't expect Uncle John and Uncle Phil to join in either, and I was darn glad when you and your father started playing catch and that you let me join in. I know I'm no good with a ball, so it was especially nice of you to let me play. Thank you for not laughing at me! But what I really liked best was when you and I went to that grain elevator and the cornfields and you told me how all that stuff works. Here in New England when people grow corn it's on a pretty small scale—really tiny—in comparison. And I loved it when you showed me that calf you're raising. He's so cute! I loved his big eyes even though they looked sort of sad.

I liked that talk we had, Mickey, and I've been thinking about what you said about the guys at school who used to call you Mickey Mouse and that some of them still do, and that they called you other names, too, the ones that you wouldn't tell me. (Of course I'm curious about what they were!) Were you teased for being small for your age and stuff? And because you like reading so much? I was teased a lot in first grade for wearing glasses, if you can believe it! So many people wear glasses, and there even were a couple of others in my class who did, but I was the only one they teased. I think some kids want to pick on kids who are different but they don't know what the real difference is that they're attacking, so they find something else and use that. Maybe I'm wrong, but I got the feeling maybe there was something more about the teasing that you weren't telling me.

I also liked meeting your friend Sam. He's very nice. I'm sorry you got upset when he asked me to go out with him to the movies and didn't ask you. I didn't want to go anyway, but even if I'd wanted to, I wouldn't have. After all, it's you I was visiting!

Well, thanks again for the powder and for the nice time! I hope maybe we can write to each other now that we're a lot older than the last time we saw each other—ten years ago!—and now that we had a good time and a good talk together.

Love,

Jennifer

❧

Dear Cuz,

Hello, Jennifer.

Sam told me that he thought he should ask you out. He thought that was what you expected and he thought I did, too, but I didn't. I don't know him very well, but so far he seems really nice. He's new in my class. He's really smart and fun, and he likes a lot of the same stuff I do. He's in 4-H, like I am, and he's gotten me to go out for baseball. I guess I will. I like baseball anyway.

I guess I did have more to say when we talked. But I decided against it. For now, anyway.

This letter is getting dumb. I'm not very good at letters, but it's okay with me if we write to each other if you can stand my dumb letters.

Mickey

✑

Dear Cuz,

Of course I can stand your letters! I don't think they're dumb at all. Well, okay, you've only written one so far, but it wasn't dumb. I hope you don't feel forced into writing, though. I hope we'll be able to find things to talk about. Books, maybe? You said you like reading, and there sure were a lot of books in your room, along with the posters of singers and baseball players. I've got posters of singers in my room, too, only mine are all women and yours are all guys, so I guess we like different ones.

Let's see. What's new here? Well, our class is doing this play at school, I mean putting it on, not just reading it. It's called The Importance of Being Earnest, which is a play on words because Ernest is a man's name, and these two guys both pretend to have that name even though they don't really. One of them's named Jack, and the other's Algernon. They use the name Ernest because two girls they know (I play one of them) say they each want to love a man named Ernest. And of course "earnest" also means serious. It's a "veddy" English play, but it's "veddy" funny, too. I know it sounds pretty corny (is it okay to say that to someone whose father grows corn?), but it's REALLY funny. It's by this English guy (well, Irish, but the play's English) called Oscar Wilde, who was what they call a fop, I guess because he dressed fancy and was kind of effeminate. Well, more than kind of, I guess, since he went to jail because he loved a man. I think it was cruel to put him in jail for that, don't you?

By the way, how's that little calf?

Love,
Jennifer

◦

Dear Cuz,

Mickey? Are you there? Earth to Mickey? Are you mad at me or sick or something? You didn't answer my last letter. Or maybe it got lost in the mail, but Dad says that doesn't happen as often as people think it does.

We've done the play now, and everyone said it was very good except there was a letter to the editor in the local paper saying it was wrong of the school to "expose impressionable teenagers"—that's what the guy wrote—to "that pervert, Oscar Wilde." Can you imagine? Wilde was a great writer, our English teacher says, and I know he even wrote fairy tales, some really beautiful ones that I read when I was about eight. And he wrote lots of other stuff, too, including a really sad poem about being in jail.

I hope everything's okay there on the farm and that the calf is okay and that you and Sam are even better friends now and having a good time. Mom wants to know if you have a girlfriend, but I told her I don't think so. Am I right?

Love,
Jen

P.S. I don't have a boyfriend, by the way.

◦

Dear Cuz,

God, Mickey, I'm so sorry about what happened to you! Your mom called and cried on the phone to my mom for about an hour last night. She says you're going to be all right, but that you've got a bad concussion and bruises and broken ribs, and that you're going to be in the hospital for a week or more. She said that Sam was beaten up, too, and that he's got a broken arm and bruises, but he's not as badly off as you. I wish I could come and see you. Mom said we might fly out for Christmas, but it's awfully expensive.

Your mom didn't say much about why you guys were beaten up. She said she couldn't imagine why you were being picked on. I don't want to make you mad by trying to guess, but I think I sort of know. Please, Mickey, you can talk to me. Whatever it is, it's okay with me. I'll still be your friend, I promise.

Next day

Hi again. I've been doing some thinking. And I've decided to tell you my big secret. I'm scared about how you'll react to it, but if we're going to be friends I think you should know, and besides— Well, never mind that. Just don't tell anyone else, okay? I don't know what my parents would do if they found out. I think they'd be upset and hurt and scared and everything like that. If I'm right about it, maybe I'll tell them someday, but not now, and besides I'm not completely sure anyway. Almost, though. Probably. Mostly I wish I knew!

I guess I'd better just say it.

It's hard to know how, though.

Well, here goes nothing!

Remember what I said about Oscar Wilde? Well, I think I might be like he was. He liked men better than women, and I think I like girls better than boys. There's this girl in the class ahead of me who I like, and there have been lots of others. Well, maybe not lots, but many, all my life. Including those singers on the posters in my room.

Anyway, about the girl I like now. Her name is Heather and she's on the field hockey team and she was also in the play. She played this

old lady called Aunt Augusta, and she was really good. We got to be
friends during the play. Then during the cast party we got to really
talking, and she doesn't care much about boys either, but her mother
makes her date. She says she likes me because I'm so feminine! I
thought girls who liked girls were always kind of boyish, but she isn't
very boyish either. A little, though. More than I am, I guess, in some
ways.

I haven't told anyone else but you about me and Heather. I'm keeping my fingers crossed that you won't hate it (or me) that I did!

Anyway, Cuz, I hope you're feeling better and that you'll be home
from the hospital soon. I hate hospitals. They're always sticking you
with needles and taking your temperature and stuff. At least they did
when I had my appendix out. I was only five, but I sure remember it!

Love,
Jen

✎

Dear Cuz,

I'm sorry I haven't written.

I'm not sure what to say next.

Thank you for that letter. Mom brought it to me in the hospital,
but I couldn't really write you till now. I just got home yesterday.
Thank you for the card, too. It made me laugh. It felt good to laugh
even though it made my ribs hurt. I hadn't had a lot to laugh about before your card came.

You're right about me, I guess. You know. Oscar Wilde. I guess you
meant that. I'm sorry I didn't react at first, but it scared me. You know,
what if my parents found your letter? I'm still a little worried about
that. In the hospital I kept it in the bottom of the night table drawer.
The nurses called the night table a "unit." They went in it to get my

toothpaste and stuff, but they didn't look at anything I kept there. And I had it under a book I'd finished reading. I don't think nurses read people's mail anyway. Neither do my parents read other people's mail, but to be safe, here at home I put your letter in this hole I cut in the wall of my room when I was nine where I keep special things. There's a picture in front of it, and I don't think my parents have found it.

I don't remember a lot about what happened, but Sam remembers more, and he came to see me and told me that the guys who beat us up were yelling stuff like "queers" and "fairies" and "pansies" when they got out of their car. We were just walking along the road. We weren't even touching each other. At least Sam doesn't think we were.

I'm better now. I can sit up without feeling like I'm going to throw up because the room's spinning around. But my head still aches a lot and my chest still hurts some when I breathe. Not as much as it did, though. I'm almost used to it.

It helps that you're like me. I didn't know girls could be.

I never knew about Oscar Wilde. I never knew about anyone else till I met Sam. I thought I was the only one, except for seeing male dogs pretend to, you know, do it, with each other. I wasn't even sure for a long time what kids meant by "queer" when they called me that. I guess I'm just a dumb hayseed.

Not anymore, though.

Do you know lots of other people like us? I mean, are there lots of other people like us? I think it would make it better if there were.

I don't feel like Oscar Wilde, at least I don't much like fancy clothes and stuff or writing plays and poems. Just reading them. Other than that, I feel pretty ordinary. I like some stuff most guys like. Not all stuff, but some. Fishing and baseball and cars. So does Sam. I'm not sure why kids always picked on me so much all my life. But I always felt different, and I guess they knew that. I don't know how they could tell, though.

Right now my head's aching like crazy, so I guess I'd better lie

down. But I hope you write more. Tell me what you know! I don't
know anything and neither does Sam, really.

Love,
Mickey

P.S. Did you really like that powder? Or were you just being
polite?

⟼

Dear Cuz,

Oh, Mickey, yes, I did really like the powder! Really, truly, and I
used it a lot. I love all that kind of stuff. Like I said, I guess not all girls
who like girls are more like boys than girls.

I don't know much to tell you. I've tried to find people like us, but
I've only found them in books, and the books are pretty grim. And
Heather's read grim stuff in encyclopedias. I don't think that can be realistic, though. I guess a lot of people hate us. I'm not sure why they do.
I don't think we do anything bad. I don't understand why there can be
anything wrong with love when it doesn't hurt anyone else. I mean,
that's what it's really about, isn't it? I don't feel that I'm crazy or that
Heather is or you are or Sam, like some of the books say. I don't think
Oscar Wilde was crazy either, or Gertrude Stein. She was an important
writer who lived with a woman named Alice B. Toklas in Paris. She
wrote books and stories and a play or two, I think. Stein did, I mean,
not Toklas, but Stein wrote a book that she called The Autobiography
of Alice B. Toklas, which was kind of a strange thing to do, but nice,
too, I think. Important artists like Picasso used to go to their house a
lot. Stein and Toklas collected famous art, I guess before it was famous.
I don't see what's wrong with a life like that, do you? I don't know if
there are very many people like us; maybe not. I don't know if there are
more famous people like us either, but since there are a couple, maybe

there are more. I wish I knew more people like us, though. It would be good to have someone older to talk to about it.

But I'm glad I have you and that we have each other, aren't you?

Love,
Jen

⌒

Dear Jen,

Guess what? Mom got me a reading lamp that's much better for reading in bed than my old one. I can get up now, but she makes me take reading naps. The other night she invited Sam over for supper, and she made all my favorite food—hamburgers and French fries with lots of ketchup and then chocolate-chip ice cream for dessert. Sam still has a cast on his arm, but he says it doesn't hurt. I was so happy I couldn't eat very much. Now I'm in bed with a pad of paper writing to you. The new lamp Mom got me is great.

Even if there aren't very many of us, I'm glad that you've read about some and that at least some of them were famous. I don't know much about famous people in other groups, but that doesn't mean there aren't any. So it makes sense that there could be more famous ones of us, too.

Did you ever think it's strange that there are two of us in the same family? I wonder if it runs in families. I wonder if there are any more in the family like us. Aunt Sadie isn't married. But she lives with Grandmother Forest and takes care of her, so I guess maybe even if she was like us she couldn't do much about it.

You never see anything about homosexuals on television or in the movies. At least I never have.

Mom says she and Dad complained to the principal of our school about the guys who beat us up. He said that Sam and I should learn to fight back. We did try at first, I remember that part! There were only two of us, and there were four or five of them. Dad says that's not fair and that the guys who jumped us were cowards because they outnumbered us. But the principal told him, "You know how boys are." Dad said he told him he does know how boys are, but fighting fair is one thing and fighting dirty is another. I hope Dad doesn't say any more, because that'll probably just make it worse for us. Sam said that the first day he went back to school, the guys who beat us up cornered him and told him not to tell anyone who they were or they'd beat him up again. He said he hasn't told anyone. I guess I won't either. But I'm sure not looking forward to going back to school.

Meanwhile, when I'm better and Sam's better, we're going to take boxing lessons if we can find someone to teach us. They don't give boxing at our school, and there's no place around here, no gym or anything, just in the city and that's too far away. Dad says he'll ask around, though.

I wish I could get more books about people like us. That's about all I can do right now, read. I can't even take care of my calf much, or help Dad with anything heavy. My sister's taking care of my calf, but that'll probably make him her calf. I don't think I can show him if I haven't done it all myself. I don't think she can either, since I started him off. I guess he's our practice calf. There's always next year, I guess.

Love,

Mickey

ᴥ

Dear Cuz,

Guess what? I found an organization, I guess you'd call it, or a club—something like that, anyway! I was in this big library downtown the other day looking for books, and they have this bulletin board. It's always covered with posters and flyers and announcements, and I hadn't even thought of looking there, but when I was walking by I saw a big poster and the names "Wilde" and "Toklas" jumped out at me. So I went over and read it—it seemed to be a sort of a club—only there was this other girl there reading other stuff and when I saw the word "homosexual" on the Wilde-Toklas poster I got nervous and walked away. I watched, though, and when the girl was gone I went back over and read what it said. I don't remember all of it, I was so flustered, but there was a phone number and I wrote it down. It said the hours were seven to nine on Tuesday and Thursday nights. Then I was too scared to call. I kept taking the number out of my purse and looking at it and putting it back in. But finally today I called, and the person who answered was very nice. I was so nervous I didn't say very much except was it really an organization for homosexuals and he said it was and he asked how old I am. So I told him fifteen and he said—I remember this part—he said, "Oh, sugar, I'm sorry, but you have to be twenty-one to join. I'm so sorry. But if you have a specific problem, maybe I can help."

He was so nice, Mickey.

So I told him I thought I might be homosexual and I even told him I was nervous. And he said it's normal to be nervous and he told me there are lots of other girls and women like me and other boys and men like him and that his organization was trying to help all of us and that he wished they could have kids join because he knew there were other kids like me.

When I hung up I cried and cried because it's not fair that there are people like us who know more than we do but we aren't allowed to be part of their group. He said the police would make them close if they did anything for kids under twenty-one and that people would think they were trying to recruit—that's the word he used—to recruit kids so they'd become gay because homosexuals can't have children and they'd die out otherwise.

That sounds pretty stupid to me. No one recruited me or you either. We were always different, weren't we? I always felt different, anyway.

It's good, though, that that group is trying to help. He said there are other groups, too, trying to do the same thing, but that most of them are in places like New York and California.

I wish they didn't have that stupid rule about having to be twenty-one!

Love,
Jen

Dear Cuz,

I'm in a pretty bad mood right now, but your letter cheered me up. Sam and I sure could use that group you found. We can't wait till we're twenty-one to be able to be with people like us. I'm sick and tired of pretending Sam and I are just "buddies." That's what Dad calls it. I'm tired of pretending we're not what we are. Boys and girls hold hands in the halls at school sometimes and no one cares, but Sam and I can't. I really love Sam, Jen. I really love him. And he really loves me. But we can't be together like we want to be. We can't go out in a car and park like the "normal" kids do, so we sneak around. Cornfields are pretty bumpy after the corn's been harvested, but we're getting to be experts at avoiding the bumps! But the whole time we're there we're scared that someone will see us and beat us up again. I want to run away, but Sam won't do it. He says we have to finish school. I know he's right, but at the same time I think he's wrong.

I'm glad at least I have you to talk to. No offense, but I wish there were a guy like us we could talk to, too.

Dad did find someone to teach us how to box, though. He's an old guy who used to fight professionally. He's still pretty good. Sam and I are getting better, except it's difficult for us to hit each other hard. Of course we have to do that if we want to learn to defend ourselves from the jerks.

I guess you can figure out that I'm back in school now. Sam and I try to stay away from the jerks, but they still yell things about fairies and queers and pansies. Homos, too; that's the one they like best. Sam thinks we might as well try dating girls. What's the use of that since pretty much the whole school has figured out what we are? It wouldn't be fair to the girls, either.

I'd better stop. This is too morbid.

Love,

Mickey

⌐

Dear Cuz,

That's so awful about those jerks at your school! But maybe you and Sam should find some girls to go out with who aren't really look-ing for boyfriends or who need boyfriends to cover up that they don't really want boyfriends. You know, girls who just aren't ready for boyfriends yet or even who are like me and Heather. Boys keep asking me out and I keep saying no, but Heather says it's a good cover, so I guess maybe I'll say yes sometime. It's too bad you and I don't live near each other or we could double-date and no one would know that in-stead of Sam and me (because everyone would know you and I are cousins), and you and Heather, it was really you and Sam and me and Heather!

Don't run away, Mickey. Where would you live? How would you get food? Where would you get money? Besides, you should finish school. Anyone who reads all the stuff you do should at least finish high school. Even if you're going to be a farmer you should do that. Be-sides, wouldn't you be a better farmer if you went to agricultural school or something?

I think it's great that you're learning how to box! I hope you and Sam can beat those jerks up someday. I think it's awful that they call you all those names. Heather gets called "lezzie" sometimes (that's for "lesbian," which I guess is obvious), but she just laughs it off. No one calls me names, but once this girl called Heather my "boyfriend, er, girlfriend." I don't think anyone would try to beat us up, though. I guess it's harder for boys.

I'm sorry that it is.

Love,
Jen

⌁

Dear Cuz,

I can't write much. I can't write for long. Jen, I'm so scared and I'm crying so much the paper's getting all wet. You remember about the cornfields? I'm sure you realized that's where Sam and I go to make out. Well, we got caught. And the person who caught us was my dad. He told Sam's dad. And Sam's dad blew up. So did my dad. He and Mom had a big scene and they told me that they're sending me to a private mental hospital to get cured. And Sam's parents are sending him to a military school in the South. Sam and I are going to try to run away. Or something. We're not sure what. Good luck to you and Heather.

Love always,
Mickey

⌁

Dear Jennifer,

By now your mother has told you what I told her today on the phone. I know you and Mickey had become close and I know he mailed a letter to you just the day before they did it. I saw it in our mailbox when I went out to mail some bills. I still don't know how they could have done it. They were so young, so much ahead of them to live for. I'm afraid they were much more confused by that cruel teasing than we ever knew, and more sensitive than we knew, too. But I still don't understand. Mickey didn't leave a note for us, and I hope the letter he wrote you will explain it to me. I hope you'll let me see it, Jennifer, or at least that you'll tell me what's in it.

Uncle George and I and Sam's parents were only trying to help. We didn't agree on the method, but the goal was the same: to help. For normal boys to be driven to—to indulge in unnatural acts— God help us, perhaps we were blind to the extent of it; perhaps it was our fault. But I still don't believe that they really were—you know. And to refuse help—

I can't write any more. But please, please, Jennifer, tell me whatever you can, I beg you.

Love,
Aunt Julie

⊖

Dear Aunt Julie,

I'm so sorry, so very sorry! I still can't stop crying when I think of them, and I'm sure you can't either. I wish I could have stopped them. But I didn't know till Mom told me and then it was too late.

Mickey and Sam really loved each other. That wasn't your fault, and it wasn't a stage or an experiment or anything. And it's why they were teased and beaten up that time. I wish there'd been someone around to help everyone understand, someone nearby. But there wasn't anyone except me, and I guess I didn't know how bad it was. Maybe what they ended up doing is my fault for not helping more.

I don't know what else to say except I'm sorry, so very sorry. I'll always miss him. So will you and Uncle George, I know.

I'm sorry. I'll write more later, maybe. But anyway, I'm enclosing Mickey's last letter for you. I got it after Mom told me what happened. I wish he hadn't done it. It was just too hard for him to be so different. He was just so sure that no one would understand. I'm sure he loved you and Uncle George. It was just too hard.

Here's the letter.

Love,
Jennifer

❧

Dear Jen,

We can't run away, we realized that. No money, no place to go. If we did and they found us, they'd separate us anyway. They don't understand. They don't even believe us. What we are will always be with us. No school or hospital is going to change that.

We want to be together always, Jen. I know you'll understand. It's not supposed to hurt if you sit in a car with the windows closed and the motor running. We're going to a place we like at the far edge of Dad's biggest field. And we'll die in each other's arms. Please think of us as happy and at peace.

Thank you for everything, Cuz. You've been my only friend.

Goodbye and love always,
Mickey

P.S. You can give this letter to Mom if you want.

❧

1980s

THE DECADE

IN 1980, AARON FRICKE, A COURAGEOUS GAY EIGHTEEN-YEAR-OLD HIGH school senior from the little town of Cumberland, Rhode Island, decided to go to his senior prom with a male date. A close friend of Aaron's, Paul Guilbert, had asked him to go to the prom the year before, but Aaron hadn't felt ready. This year, though, Aaron decided to ask Paul to be his date even though Paul had left Cumberland High because of the homophobic reaction his earlier attempt had unleashed.

First, Aaron came out to his parents. That was difficult, but it went well. Then he explained his reasons in a letter to his school newspaper. That didn't go so well; it wasn't printed. Then he asked Paul, and Paul accepted. But when he told Cumberland High's principal about his plans, the principal refused to give him permission to go to the prom with another boy.

Aaron, with the help of the seven-year-old National Gay Task Force, decided to sue. There followed a lot of publicity plus a lot of harassment, including a punch in Aaron's face at school, resulting in a cut below his eye that needed five stitches. But after two days of hearings in federal district court, a judge ruled that Aaron had a First Amendment right to go to the prom with a male date. (The First Amendment is the one that establishes freedom of speech, the press, religion, and assembly, plus the right "to petition the Government for a redress of grievances.")

On the night of the prom, reporters met Aaron and Paul outside the building, Aaron and Paul went inside—and no one threw them out. By later in the evening, toward the end of a song called

"Rock Lobster," boys were dancing with boys and girls with girls—
and Aaron and Paul's brave gesture was reported as news across the
country. Later, Aaron told his story in a book called *Reflections of a
Rock Lobster*.

Although the eighties began with that tremendous act of courage,
although more high school kids than ever before were beginning to
come out at home and in school, and although there were important developments in gay civil rights in that decade, AIDS defined the
eighties for many gay and lesbian people. That's not surprising, since
in the first ten years or so of that devastating epidemic, many thousands of gay men died, victims of the virus that causes AIDS. Think of
it—*thousands*—so many that some gays and lesbians lost many or
most of their friends. It's hard to imagine spending countless hours
week after week visiting hospitals and going to funerals, but that's what
many people in our community did during that frightening and tragic
time.

It was in the early eighties that some gay men began noticing odd
purplish marks on their bodies. These were eventually diagnosed as
Kaposi's sarcoma, a rare form of cancer that until then had primarily
hit elderly Italian and Jewish men. But soon, as more and more gay
men of various ages and background got Kaposi's, the press began referring to it as "the gay cancer." Some gay men came down with an unusual form of pneumonia as well.

Kaposi's sarcoma and *Pneumocystis carinii* pneumonia, as is now
well known, are early signs of AIDS.

The next years were filled with controversy over the disease. Some
gays believed AIDS was the result of a straight conspiracy to introduce
a fatal disease into our community, eventually wiping us out. Some
straights believed it was a plague sent by God to punish gay immorality. Neither, of course, was true. But it is true that, especially at first,
AIDS in the United States was most prevalent among gay men (lesbians can get AIDS, too, but far fewer have). Bodily fluids, including semen, can transmit the AIDS virus—and it's true that many gays had

furtive, anonymous, unprotected sex in public toilets, bathhouses, and parks, often with many casual partners. Sometimes this was for money (especially on the part of young runaways), sometimes for the comfort, human contact, and pleasure sex can bring, and sometimes because of the difficulty of forming stable gay relationships in a hostile society. It is by no means true that all gays behaved this way, nor is it true that some straight people didn't and don't also have casual sex. It's also not true that all gay AIDS victims contracted the disease because of promiscuous behavior. But it is true that a great many did.

In 1984, HIV, the virus that causes AIDS, was discovered. That was a tremendous breakthrough; HIV destroys the body's immune system, opening the door to AIDS and the infections and illnesses that eventually kill AIDS victims. The discovery of HIV helped researchers hunt for ways to prevent, treat, and cure AIDS—but while the scientists studied and agitated for much-needed funds to support their work, the rapidly growing number of AIDS patients had to be helped.

The gay community rallied as never before. AIDS walks, red ribbons, speeches, and articles increased the public's awareness of the disease and gradually reduced the hysteria it caused. Starting in 1986, the NAMES Project's enormous quilt made of hand-sewn squares celebrating the lives of deceased AIDS victims did its part in helping to ease the grief of bereft lovers, parents, siblings, and friends. Gay organizations new and old embarked upon education programs and tried, often in angry confrontations, to convince the government and drug companies to fund AIDS research. They also agitated for an end to the discrimination that was visited on AIDS patients—eviction, loss of employment, refusal of insurance coverage, and denial of hospital visiting rights to the lovers of dying patients because they weren't relatives or legal spouses. Ironically, as the epidemic spread, straight AIDS patients were deprived of many of the same rights, which of course had also long been denied to AIDS-free GLBT people when their sexual orientation became known.

Finally, by the late 1980s, the government began devoting more money to AIDS research. But—tragically, because many people contract HIV when they are quite young—there still was (and in many places still is) enormous resistance to providing AIDS prevention information in schools.

AIDS brought out the best and the worst in the gay community. On the one hand, countless gay men and lesbians tenderly nursed their sick and dying friends. On the other hand, some people with HIV withheld that information from their sex partners, thereby spreading the disease. Rumors abounded, too. Many people feared that they could contract HIV-AIDS from toilet seats or dishes and utensils, even after it was known that the virus doesn't live long outside the body and that in addition to semen, only blood, vaginal fluids, and breast milk can transmit the virus. People can get HIV only if they have unprotected sex, use dirty hypodermic needles, or come in contact with contaminated blood through a wound or via a transfusion. (Hemophiliacs and others who require blood transfusions were among the early AIDS victims before this country's blood supply was carefully monitored, as it now is.) Infants whose mothers have HIV can get the virus from breast milk, and can also contract it in the womb through shared body fluids.

If there has been a good side to AIDS in addition to the way the gay community rallied to fight it, it's that, as time went on and AIDS education spread, increasing numbers of gay men began practicing safer sex. As a result, in time, the incidence of HIV-AIDS among gay men began dropping. Now most people, gay and straight alike, know that the best way to avoid HIV-AIDS is to abstain from sex unless one has a single, HIV-negative partner, and that the next best way is to practice safer sex by using latex condoms or other forms of protection, such as latex gloves, unperforated plastic wrap, latex squares, or dental dams. Unfortunately, though, now that there are effective means by which HIV-positive people can stave off AIDS indefinitely, more people—especially young people—are again having unsafe sex. You can't assume that if you get HIV you can save yourself from AIDS by taking pills. They don't work for everyone, they're very expensive, many have very unpleasant side effects, and they don't cure AIDS. *The bottom line is that there is no cure.*

Fears of a possible new, drug-resistant HIV virus surfaced and then died in New York City in 2005. But it led to predictions that such a virus might very well emerge in time. It's *always* going to be important to practice abstinence or safer sex, and equally important to shun combining sex and recreational drugs, for drugs can make one feel invulnerable, which in turn can make safer sex seem unimportant.

In addition to more people practicing safer sex, another possible "good" side to AIDS—perhaps really more of a mixed blessing, since it also tended to support the misconception that all gays are promiscuous—was that, as the disease spread, many straight people were forced to recognize that the gay population was larger than they'd thought. The popular movie star Rock Hudson died of AIDS, and so, although there were those who denied it, did the famous pianist Liberace. The automatic assumption, of course, was that because these people had died of AIDS, they were gay. Rock Hudson, who was gay but closeted, had been admired as a sexy straight man; the revelation that he had AIDS shocked his fans. Unlike Hudson, Liberace had been as flamboyant as the gay Irish playwright Oscar Wilde, and had been involved in legal battles because of allegations of homosexuality (which he'd denied), so statements that he'd died of AIDS weren't quite as surprising.

Because of AIDS, other closeted celebrities also were revealed as being gay, and that in turn showed people that gays had made valuable contributions to American society. Gays who weren't in the public eye were also often forced to come out to their families, straight friends, and co-workers when they contracted the disease. That showed the straight public that many ordinary families had gay members, and many businesses had gay employees.

But sadly, although some AIDS victims were nursed lovingly by their families, others were ostracized at a time when they needed family support the most. The disease also took a terrible toll in the arts communities and cut short the lives of many talented and productive gay people, both famous and not famous. It led to rifts within families and tragically ended the deep relationships of many loving gay couples, often leaving their surviving partners to die alone of the same disease.

Still, despite the enormous suffering HIV-AIDS caused, running beneath the epidemic through the eighties and beyond, the battle for gay rights continued. Although AIDS often overshadowed news of them, there were a good many important advances—enough to make the religious right introduce a "Family Protection Act" into Congress several times in the early eighties. This act would have denied all of us freedom of association and the right to collect student aid, welfare, social security, and veterans' benefits. Luckily it never passed, and overall, the advances in gay rights outweighed the threats and the setbacks. The eighties saw a few more gays elected to public office, the ordination of a few gay clergy, more antidiscrimination laws, and efforts to legitimize gay relationships in legally sanctioned domestic partnerships and marriage.

The first Gay Games—Olympic-style competitions for gay athletes —were held in San Francisco in 1982. Gay social clubs devoted to such pursuits as hiking, sports, board games, and other activities, plus gay community centers and bookstores, sprang up here and there, providing alternatives to the bars. Gay characters and issues began appearing more frequently in films, on TV, and in books—including books for teens—and increasing numbers of those portrayals were honest and positive.

In 1984 at Fairfax High School in Los Angeles, science teacher and college counselor Dr. Virginia Uribe formed a group called Project 10 to run workshops about teens and homosexuality for school personnel and to organize support groups for GL high school students. Project 10, which is still active today in thirty to thirty-five

California high schools, also sought to encourage schools to add accurate references in their curriculums to homosexuality itself and to homosexuals who have made outstanding contributions in various fields.

Soon, as an offshoot of Project 10, a small group of students at Fairfax High started a club named after murdered San Francisco supervisor Harvey Milk. According to Dr. Uribe, whom I asked about the club, they wanted a group that was more of a social and educational organization than Project 10's support groups, which concentrated on discussions of the problems faced by gay youth; they wanted a club where gay and straight kids together could listen to speakers and watch films that had to do with the gay experience. Dr. Uribe explained that the kids wrote a constitution and went to their supportive principal, Warren Steinberg, for permission to go ahead. Steinberg sent their plan to the school's legal department and learned that there was no barrier to forming the club as long as it was open to all students, both gay and straight, but warned it could be subject to controversy. Perhaps for that reason, Fairfax's Harvey Milk Club never really took off, but because it was open to both gay and straight students and concentrated on social and educational activities rather than on the problems of being gay, it can be seen as the "ancestor" of the gay-straight alliances (GSAs) and similar clubs that today exist in more than three thousand high schools across the country.

In 1985, a two-classroom public high school, also named after Harvey Milk, was opened for gay students in New York City by the Hetrick-Martin Institute. Its mission: to provide an education to kids perceived as being gay or lesbian who couldn't make it in regular schools because of harassment and bullying. Today, the expanded Harvey Milk High School is open to all kids whose education has been hampered for those reasons, but by far the majority of its students are GLBTQ. A similar but private high school, called the Walt Whitman Community School, operated in Dallas, Texas, from 1997 to 2003.

Despite AIDS, the gay liberation movement was rapidly expanding. And despite a gradually rising backlash throughout the country caused by our increased visibility as the eighties moved into the nineties, more and more gay and lesbian youth, no longer content to suffer in silence, were finding one another and courageously starting to speak out.

MY FATHER'S BUDDHA

MY FATHER HAS A BUDDHA IN THE FRONT YARD.

It's a small stone one, with a little garden around it, and our yard's right near the street, so people sometimes stop and look at it. Once we even found a couple of sticks of incense near it and, another time, about fifty cents in change.

We're not Buddhists or anything. My dad was what they call a draft dodger during the Vietnam War. He didn't think the war was right, and he'd been brought up a Quaker, so he was a conscientious objector. But my uncle Frank (who I'm named after, by the way), was in Vietnam, fighting to save the Vietnamese from Communism. Or so he thought; unlike my dad and my grandparents, he believed the war was a good thing. They must've had arguments about that, but they've always been really close, and they all sure seem to have loved Uncle Frank, so they probably never got very mad about it.

Well, this one day Uncle Frank was in some enemy village, I guess, where there was this small Buddha, and the Vietcong—that was the enemy—attacked, and he just happened to be near the Buddha, so he squatted down behind it, sort of using it like a duck blind, you know, to shoot from. And a bullet came along and went right into the Buddha. You can still see the hole.

If the Buddha hadn't been there, that bullet would've hit my uncle. After that he tried to pretend to shoot instead of actually shooting. I don't think he could always pull that off, but he tried. He wrote my dad saying it was because he owed something to the people whose Buddha it was even if they were supposed to be the enemy. He told Dad he realized that the Vietnamese on both sides of the war had Buddhas, and that the real Buddha probably didn't like wars. He thought maybe the real Buddha had saved him to show him that, and he said the war didn't make sense to him anymore.

Uncle Frank was killed in Vietnam anyway, later. But after he was killed, some of the guys in his squad or patrol or whatever it was found "his" Buddha and somehow managed to send it to my dad. And Dad put it in the yard as a thank-you for letting Uncle Frank live a little longer and for changing his mind about the war.

That's not what this story's about, though.

This story is about me, my friend Josh, and our friend Calvin, who has AIDS.

Sorry. Had AIDS.

Calvin taught part-time at the high school Josh and I don't go to, and the rest of the time he helped run an organization that works for what they call gay liberation. It's pretty militant; they have marches and stage sit-ins at government offices and stuff. Josh and I don't know much about it because you have to be something like eighteen or maybe even twenty-one to join. But we used to go and see Calvin a lot after school and just talk, because he and Bruce are the only other gay people we know.

Oh, sorry. Bruce is Calvin's lover. Was.

Josh and I met Calvin and Bruce one Saturday night when we were walking home from the movies. We'd gone to see this foreign film that had a gay character in it—I don't remember what it was called—at this art theater in a not very good part of town, and we were walking home and Josh was pretending to be a drag queen—he can be very butch but he likes to kid around—you know, flapping his wrists and talking in a high, squeaky, falsetto voice. He'd tied his coat around his waist, and it was hanging down kind of like a skirt, and he was, well, mincing, I guess you'd call it.

All of a sudden this car screeched to a stop next to us and these two big guys jumped out. One of them grabbed me and held me in this viselike grip, and the other one jumped Josh and started beating him up. "You're next," the one holding me said—I was trying to hit him and trying to break away and yelling I don't know what-all—"unless you can prove you're not a faggot, too."

"I am a faggot," I yelled. "Let go of my friend."

"Jeez, you don't look it," the guy said. "But I guess it figures anyway, you being with him." He let go of me with one hand and lifted that hand up in a fist—I can still see it—and was about to hit me when someone rushed out of this derelict-looking building that I later saw had a couple of posters with letters on them standing for the name of what we later learned was the gay organization. The someone ran right up to the guy who was holding me and punched him in the mouth. At the same time, another person ran to the guy who was beating Josh— and before we'd really taken it all in, our two saviors had dragged me and Josh into the derelict building and our attackers had stumbled to their car and driven away.

You guessed that our two saviors were Calvin and Bruce, right?

Josh's nose was bleeding pretty bad, and he was hurting so much we thought he might have a couple of broken bones, and Calvin—he was the one who'd helped me—kept saying, "I think we'd better call the cops and an ambulance," and Josh kept saying, "No, please don't. I'm okay," and I kept saying, "Thank you," and Bruce said, "How about we call your parents, then?" and that made everyone stop talking except Josh, who said, "Please don't" again, only even more emphatically.

"Why not?" Calvin asked, but he and Bruce looked at each other in a way that made me know they knew. About us, I mean.

"Because they'd be mad that we're in this part of town," Josh said through his teeth—he was still in a lot of pain.

"And they'd want to know why we were here," I said.

"And," said Bruce, "you're here because . . . ?"

"They're here," said Calvin, "because they're gay or think they might be, and they've just been to the Beaux Arts Theater." He'd been mopping up the blood on Josh's face with a handkerchief, and he stopped now, reached for a bunch of paper towels Bruce had gotten from someplace and was holding out to him, and went on mopping. "What did you think of the film? When we saw it, I thought it looked pretty low budget. Too bad, though. The story's pretty good."

So we spent the next hour losing track of time while we discussed the movie and how rotten it was that there weren't really any decent movies—or any movies that we knew of, anyway—about people like all of us. And then we cooked up an almost-true story for Josh's and my parents, none of whom knew we were gay, about why we were out so late and about the bullies who'd beaten Josh up. By then at least we'd decided he probably didn't have any broken bones, because he was feeling much better and he could move around and everything.

That's how we met Calvin and Bruce.

It turned out they'd been lovers for more than ten years. Calvin wanted to start a group for gay kids at the high school where he taught, but of course he couldn't even try if he wanted to keep his job and not risk being arrested as a pederast. Bruce was head teller at a bank. They'd both been what they called "in the movement" for a long time. Bruce had been in the air force, but he'd been thrown out when someone discovered he was gay.

After that night Josh and I used to go to their office whenever things got bad for us, which really wasn't all that often because we hadn't told much of anyone we were gay. We also went whenever we wanted to talk about stuff like whether or not to tell our parents, or about guys we had crushes on, or just when we wanted to be with people who knew who we really were and were like us. That was pretty often. We even went to their apartment—it was above the office—a few times on Saturdays for a spaghetti lunch. They had this really enormous cat named Sappho for a Greek probably lesbian or bi poet, and about a ton of books on shelves made of long boards with bricks in between them. Lots of them were religion books, including a bunch about Buddhism with Calvin's name in them. There were tons of classical records, too. We learned a lot from Calvin and Bruce about music, and they lent us some books with gay characters in them that we had to hide from our parents. And I looked at the Buddhism books and read some of the notes that Calvin had put in them back when he'd been in college. One idea, about how in order to be at peace you have to not want anything, really stuck in my mind. I want so much out of life that that idea struck me as weird and as something I could never do.

Calvin and Bruce were sort of like a couple of big brothers to us, you know? When Josh fell in love with this kid, Andy, and didn't know what to do about it, he talked to Calvin about him more than he talked to me, and when he told Andy how he felt and Andy said he didn't feel the same way, if it hadn't been for Calvin, I think Josh would have— Well, I don't know what he'd have done, but something pretty drastic, I guess. And when I had this huge crush on Brian Lang, Calvin used to drive me past his house so I could see if he was home, and he explained ice hockey to me because Brian was on varsity.

Well, anyway, that was junior year. Toward the end of it, we noticed that Calvin was looking kind of thin and pale, and then there began to be days when he didn't come into the office much. Then, in the beginning of the summer, he went into the hospital with pneumonia, some kind of fancy-named pneumonia that Bruce said he'd had a couple of times before. Bruce looked more and more worried, and he wouldn't let us visit Calvin in the hospital but he took messages to him from us, and this one time Josh and I sent Calvin a huge bunch of flowers.

(By the way, I'd given up on Brian. He'd never really known I was anything more than a weird kid who went to all his games, and that got too hard to take after a while. Besides, by then there was another guy I liked, Greg—but he's not what this is about, except that, because of him, Calvin taught me a lot about cars, because Greg had this old wreck he was always working on.)

By the end of the summer, when Bruce was bringing Calvin home from the hospital for something like the third time, Josh and I snuck up to their apartment with this huge steak and two packages of frozen French fries, and lettuce and tomatoes and other salad stuff, and bottled dressing, and ice cream—chocolate, butter pecan, and peppermint stick. We made this big sign saying SURPRISE! and another saying WELCOME HOME! and we hung the signs from the ceiling in their little front hall, and we blew up a ton of balloons and fastened them to everything we could fasten them to.

Finally, after we'd been working at keeping Sappho from batting at the balloons for what felt like forever, we heard the office door open and heavy footsteps coming up the stairs to the apartment.

It sounded like only one person was coming up, and we looked at each other, scared that Calvin had died or something.

But then the apartment door opened, and it was almost worse.

Bruce was carrying Calvin, who looked so awful we hardly recognized him. And both their eyes were wet with tears.

Bruce just stopped in the doorway and stared at us. Then he said, "Oh, God!" And when he said, "No, kids, sorry, not now," his tears spilled over.

But Calvin held out his arm, which looked more like a stick than an arm, and said, "You sweet children! Thank you! I love you."

I knew we'd made a terrible mistake along with doing a nice thing. We'd made stupid assumptions and we'd been tactless. But we hadn't known how bad Calvin was.

Or what it was he had.

What he had, of course, was AIDS. Somehow, even though the gay paper we'd read occasionally in the office was full of it and even though sometimes the regular paper mentioned it, we hadn't thought of it in relation to Calvin's being sick. AIDS was something other people got. People who slept around a lot. Of course we didn't know then that it takes a long time for AIDS to develop inside people. Or that you can get it from sleeping once with someone who has it. We didn't know anything except that we'd interrupted what should have been a private homecoming that looked as if it might be the last one. But at least we figured that out fast, and we each gave them both as good a hug as one can give two people when one of them is carrying the other, and we crept down the stairs and outside.

Later, Bruce told us that the meal had been delicious, and we didn't let him know we were pretty sure they hadn't eaten it, at least we were pretty sure Calvin hadn't.

"It's AIDS, isn't it?" I asked bluntly—I'm not known for my tact—a couple of days later, when we dropped in at the office. Calvin, of course, wasn't there. He was upstairs in bed.

"Yes," Bruce said.

"Is he dying?" Josh asked gently.

"Yes. And"—Bruce got up from his battered desk and went over to the window—"he's so scared," he whispered.

"God," said Josh, "who wouldn't be? I mean, look at him, how sick he is! He must feel horrible!"

"Yeah," Bruce said, "he does. But the trouble is it's going to be superhard on him when he goes. He's fighting it; there's no peace for him. He's worried about leaving me, and the organization, and you two kids, and the kids at the high school, and hockey and baseball on TV, and the sky and the sun and the big maple tree on this street, and . . ." Bruce covered his face with his hands, and Josh got up quickly and held him for a long moment till he broke out of Josh's embrace and said, "Sorry. I'm sorry."

"Don't be," Josh said. "Please."

I'd been watching all this and aching for all of us, especially Calvin, and I'd been thinking, too, of what Bruce had just said about there being no peace for Calvin, and suddenly I had an idea.

I told Josh about it on the way back to our neighborhood, and we spent a long time outside my house looking at the Buddha. It was late summer by then, and the leaves on the dwarf weeping cherry tree or whatever it was that curved over the Buddha's head were red, and there were yellow chrysanthemums and pale purple asters around its base, along with foliage from flowers that had pretty much stopped blooming.

"Maybe," Josh said doubtfully.

"It's worth a try," I said, and went inside.

Two days later, Bruce drove onto my street with Calvin and a wheel-chair. He'd told Calvin he had a sort of surprise for him, and Calvin had thanked him and said he was sorry but he didn't feel up to a sur-prise, and Bruce had told him it was from us and how could he let us down, and finally he'd agreed.

When the car stopped where the street curves about a block from my house, which is where Josh and I were waiting, I unloaded the wheelchair and Bruce lifted Calvin out of the car and into it, and Josh put the blue plaid blanket Bruce had bought for the wheelchair over Calvin's thin knees. Then we all walked slowly in a procession down the side of the street my house is on. It was one of those bright, fall-like afternoons when the sky is a vivid blue and the air is crisp and clear but it isn't really cold yet. My heart was beating like a hundred ham-mers, and I could see that Josh's shoulders were sort of hunched the way they get when he's tense or nervous. Bruce looked grim, as if he was sure our plan wasn't going to work.

The closer we got to my house, the more I agreed with him. How could I have been so dumb?

But when we got to the edge of my yard and came around the curve to where you can see the Buddha and the garden, I heard a gasp from Calvin. I grabbed Josh's arm, and Bruce kept on grimly pushing the chair—and when we got to the garden itself, Calvin said softly, "Bruce, stop. Oh, please, stop."

Bruce stopped, and pulled up the brakes on the wheelchair. The three of us, Josh and Bruce and I, stepped back a little way and watched as Calvin, with tears streaming down his face, sat there for a long time looking at the Buddha. His face slowly relaxed into the calmest and most peaceful expression I have ever seen.

Two nights later, Calvin died, easily, in Bruce's arms.

"I'M NOBODY! . . ."

SHE LOOKED BOTH WAYS BEFORE CROSSING, BUT NOT FOR CARS.
There was no sign of Duncan. That was good.

There was also no sign of Michael. That was not good.

There continued to be no sign of Michael all the way to Clarence Street, where there were, unfortunately, plenty of signs of Duncan. He hadn't been behind the convenience store, poised to pop out at her, whistling, ready to grab whatever part of her he could reach. He hadn't been behind the shaggy forsythia at the edge of Doc Carver's yard, yelling, "Hey, Lily-filly, want to see my willy?" Doc Carver sometimes looked out of his front window at them, but he never came outside.

This time Duncan was near the abandoned garage at the corner of Clarence and Marsh, big as life and twice as ugly, as Mom would probably say if she knew about him, but she didn't. There he was, just when Lily thought she might be able to get all the way home from school, for once, without him.

But of course that was too much to ask.

Much too much.

And this time Duncan wasn't alone.

As soon as she got to the corner, they came out, Duncan and a bunch of his friends, six or seven; she was never sure how many of them there were. They surrounded her quickly, before she had time to even think about screaming, and, forming a tight band around her, made her walk in their midst to the back of the empty, closed-up garage. There they silently opened up their circle, and she saw . . .

She saw . . .

Lily saw Michael lying in a bloody heap on the ground.

Agony for him and fear for both him and herself clutched at her insides as she fell to her knees beside him, gasping. But Duncan grabbed her wrist before her hand could touch Michael, grabbed her wrist and yanked her to her feet, snarling, "See, baby dyke? See what we do to faggots? Now we're gonna fix you, teach you how to be with men. You want to be a real woman deep down inside, you know?"

Lily heard herself whimper, heard herself try to say "No, please," felt her head shake and her free hand go out to protect herself . . .

But it was too late. Duncan had already ripped her shirt and twisted her around, forcing her down to the ground.

For three days she lay silently in her room while her mother sat beside her, sometimes rubbing her back, sometimes singing songs she hadn't sung since Lily was a baby, bringing her food that Lily didn't, couldn't eat, begging her to talk, to tell her what had happened, at least to tell her who had raped her.

For that much her mother had guessed when Lily had crawled home, bruised and beaten, with her pants bloody and her breasts and mouth bruised. The doctor at the hospital, the nurse, the rape counselor, they'd all begged her to talk, to tell them how it happened and who had done it, but all she could say was "Clarence Street, behind the old garage, find Michael, help him."

They'd done that much, but Michael, who now lay in his hospital bed as silently as Lily lay in her bed at home, wasn't able to speak, and no one knew if he'd ever be able to speak or move again.

Her mind felt fuzzy, and sometimes she wasn't sure she really remembered what had happened. Other times, though, she smelled Duncan's sweat again, and the oily dirt smell that clung to the ground outside the garage where she'd lain, and saw Duncan's face clearly, bent above her own, snarling, laughing, laboring, sweating, bobbing up and down as he pounded into her. The others did the same, with Duncan's face still above hers, only upside down because he was behind her then, helping to hold her.

Finally, she screamed.

It was at night, really, but she wasn't aware of that. She was only aware that Duncan's face had come back to her so vividly she had to do something to make it go away. She pushed at it, at the vision of it, with her hands, surprised that her hands could move, for of course someone had held them back before. But even though they could move, they couldn't push his face away, so she did the only other thing she could: she screamed.

The scream brought her some relief, at least she felt a little less helpless, so she screamed again, and it was almost as if Duncan, or the vision of Duncan, moved away from her in surprise. The scream also brought her parents and her older brother, and they all hugged her and talked to her and tried to soothe her. But she couldn't stop screaming for a very long time, not until she heard her father say, "Should I slap her? I think sometimes that's supposed to work."

And suddenly that seemed funny to her, hilarious, so she laughed, only it turned out to be like the scream: she couldn't stop.

Finally her father, tears running down his cheeks, did slap her, and she stopped then, staring at him, till he caught her in his arms, cradling her and saying over and over as she cried—as she finally cried—"My baby, my little girl, Daddy's here, Daddy's here."

She clung to him, sorry for him, not wanting to tell him that he couldn't really help her anymore, that she was no longer anyone's little girl, that she never, never would be anyone's little girl again.

The next morning, Lily got up, dressed, and went downstairs to the kitchen, where her family was sitting around the breakfast table eating eggs and bacon and toast and drinking coffee and juice and tea. She said, "Good morning," surprised at the fact that her mouth, though it still felt swollen and bruised, could form words and that her throat and lungs could somehow push them out.

They all looked so startled and then so happy that she wanted to laugh again, but she remembered in time that if she did, she might not be able to stop, so she just pulled her chair out and reached for a piece of toast from the plate in the middle of the table.

It tasted surprisingly like nothing. She couldn't taste the coffee her mother gave her either, or the juice; she could feel their wetness and the toast's dryness, but nothing had any taste. Maybe Duncan hurt my taste buds, she thought, but then she decided it was probably psychological.

"I want," she said very slowly and clearly, "to see Michael."

Her parents looked at each other, and her brother reached out and took her hand.

"Lil," he said, "Lil, Michael's very badly hurt."

"Is he dead?" she asked, too loudly.

"No," her father said quickly. "No, hon, he's not dead. But he's in a coma."

"I want to see him," Lily said again. Her voice sounded distant to her, as if it came from someone else.

"Okay," her mother said. "Okay, I'll take you to see him."

But later, when her mother opened the front door to take Lily outside, Lily stepped back, suddenly blinded by the light even though it was a cloudy day, and she realized she wasn't going to be able to go. She could almost see Duncan and his friends behind the bushes in front of the house, or crouched behind the car. The wind brought an oily smell to her from the driveway, and suddenly she was lying in the dirt again, smelling it, smelling Duncan's sweat, seeing his face.

"It's okay, honey," Mom said softly, putting her hand under Lily's elbow. "It's okay. I'm here, you're safe."

But Lily heard herself draw her breath in sharply, and she pulled away from her mother and ran back upstairs to her room, where she spent the next two days silently willing Michael to wake up and call her.

On the third day her mother and father brought a policeman upstairs to see her. Her parents sat on the other side of her small room while the policeman asked her questions and she didn't answer them.

The worst question was "Lily, who hurt you?"

The next worst question was "Who hurt Michael?"

And the last worst question was "Do you know why you and Michael were attacked?"

She couldn't answer the first two, because, if she did, she knew Duncan would find her again and kill her. That's what he'd said. He'd held his shiny knife to her throat and said, "If you tell anyone about this or mention my name to anyone, I'll find you and kill you."

And she couldn't answer the last question because she'd never told her family and Michael had never told his family that they were gay.

They'd known each other since first grade and played together for what seemed all their lives, and they'd seen each other through the slow realization that they were different from the other kids and the longer, slower realization of what that difference was. But they were always able to rejoice in each other, comfort each other, because they were the same—like the people in the Emily Dickinson poem, Michael had said when they'd read it in English class in eighth grade:

> I'm nobody! Who are you?
> Are you nobody, too?
> Then there's a pair of us—don't tell!
> They'd banish us, you know.

The other kids had already done that; they'd banished Lily and Michael, especially in middle school and then in high school.

Duncan had come along last year, new to the school but an instant leader, swaggering and joking and making kids laugh at other kids. People said he'd been in foster homes; his father was a drunk and maybe his home life made him a bully, but after all, boys will be boys—that's what they said, the principal and the teachers. And they told Michael not to react or "ask for it," not to walk the way he walked or wear so much jewelry to school, and they told Lily to stop being so assertive, to stop opening doors for other girls, and to go to the dances, to find a boyfriend—not Michael, for goodness' sake! If she and Michael would only act normal, then surely Duncan would stop pestering them.

Pestering. That was the word the principal had used, last time.

Lily didn't see any point in telling the policeman that, and, finally, he left.

The next day a woman came, a social worker, Lily thought she must be, and this time her parents didn't stay in the room. The woman had very black hair, short and sleek, and friendly dark eyes. Her hands looked strong, with stubby fingers and short nails that looked as if she might have bitten them once but had now stopped and was trying to let them grow. And she wore a dark red shirt with a black pattern on it, perhaps vines, perhaps just squiggles.

Her voice was rich and soft. "Lily," she said, "I'm Rose. Can you believe it? We're both named after flowers. I don't think I'm anything like a flower, myself; how about you?"

Lily was so surprised she felt herself smile, and she said, "No, I don't think I am either."

"I always wanted to be called Carol," Rose said. "I told people I liked that name because it sounded like Christmas, and that was true, but secretly I liked it because I knew it was a boys' name, too."

Again, Lily was startled, and she found herself saying, "I always wanted to be called Toby. That's what Michael called me. Toby." She realized what she'd said then, and she whispered the last word.

But it did feel good to say it.

Rose smiled. "Toby," she repeated. "I like that."

It was then that Lily noticed the notebook Rose had in her lap. But she also noticed that Rose hadn't opened it.

"What did you call Michael?" Rose asked.

Lily hesitated. But there was something about Rose that she trusted. "Michele," she whispered. "Sometimes."

Rose nodded.

"I've been talking to some people at your school," Rose said softly. "Some of the kids, and teachers. They seemed to think you and Michael were teased a lot. Maybe worse than teased. Some of them said they were sorry they hadn't realized how bad it was." She looked expectantly at Lily.

"It was pretty bad," Lily said hesitantly, after a minute.

"Can you tell me about it?"

But Lily found she couldn't.

Whenever Lily asked about Michael, her parents told her he was still in a coma, and after a while she decided that he was probably dead and they didn't dare tell her. After a while, too, Lily's parents told her she should probably start thinking again about school, maybe call some classmates and get some assignments. Rose had come back a few times by then, and so had someone else, a man called Henry, who Lily decided was a psychiatrist in disguise, or a detective, since he kept asking her who had raped her and who had hurt Michael. She hadn't been able to answer him or talk to him at all. Finally one day, when she was really a lot better anyway, she said to her parents, "I know you're trying to help, but I can't talk about what happened. I really, truly can't. I'm sorry."

Not long after that, they told her she would *have* to go back to school very soon. So one day she decided she would. She got up at seven o'clock and put on clean jeans and her favorite red long-sleeved polo shirt and found her big notebook and her backpack and went downstairs to breakfast.

"Wow!" her father said jovially. "Look at this! Looks like our old Lilybelle!"

She cringed at the nickname she'd always hated, but she knew he was trying to be nice, so she smiled and said, "Yup, it's the old me, ready to go off to the Word Mill." That was another family joke, sort of, calling school the Word Mill.

Food still didn't taste, so Lily hadn't eaten much for a long time, but she managed to swallow two pieces of toast and drink half a glass of juice before she strode briskly to the front door, sure that if she walked fast enough she'd be able to go through it, and outside.

But again she couldn't. Even though her mother said she'd go with her, as soon as Lily opened the door it was as if an invisible wall hit her and she couldn't move. Duncan visions, Duncan smells, Duncan clones, loomed behind every shadow saying, "Lily-filly, want to see my willy?" and "Baby dyke, we're gonna fix you, teach you how to be with men."

Angry at herself—no, furious—Lily turned around and fled back upstairs to her room, where she slammed her fists against the wall over and over again till her brother came in and grabbed her arms, stopping her.

Every day it was the same. Every day she tried, and every day her family watched her hopefully, and every day the Duncan clones rose again and she couldn't get beyond the open front door. And every night she lay in her bed thinking of Michael lying either in his grave or in his hospital bed.

One night, more than a month after it had all happened, she had a weird dream, a dream in which Michael came to her, sat on the edge of her bed, took her hand, and said, "Toby, you have to speak for both of us now. I can't talk, but you can. We can't let them get away with it, Duncan and his friends. We can't, Toby. I know you're scared, I know you're afraid to tell. I know you don't want to go out because you're afraid if you do you'll have to tell and then they'll get you again. But you can't spend your whole life in your room. If you do, Toby, Duncan's going to win. He's going to win, and we can't let that happen. We're not nobody, like we thought. We're only nobody if we let guys like Duncan make us nobody. We can't let that happen. Please, Toby, please. Please do it for both of us."

When she woke from that dream, Lily's face was wet with tears, and she sat bolt upright in bed, feeling the pressure of Michael's hand in hers as firmly as if it had really been there. Soon afterward, a great calmness came over her. She fell asleep again, warm in the feeling of Michael's closeness, and she slept more soundly than she had in weeks.

In the morning she woke up hungry. While she was getting dressed, trying to quell the turmoil in her stomach, she heard the phone ring, and a few minutes later, her mother came into her room, tears streaming down her face.

Lily knew then, but she let her mother lead her to the bed, sit her down, take her hands, and say gently, "Lily, I don't know how to make this easier, but that was Michael's dad. Michael died at about three this morning." She put her arms around Lily and pulled her close. "Oh, honey, I know how much you must have hoped he'd get well! But he couldn't have, Lily; he was too badly hurt. He wouldn't have been able to walk, or maybe to speak, or—"

"Shh, Mom." Gently, Lily touched her mother's face. "Shh. It's all right. I know. I knew. It's all right." She looked into her mother's eyes and smiled. "He's here," she said, putting her hand over her heart. "Michael's with me here. He always will be. It's all right now."

An hour later, Lily, with her parents following behind in the car, walked to school, along Clarence Street and past the convenience store, past Doc Carver's, past the abandoned garage on the corner of Clarence and Marsh, in through the big double doors of Brixton High, and straight to the principal's office. Her parents wanted to go in with her, but she asked them to wait outside.

"Mr. Forsythe," she said clearly when the surprised secretary let her in. "I'm ready to talk about what happened to me and to Michael. I'll go to the police later, but I want to talk to you first. Duncan and his friends . . ."

1990s

THE DECADE

"IT WAS THE BEST OF TIMES, IT WAS THE WORST OF TIMES."

Charles Dickens began his famous novel *A Tale of Two Cities* with those oft-quoted words, referring to the French Revolution. But one could say the same thing about the gay rights movement in the nineties. On the one hand, GLBT people were more visible than ever before, and there were tremendous strides in all areas: antidiscrimination laws, domestic partnerships, same-sex marriage, the media, entertainment, education, politics—you name it! Perhaps the most exciting and encouraging development on the legal front occurred in 1996, when, in a case called *Romer v. Evans*, the U.S. Supreme Court ruled that Amendment 2 to Colorado's constitution, which had been passed by the state's voters, was unconstitutional. The amendment would have made it impossible for gays and lesbians in Colorado to fight anti-gay discrimination in the courts and for Colorado to give them "protected status." People who favored the amendment said, as they have said repeatedly when fighting against civil rights for gays, that gays were seeking "special rights." But the Supreme Court said Amendment 2 really sought to deny gays and lesbians *equal* rights, not grant them special ones.

But wonderful though the outcomes of *Romer* and other advances were, the backlash accompanying our increased visibility continued to grow, and there were many steps backward. Tragically, there were terrible hate crimes in the nineties, including the murder of Matthew Shepard, a college student in Laramie, Wyoming, who was beaten, tied to a fence, and left in the cold to die. He was still alive, but only barely, when he was found; he later died in a hospital.

Although wider and more inclusive news coverage may have made the climate in the nation's schools seem worse than it was, it did appear that there was an increase in name-calling and bullying of GLBT kids. (Yes, finally, GL*BT*, for it was in the nineties, especially the late nineties, that bisexual and transgender people, including youth, began coming out in greater numbers than ever before, forming new organizations, and working to make antidiscrimination laws and regulations more inclusive.)

One of the most dramatic and widely publicized school harassment cases involved a gay Wisconsin boy, Jamie Nabozny, who was bullied in both middle school and high school. Jamie was called names, spat on, hit, mock-raped, urinated on, and kicked so severely in the stomach that he suffered internal bleeding. Even though both he and his parents complained to school authorities many times, Jamie, like many other GLBT students, was told that unless he stopped "acting gay" the abuse would probably continue, because—once again—"boys will be boys."

Not surprisingly, Jamie tried several times to kill himself, and finally, in the eleventh grade, he dropped out of school and moved to another state, where he studied successfully for a GED. He also started working to help other gay youths. And, with great courage, he sued his former school district.

In 1995, Jamie's suit was dismissed by federal district court in Wisconsin, but in 1996 an appeals court ruled in his favor, and, in an out-of-court settlement, Jamie was awarded $900,000.

Jamie Nabozny was the first gay student to sue a school district for ignoring abuse, and his brave action still stands as a warning to all schools that ignoring such abuse is unacceptable legally as well as morally.

But the nineties were the best of times, too. The "Gay Nineties," as some people, borrowing a term from another time and situation, have called the decade, strengthened our already strong GLBT community and prepared us to enter the twenty-first century with renewed vigor and optimism.

It's in education that perhaps the greatest strides were made, if only because schools had come fairly recently into the fray and had the farthest to go. Of course, there had always been gay kids and teachers, but until the late eighties, very few of them emerged from the closets the education system had built and encouraged. Schools, terrified of charges of child molestation and of endangering the morals of minors, and colleges (especially single-sex colleges), afraid of being viewed as "hotbeds" of homosexuality, had traditionally been quick to fire, suspend, or expel anyone, student or teacher, whom they suspected of being gay. Those fears, although diminished, still exist in some institutions and are still sometimes acted upon. But even so, it was in the nineties that growing numbers of school systems and colleges at last added "sexual orientation" to their antidiscrimination policies and became safer, friendlier places for GLBT students and teachers.

Gay-straight alliances blossomed all over the country in the nineties. Pink triangles appeared on the doors of some classrooms, signifying that those rooms were safe places for GLBT students, and schools began recognizing and participating in events such as Coming Out Day, Pride—including Youth Pride—marches, and the National Day of Silence, when GLBT and straight high school students refrain from speech in order to protest the silence and invisibility that prejudice forces on GLBT people. The climate of the nineties for gay kids was as different from that of the fifties as night is from day.

How did this happen?

There were many contributing factors, not the least of which were, again, our greater visibility and an effort on the part of many people to recognize, respect, and honor minority groups in general. But a pivotal event for gay and lesbian youth had occurred back in 1989. It was then that a report on youth suicide issued by the U.S. Department of Health and Human Services revealed that suicide was the number one cause of death among gay and lesbian youth, and that young gays and lesbians were two to three times more likely to attempt suicide than their straight peers. That report, which covered suicide among straight kids also, wasn't widely circulated—some say it was suppressed—but even so, it did lead to positive remedial action by some health care professionals.

In that same year, a Gay and Lesbian Civil Rights Bill was passed in Massachusetts, and it, plus the suicide report, led to the formation of the Massachusetts Governor's Commission on Gay and Lesbian Youth. In February 1993, the commission issued a landmark report that paved the way for huge advances in the lives of gay and lesbian kids all over the country and to ongoing efforts to make schools safe for them. The establishment of gay-straight alliances, which are usually open to students of any sexual orientation, was a major part of those efforts, as were regular consciousness-raising and sensitivity training sessions for school personnel.

The Gay, Lesbian and Straight Education Network (GLSEN), founded as the Gay and Lesbian Independent School Teachers Network in 1990 by private school teacher Kevin Jennings, was another major development. Its goals were originally to help GL teachers and to work against homophobia, but the organization grew rapidly, expanding to include public as well as private school teachers and then to support GLBTQ students and GSAs. Soon also, nonschool-affiliated support groups for GLBTQ kids sprang up here and there across the country, especially in major cities; there were even a couple of snail-mail pen pal groups! And as the Internet expanded and more and more kids had access to computers, young GLBTQ people were able to find support and companionship on the Web as well.

But the path to success in making schools safe for GLBT youth was not always a smooth one. Some administrators and school boards resisted vehemently and still do, and there have been bitter fights, especially over the formation of GSAs.

One of the lengthiest and most bitter occurred in Salt Lake City,

Utah, when in 1995 the principal of East High School refused Kelli Peterson, Ivy Fox, Keysha Barnes, and a few other students permission to form a GSA. Eleven years earlier, a law called the Equal Access Act had been passed by Congress; it established that when a public secondary school accepts federal funds, if it allows one noncurriculum-related club to meet on school grounds, it must allow *any* noncurriculum-related club to meet. (A noncurriculum-related club is one that doesn't have anything to do with a school subject—a photography club, for example.) East High did have noncurriculum-related clubs, and after it was pointed out that therefore it had to allow a GSA, the school district in 1996 decided to ban *all* noncurriculum-related clubs in order to keep the GSA one out. It also changed the designation of some noncurriculum-related clubs to curriculum-related.

In 1996, too, in an attempt to clear the way for the banning of East High's GSA and probably future GSAs as well, the Utah state legislature passed a law allowing schools to choose to ban clubs that "encourage criminal or delinquent conduct, promote bigotry, or involve human sexuality."

In 1998, the East High Gay/Straight Alliance and two of its student members sued the Salt Lake City School Board, saying that the district was in violation of the Equal Access Act and the First Amendment. But a federal district court judge dismissed the suit in 1999, first on Equal Access grounds, because the school was by then allowing the GSA to meet, and then, when the school said it would not prevent students from expressing pro-gay views, he dismissed the First Amendment allegation as well.

At that point, the students tried to form a curriculum-related club they called PRISM (People Respecting Important Social Movements), which amounted to a GSA. But the school banned it—and the students went back to court.

The court issued an injunction that allowed the club to meet while the case was in progress, and at last, in October 2000, the school board gave permission for PRISM and other clubs. The lawsuits were dropped; finally the determination, courage, and sheer hard work of those students in Salt Lake City had been rewarded.

Other students, who have managed to convince their school officials to allow them to form GSAs or who have met with no official resistance, have nevertheless sometimes been taunted and harassed by their peers. Sometimes their posters have also been torn down and their bulletin boards have been trashed, but most have continued their struggle anyway—and most have eventually won.

The nineties saw a bitter battle over the anti-gay policy of the Boy Scouts of America, a battle that to some extent is still going on as I write this. In 1990, nineteen-year-old Eagle Scout James Dale was expelled from the Boy Scouts when Scout officials found out he was gay—even though he had been awarded more than thirty merit badges in his long scouting career. Dale fought his expulsion for years, and in 1999 the New Jersey Supreme Court said that according to that state's antidiscrimination law, the Scouts couldn't discriminate against gays. But meanwhile, in 1998, the California Supreme Court had ruled that since the Boy Scouts are a private organization, they *could* discriminate against gays, as well as against atheists, who had been at issue, too. The Scouts appealed the *Dale* decision, but in June 2000, the U.S. Supreme Court also ruled in favor of the Scouts' policy.

Since then, however, many individuals, secular and religious organizations, charities, school districts, and some major corporations and police and parks departments—even the movie director Steven Spielberg—have broken all ties with the Boy Scouts in protest. And even before the U.S. Supreme Court decision, a twelve-year-old Scout, Steven Cozza, and a scoutmaster named David Rice founded Scouting for All, an organization and Web site dedicated to changing the discriminatory policy and opening the Boy Scouts to all young people, regardless of their spiritual beliefs, gender, and sexual orientation. Scouting for All continues its mission today, with Steven's dad, Scott Cozza, as president.

Other well-known and popular youth organizations, such as the

Girl Scouts, Boys & Girls Clubs, 4-H, and the YMCA, do not discriminate on the basis of sexual orientation, but despite that fact and despite
efforts by some local Boy Scout councils to change the national organization's policy, in February 2002, the Boy Scouts of America resolved
that neither gays nor atheists can be Scouts or lead them.

Perhaps reflecting the new public awareness of the existence of GL
youth, and certainly a welcome by-product of the growing visibility of
gay people in general, during the late eighties and the nineties there
was a tremendous increase in GL literature for young adults, both fic-
tion and nonfiction. Some novels showed how straight kids adjusted to
having gay or lesbian friends or relatives, how straight kids dealt with
older siblings, teachers, and relatives with HIV-AIDS, or how straight
kids fought anti-gay bigotry. Others showed gay kids coming out and
falling in love, but usually as secondary characters; only a few young
adult novels had gay or lesbian protagonists, and even fewer included
bisexual or transgender characters. Nonfiction books for young adults
covered such subjects as coming out, homophobia, gay history, AIDS,
gay rights, suicide prevention, and law. Many included lists of re-
sources for young gays and lesbians. There were also a few biographies
of gays and lesbians in the arts, sports, politics, and other fields—and a
few autobiographical sketches by gay and lesbian teens themselves appeared in other books. Responding to the fact that many GL couples
were having or adopting children, picture books for and about those
children began appearing as well.

Many of these books were challenged by school boards and/or parents who argued that homosexuality is immoral or an inappropriate
subject for school-age students; they urged that the books be removed
from library shelves or dropped from school curriculums. Some of the
people who complained actually removed the books themselves or
used markers to black out passages they felt were offensive. The
groundbreaking picture book *Daddy's Roommate* by Michael Will-
hoite, about a little boy whose father is a divorced gay man living with
his male partner, was the second most frequently challenged book be-

tween 1990 and 2000; *Heather Has Two Mommies* by Lesléa Newman, about a little girl being raised by lesbian parents, was the eleventh.

Other gay books under fire in this era included the nonfiction books *Two Teenagers in Twenty* by Ann Heron and *When Someone You Know Is Gay* by Susan and Daniel Cohen, plus the novels *The Drowning of Stephan Jones* by Bette Green, *Baby Be-Bop* by Francesca Lia Block, and my own *Annie on My Mind*. *Two Teenagers in Twenty*, *The Drowning of Stephan Jones*, *When Someone You Know Is Gay*, and *Baby Be-Bop* were removed from the Barron, Wisconsin, School District in 1998 as a result of a request by a resident; four other books, three of them gay, were also challenged but not removed. A lawsuit protesting the removals was settled in 1999 with the stipulation that the books be made available to students.

Annie on My Mind was burned in 1993 in Kansas City and removed from school library shelves in a number of school districts in and around Kansas City in both Kansas and Missouri. A lawsuit brought by a group of brave, determined students in Olathe, Kansas, was finally decided in 1995, and the judge ordered that the book be returned to library shelves. Once again, as in Salt Lake City and other places as well, teens had shown that they would not tolerate the violation of their rights—and that they could fight such violations and win.

In many ways, it was gay and lesbian youth and their supportive straight peers who shaped the Gay Nineties and continued the battle for the rights of GLBT people. In the nineties, GLBT youth emerged as a strong and proud force for change, willing and eager to help themselves and to make their own valuable contributions to the movement.

PARENTS' NIGHT

THIS YEAR MY DAD DIDN'T GIVE ME A ROSE ON MY BIRTHDAY.
When I was born, he sent Mom yellow sweetheart roses and
had the florist put one in a separate vase for me. Every year after that
he gave me yellow sweetheart roses on my birthday, and when my sister, Josie, was born, he did the same for her, only with carnations. He
kept on with my rose, too, even though by then I'd begun refusing to
wear the frilly pink dresses he liked, with spotless white tights and old-
fashioned pink hair ribbons.

"Hair ribbons!" my girlfriend, Roxy, shrieked when I told her. "Oh,
God, hair ribbons!" She laughed so hard that pretty soon she got me
laughing, too. Roxy's like that—happy, infectiously cheerful.

"Come on," I said, grabbing her. "Didn't you ever have to wear hair
ribbons?"

"No, Karen," she said. "I didn't. I had to wear blue barrettes."

"Barrettes!" I shouted, the way she'd said "hair ribbons." I started
to laugh, but then she kissed me and for a long time we didn't talk anymore.

That was in September, when we'd just come back from a summer
vacation away from each other. We were drunk with love, high with
it—we still are, but it was extra special at first, when we weren't worried about anyone, especially my dad, finding out. School? Ours isn't
perfect, but there's this group there called the Gay-Straight-Bisexual
Alliance, which we'd both joined only a few months after Roxy'd come
to our school the January before.

But back before I'd gotten to know Roxy or figured out I was gay,
my friend Ab—Abner—and I were talking about a dance everyone was

going to. "The last thing I want to do is prance around with some stupid boy and pretend I like him," I said, and Ab said, "You really do like girls better than boys, don't you, Karen?" It hit me then that I always had, and that I wouldn't mind at all dancing with a girl. Ab remarked, very softly, "We're two of a kind, then; I like boys better than girls. You know. That way. Sexually. To be in love with."

Right away a picture of Roxy jumped into my mind, with her wavy red-gold hair and deep sea green eyes and her wonderfully soft smile. As soon as that happened, I said, "Oh, wow!"

Ab looked at me with a sort of sideways grin he has. "I'm gay, Karen," he said. "And I'm in that new group, the Gay-Straight-Bisexual Alliance. It's pretty good. Maybe you should come to a meeting. A bunch of us are going to the dance. We're probably going to dance with each other. Want to come?"

"No," I said, because I wasn't sure if Ab was right about me, but then he told me most of the kids in the group weren't sure about themselves either. I still wasn't completely convinced, but I decided to go to the dance.

Luckily, Roxy was there.

When I first saw her, I was dancing with Ab, but when I noticed she was looking my way, I muttered "See ya" to him. I danced over to this girl, Ann, who he'd introduced me to. She was in GSBA, and she was more or less dancing alone; I made this big point of relating to her. No, I don't know where I got the nerve. All the time I was grinning at Ann, I was praying, "Notice, Roxy, notice; notice that I like girls." Somehow I forgot that might disgust her—dumb, right? But a couple of straight girls were dancing alone or with each other, too, and none of the straight kids seemed to notice the GSBA kids much. (Well, one guy yelled "Faggot" a couple of times, but a teacher threw him out.) I didn't think Roxy really saw me.

But a little later when I was getting a Coke, she came up to me.

I got all sweaty when I saw her heading for me, and I knew I wasn't going to be able to think of a thing to say. But she just smiled and said,

"You look great dancing. Is it really true no one minds if girls dance with girls at this school?"

"Well, I—I . . ." I stammered—eloquent, right? "Sometimes. I mean I don't really know. This is the first dance I've been to here. But it looks like no one minds, doesn't it?"

Roxy laughed her infectious laugh. "Yes," she said, and she actually took my hand. "It does look like that. I don't see any boys dancing together, though. I'm glad we're not boys, aren't you?"

I gulped and said, "Yeah," and we danced. We went on dancing together the whole night, and I almost didn't notice when Ab sailed by and mouthed "Lucky" at me.

Well, that's how I got to know Roxy. We had one lunch period a week at the same time, and we had a couple of classes down the hall from each other, and of course there was after school. We both went out for the same sports, not because we both liked the same ones but so we could be together. We left notes in each other's lockers. And pretty soon we were so close, we almost breathed the same breath. I knew what she was going to say before she said it, and she knew what I was thinking. We didn't always agree, so we argued a lot, but we always ended up laughing and then learning from each other—we still do. We both joined GSBA, and pretty soon the other kids there began calling us "The Lovebirds." Without really saying anything about it, suddenly we, plus Ab, were the only kids in the group who were sure enough we were gay to be out.

Out in the group, that is. Not out to teachers or kids outside GSBA, as Ab was, not out to straight friends, not out to siblings, and especially not out to parents.

In September, after school started again, Dad kept saying I should make other friends, and Mom kept asking me about boys.

Finally Mac, who's the faculty adviser to GSBA, said, "Karen, your parents aren't going to get off your case unless you explain things to them."

I'd been complaining about how hard it was for me to pretend to my parents that Roxy and I were just ordinary best friends. I'd told them Ab was my boyfriend, and Mom had been urging me to get him to fix Roxy up with someone so we could go out together as two couples instead of as a threesome, which is what we usually did. "It isn't fair to Roxy, dear," Mom said. "Think how you'd feel if she had a boyfriend and you didn't." Mom's a social worker, and she prides herself on understanding what goes on inside people. "Don't you want Roxy to have a boyfriend?" she asked. "Doesn't Roxy want one?"

I wanted to scream "No!" but I had to say "Yes" to both questions. I muttered something about Roxy's being shy, and Mom said we'd have to help her get over that and how about giving a nice little party.

"She's a social worker, Karen," Mac said when I told the group. "She must know something about homosexuality."

Roxy reached for my hand. "Knowing and accepting aren't the same thing. You should see her, Mac! She spends two hours a week at the beauty parlor, and she buys all her clothes at Lord & Taylor, and when she meets a woman friend, she sticks her cheek against her friend's and her butt out behind—God forbid she should touch another woman's body—and she and the other woman kiss the air."

"I love it!" Ab chortled. He grabbed the hand of a guy named Jonathan, who sat next to him, and they stood up and demonstrated, perfectly.

Everyone laughed, and we went on to something else, but at the end of the meeting Mac said, "I have an announcement," and we all got serious again, because Mac's rarely that formal. He's the only teacher in the whole school who's out, which must take incredible guts, and he started GSBA, so to us he's pretty much of a hero. He was usually so upbeat that the solemn face he put on then made me afraid he was going to tell us he was HIV-positive or something. But all he said was "Okay, gang. You probably know Parents' Night is coming up . . ."

We all groaned, which is the usual thing kids in our school do when someone mentions Parents' Night—"Showtime," Ab calls it. It's bad enough to have to clear out the desks and lockers, and make sure there's evidence of Exciting and Meaningful Projects in the classrooms, and only great-looking artwork on the walls—but there are also parent-teacher conferences, and some kids have to serve as guides and escort the parents around the school.

Mac held up his hand. "I know, I know," he said sympathetically. "But the gimmick this year is that the gym's going to be set up with booths for all the student organizations and clubs, and I thought we should have one, too."

There was a stunned silence. Nobody said anything for a while, but finally Ann, the girl I'd danced with when I was trying to get Roxy's attention, said, "What's supposed to be in the booths?"

"A couple of members of the organization, and something to show what the organization does," Mac answered. "The drama club will have programs of past shows—that kind of thing."

"We could put out those book lists you've been giving us," said Roxy.

"And the list of gay organizations in the city," said Ann.

"And AIDS stuff," Ab suggested.

Jonathan grinned. "Hey, we could hand out condoms!"

"Don't think that didn't occur to me," said Mac. "But I have a funny feeling that might not go over big with some of the parents. The last thing we want to do is antagonize anyone."

"But AIDS stuff is a good idea," said Roxy. "The lists, too, of course."

"Good," said Mac. "Any volunteers," he asked casually, "for sitting in the booth?"

"You," said two or three people at once.

"I'll be there," said Mac, "or nearby, but the point is for the parents to see what the *kids* are doing. I know what I'm asking," he added. "Believe me, I know."

"It should be someone who's out," the girl next to Ann said.

All eyes went to Ab, and then to Roxy and me.

"Not necessarily," said Mac. "Remember, our big point has always been that no one has to be out, or sure of their sexual orientation."

"Yeah," I pointed out, "but most kids figure we're all gay, and the parents probably will, too. You know what people are like."

"Yes," Mac said. "I know."

Everyone was still looking at the three of us.

Ab shook his head. "My dad would throw me out of the house. I know he's coming to Parents' Night. I'm sorry. I'd really like to do it, but I can't."

"You mean you're not out to your folks?" asked one of the other boys. "Jeez, you're out to everyone in this whole school!"

"I know, I know. But at home I'm a master of subterfuge." Ab gave a little bow, and we all laughed, but uncomfortably.

"That leaves us," I said to Roxy. "But we're not out to our parents either," I said to everyone else.

"No one has to make a decision now," Mac told us. "But do think about it, everyone. And remember, it really doesn't have to be anyone who's out, or anyone who's sure of their sexuality."

"But no one who's not sure is going to dare," Roxy said later, up in my room; my parents were still at work. She hesitated. "My dad's got one of his trips that week, I think, and Mom's going with him." Roxy's dad was in the travel business, and she and her older sister often had to stay home alone.

"Lucky!"

"I'm not absolutely sure yet." Roxy smiled bravely. "But look, if I have to do it—be in the booth by myself, I mean—it's okay. Maybe it would be better."

"I can't let you do that," I said. "God knows how people are going to react."

"Mac'll be there." She kissed me. "Don't worry."

I kissed her back, deciding quickly. "I'll be there, too."

· · ·

But how, I asked myself after she left, am I going to tell my folks? I knew I couldn't just suddenly appear in the booth without warning them.

I went over lots of scenes in my mind, starting with the one where I come down to dinner and say, "Mom, Dad, Josie, I've got something to tell you. I'm gay. I'm a lesbian"—whereupon Mom throws her hands up to her face and bursts into tears and Josie stares at me like I've just grown another head, and Dad shoves his chair back and says, "I'm going out"—and ending with the one where I say quietly on Sunday while we're all reading the paper, "By the way, I'm going to be in one of the student organization booths on Parents' Night," and Mom says cheerfully, "That's nice, dear. Which one?" and I say "GSBA," and Dad says, "What in blazes is that?" I say "Gay-Straight-Bisexual Alliance," and they *all* stare at me like I have two heads. Mom says, "Do you think that's wise, dear?" and at the same time Josie says, "Gay as in homosexual?" Dad bellows, "I don't want any daughter of mine mixed up with a bunch of queers. You want to do social work, you go to school for it, like your mother. *Then* we'll talk about it."

But as it turned out, I didn't have to play any of the scenes I'd imagined.

Three nights later, at dinner, Mom said, "I had to turn down two more cases today. I really wish my supervisor would get it through her head that I just can't handle AIDS cases."

Now, this wasn't a new topic. Mom's okay as a social worker, I guess, but she's developed this one serious blind spot: She'd refused to handle AIDS cases ever since her supervisor first tried to give her one; she said she had to protect our family's health. This had started back before I knew much about AIDS. Later, when I knew more, I made a feeble attempt at telling her she couldn't catch AIDS unless she slept with her clients or got their "bodily fluids" in a cut or something, but she just said, "Medical science isn't infallible; there's a lot people still don't know. I can't risk your health." At that I'd given up.

But tonight, since all I'd been thinking about was that darn booth and how sick I was of hiding from my parents anyway, I just fell apart.

I tried to be calm at first. "Who gets the AIDS cases you give up?" I asked. I could hear that my voice sounded funny, and I guess everyone else did, too, because Mom, Dad, and Josie all stopped eating and stared at me.

"Why, I don't know," said Mom. "But they do get reassigned, eventually."

"Oh, great," I said sarcastically. "And until they do, some poor gay guy languishes in his rented room, too weak to go out and get food or cash his welfare check or whatever."

Mom and Dad looked at each other.

"Karen," Dad said to me, "your mother is a very good social worker. She is also a very good mother, and she's told you before why she won't take AIDS cases. You should be grateful."

I laughed. "Isn't that just a little bit hypocritical? I mean," I went on, turning to her, "if you really believe you're going to catch it, aren't you condemning some other social worker and her family to certain death by letting the cases be reassigned?"

Mom looked startled, and then I swear she turned pale. "I know the risk isn't great, Karen," she said evenly, but I could hear that she was furious. "And I believe most of the workers who accept AIDS cases don't have families. Some even volunteer. I just happen to prefer working with normal people who need social services through no fault of their own."

Then I really exploded. I could feel it coming, but there wasn't any way I could stop it. "Fault of their own!" I yelled. "Normal people! God, how unfair. What you're really saying is that if my gay brothers and sisters get AIDS, it's their fault and they deserve to get sick!"

There was a deadly silence. I mean deadly. The kind that chokes you.

"I thought it wasn't just gay people," Josie said, looking around anxiously. "They said in health class that it's drug addicts using dirty needles, and people not using condoms, and you don't have to be—to be gay, Karen. Normal people can get it, too, and kids can, and people have gotten it from bad blood transfusions, and—"

"What do you mean, your 'gay brothers and sisters'?" Dad boomed, ignoring Josie.

Suddenly I was freezing cold, and my heart was beating so hard I felt dizzy. I took a deep breath and looked Dad straight in the eye. "I mean I'm gay, too," I said as calmly as I could. "I didn't want to tell you this way, yelling it, and I'm sorry I did, but I'm tired of hiding. I'm a lesbian, and Roxy and I, we're not just friends like you think, we're—"

"That's enough," my father snapped. "Josie, please go to your room."

"But, Daddy—"

"Do what your father says," Mom ordered. She'd sort of moaned when I'd said the word *lesbian*, and now I could see that she was fighting tears.

I got up and tried to put my arms around her, but she pulled away.

"I—I'm sorry," I said, going back to my chair. "I'm sorry. But that's how it is—how I am. I can't do anything about it; I don't want to. I never fit in before, because I didn't know where I belonged or what made me different. Now I do. And I wanted you to know. I'm in this group at school . . ."

I told them about Parents' Night and the booth and how Roxy and I were going to be working in it, but when I'd finished, my father got up from the table, looked at me coldly, and thundered, "You are not going to be in that booth. And you are going to drop out of that—that organization. If I have to take you out of that school and send you to another, I will." He stormed out of the room.

My mother let go her tears, and followed him.

I didn't drop out of GSBA, and luckily my parents didn't mention it again. Two days later was my birthday, and we had the usual family party, with cake and ice cream and presents. My parents had been pretty strained and distant, but they went ahead with all the traditional stuff almost as if nothing had happened, singing "Happy Birthday" and marching in with the presents and the blazing cake. I oohed and aahed, and there was a certain amount of false laughter. But there was no yellow sweetheart rose from Dad, and he was the most strained and the quietest of all of us. You better believe I noticed, and after dinner I went to my room and cried.

Time went on and things slowly settled down on the surface, except I noticed a list of names near the phone one day that I figured might be psychiatrists, and I almost threw it away. No one said anything about it, though, so I didn't. Then one Saturday a couple of weeks later Dad went fishing with a friend of his at some ungodly hour like 5 a.m. Josie slept late, so I had Mom to myself when I went down for breakfast. She said, "Good morning," cheerfully and made us both bacon and eggs, and we talked about the weather and how many fish Dad might or might not catch. But when she started on her second cup of coffee, she finally said, awkwardly, "Karen, I'm sorry about the—that argument."

"I am, too," I said. "I'm sorry I attacked you. I don't agree with you about AIDS, and it's something that matters to me. But I guess you have a right to your opinion."

"Maybe I don't," she said, "if my opinion is wrong. I've been doing some reading, and I'm a little ashamed of myself. I—I think I've lost sight of why I became a social worker in the first place. I've always been—uncomfortable, I guess you could say—about homosexuality. But . . ."

"There are parents' groups," I told her tentatively.

"Yes," she said with a sort of embarrassed smile. "I know. Parents, Families and Friends of Lesbians and Gays. I've talked with a very nice woman, several times. She's helped a lot. Karen, I—I'd rather you weren't gay. And I don't quite believe you are; you're so very young. But if you are, if you turn out to be, I want you to know I still love you, and

I'll do my best to support you. I like Roxy," she added shyly. "And I'm glad you—you've got her."

"Me, too," I said. Then carefully, I added, "Are you and Dad coming to Parents' Night?"

"I am. And I've been trying to get Dad to come, too. Are you going to do that booth?"

I took a deep breath. "Yes," I said. "With Roxy."

Her lips tightened, but she nodded and finished her coffee.

By the time Parents' Night came, though, I still didn't know if Dad was coming. He'd caught several big trout on his fishing expedition, and we'd had them for dinner that night rolled in oatmeal and fried the way he liked them. I helped Mom cook them, and he seemed pleased at that. He wasn't really hostile anymore, but I kept catching him looking at me like I was some stranger. A couple of times I wanted to say, "Hey, Dad, I'm still the same person I always was; it's just that you know me better now." But I didn't dare.

The afternoon of Parents' Night, I had a bad case of nervousness when Roxy and I and the other kids set up our booth. Some of the straight kids looked at us kind of funny, but I guess Mac's being there kept them from saying anything. When we got back to the gym that night, though, a while before the parents were due, someone had painted FAGGOTS AND DYKES over the words GAY-STRAIGHT-BISEXUAL on our sign.

"Ignorant bastards," Mac muttered, and Ab, who'd brought the AIDS literature, said, "I'll fix that," and he ran off to the art room. By the time the doors to the gym opened and the parents started coming in, the sign said the right thing again.

"Are you as nervous as I am?" I whispered to Roxy when Ab had left.

She nodded, and Mac pretended his hands were shaking and his head and his whole body, and that made us laugh. A few minutes later the principal came up to us and said, "You folks get the prize for brav-ery. Good luck, and let me know if there's any problem." That was pretty nice.

There wasn't much of any problem. A few parents came up sort of hesitantly, like they were surprised or embarrassed, and that helped me feel less scared. One or two walked by grinning or giggling as if we were aliens or something, and one man stopped in front of the booth, shaking his head and saying "I don't believe this" over and over, but no one paid much attention to him. Lots of people took AIDS literature, a couple of people said they were glad we were there, and a few people took the book and organization lists.

And then I didn't see much else, because I spotted my parents coming into the gym.

Right. My *parents*. Plural. Mom was smiling bravely, and hanging on to Dad's arm as if she were trying to show the world he belonged to her and they were a happy, well-adjusted couple. Well, okay, I figured I'd do that kind of thing, too, with Roxy, if I could. Dad's left arm, the one that wasn't linked with Mom's, was behind his back. Without even glancing at any of the other booths, he led her right up to ours.

Talk about cold sweats!

I put as much of a smile on my face as I could and started to say, "Hi. Thanks for coming."

Dad looked very embarrassed, and as nervous as I felt. He sort of scanned the gym as if he were checking for people he knew, and he gave Mom a desperate look. She nodded in a stiff kind of way, and Dad bent down awkwardly so his head was sort of half inside the booth, and he kissed me.

Then he took his other arm from behind his back and handed me a yellow sweetheart rose.

"Happy birthday, kiddo," he whispered. "I'm a little late with this, but I promise I won't be again. I—I've got a lot to get used to, but—well, you're still my daughter. I just need some time." He smiled, a little crookedly, but hey, it was still a smile.

I couldn't move, and I felt tears well up in my eyes. While I was still trying to figure out what to say and how to keep from blubbering all over the booth, Dad reached over to Roxy and gave her shoulder a clumsy pat. "I'm glad you and Karen care for each other," he said awkwardly.

He looked around the booth and picked up the lists and some AIDS pamphlets. He handed the AIDS stuff to Mom, winked at me, and then they walked off, heading for the next booth.

And I stood there with the tears spilling over and Roxy gripping my hand till Mac gave me a handkerchief and Roxy whispered, "Hey—crying's bad for business," and we went back to work.

THE TUX

S O, LISTEN: AFTER SCHOOL THREE GIRLS GO INTO THIS TONEY CLOTHES rental-and-sales shop we have in our town, where you can rent a tuxedo or buy a formal gown and get all the stuff that goes with both. Anyway, it's prom time, and the place is having a special deal for the local high schools, and it's full of kids when the girls walk in. They're kind of laughing and joking and . . .

Oh, who am I kidding?

There's no punch line; this isn't a joke. Well, maybe it's kind of funny, but it's not a joke, it's, like, real.

The girls are me; my girlfriend, Sara; and our friend Rachel. I'm Laine. It's short for Elaine, which I hate.

We're there so Sara can rent a tux.

Why she wanted to wear a tux to the prom was a mystery to me. I mean, she's no way butch; if either of us is butch it's me, and I'm not all that butch. I'm maybe, like, "futch," which is what my great-aunt Barbara says is a word someone invented back in the sixties to describe a dyke who's not either butch or femme, but a little bit of both. The other thing is that I'm what Rachel calls "zaftig," which can be a nice way of saying fat. Rachel's Jewish, in case you didn't guess that from "zaftig," and by the way, she's also so straight you could draw lines with her if she lay down on a big piece of paper. Straight but not narrow, like the political button says.

We made Rachel come with us. Let's face it, even though the hets— um, that's straight people—have been letting us go to proms since that kid from Rhode Island—what's his name?—Aaron Something?— made a big stink about going with his boyfriend, still, proms are so not gay. Sara and I figured we needed someone with us in that rental-and-sales place to help us navigate in, like, hostile waters.

We were right.

Half the football team was in there, and almost the whole cheer-leading squad.

"It's our lucky day," Sara whispered to me, rolling her eyes.

"Yeah, right," I whispered back, trying to tell my face that jocks weren't worth the embarrassment of looking nervous right there in front of everyone.

"Hi, Craig, Joe, Max, Diver," Rachel caroled brightly.

Various big lugs grinned and nodded, and said "Hi" and "Hey," and "Whassup?" and stuff like that.

Did I mention that Rachel is gorgeous?

Rachel is gorgeous.

Mom used to kid that she's a "Jewish-American princess" back when we were in, like, third grade, because of her looks, not because of her attitude, which is not stuck-up or anything like that. Maybe she's the good part of being a princess, you know? Kind, and friendly, and cheerful even if she's sad, which she sometimes is because she's also really smart, and when you're that smart I guess you see a lot of stuff in the world that makes you sad. I was secretly in love with Rache from sixth grade to eighth grade, when I met Sara. Luckily, after that, we went back to being friends.

"So, Lisa, you getting that blue gown you saw?" Rachel was asking one of the cheerleaders. Rache had been rooting around in the racks of dresses.

Sara poked me. "That's the one I saw, too. The one that would look good on you."

"Yeah, right," I said again, even more sarcastically this time.

I look even worse in skirts than I do in pants.

"You have to wear *something*, Laine," Sara said. Then she giggled, and I knew that both of us were having the same fantasy: her in the tux she wanted and me in nothing and both of us dancing and everyone clapping. Well, maybe she didn't have the exact same fantasy, but I bet hers was close.

"This one's not bad," Rachel said, shoving a blue sort-of velvet—I don't know a whole lot about stuff like this so you're going to have to use a lot of imagination here and there—a blue sort-of velvet top at me. It had a turtleneck and no sleeves. Now I've got pretty good biceps, so I chalked up a plus for no sleeves. Maybe not for the turtleneck, though—I mean, like, hello? For a June prom? For *anything* in June?

"It comes with this." Rachel showed me a long, lighter blue skirt made of some shiny, smooth material. Silk, satin, whatever. One of them.

"I'd trip over it."

"Duh," Sara said, grinning. "You would."

"It's not *that* long." Rachel held it up in front of me, and it stopped an inch or two from the floor. "Perfect," she said, and she shoved me and it toward the back of the store, where there was a little alcove with a couple of floor-length mirrors and the dressing rooms in it. A couple of the dressing rooms were marked "M," and a couple across from them were marked "F."

Between them stood Craig and Max, with Diver.

Diver's called Diver not because he's an underwater freak but because he dives for the ball like I guess no one else ever has in the entire history of football.

Diver's also not what anyone could call "a Friend of Dorothy," which is what Great-aunt Barbara says used to be code for being gay. Well, I guess I should say he's not known for being a Friend of Friends of Dorothy. Whatever.

"Eeee-Laine!" Diver goes.

Yeah, he always calls me that. It cracks him and his buddies up every time. Sometimes they string it out long and loud and sometimes they squeak it so it's like "Eeeek, a mouse!"

I've been trying for years to find something similar to do with his name, but the best I've been able to come up with is "Glubber"—you know, for "Glub, glub"—but although that would work if he really *was* a diver, it doesn't work for football.

Anyway, I just shoved past him and his pals and went into one of the "F" dressing rooms.

I stripped off my flannel shirt, and Diver poked his head in through this ridiculous "privacy" curtain. Privacy, my ass!

"Holy shit, guys, some tits!" Diver called, whereupon Rachel and Sara grabbed him and pulled him away, and just before Sara pulled the curtain shut again and Rachel stood in front of it, like my own private guard dog, I heard someone say in a real loud salesperson voice, "Out!" When I came back out of the dressing room, looking like a stuffed trout that was turning blue from lack of O_2 (the damn dress was too small for me, as you probably figured out), I saw the absence of Max and Diver. Sara and Rachel were gone, too, but Craig and Joe were still there, and Craig was standing in front of one of the mirrors in this I had to admit really snappy-looking tux with a gray and black and white vest and matching tie over the whitest shirt in the world with these little round black button things that I was soon to learn are called, I guess appropriately, "studs."

"Man," I said without thinking, "that is so cool!" I imagined my own head on top of the shirt and the vest and the tie and the jacket, and before I could stop myself I said, "That's what I want, one like that one!"

Out of the corner of my eye I saw Craig grin and Joe clap his hand over his mouth and make his eyes bug out.

A saleswoman who must have been about a hundred years old materializes right next to me with a hanger that's wearing the same dress I'm wearing; Sara's right behind her beaming her encouraging-insistent smile—the one that encourages me to do what she wants me to do. "Luckily we have this in a larger size, miss," the saleswoman says, the words slipping out of her snide mouth like melted butter. She gives me this phony smile and says, "The blue matches your eyes."

This time it's Sara who claps her hand over her mouth, but then she takes it down and says, "Go on, hon, try it."

I love it when she calls me "hon," and she knows it, the little schemer. I melt, and like a good dog I take the damn dress from the saleswoman and pop back into the dressing room, yanking the curtain shut and just missing the saleswoman's nose.

When I came out with the larger dress on, I saw that I still looked like a trout, not anymore like an O_2-starved one, but like one who's had a lot too many worms or flies or whatever trout eat, and I also looked like I was in drag. Who am I kidding? I said to myself. I won't ever look like Dapper Craig, but I'll look *better* in a tux than in any dress. There must be fat guys who wear tuxes. Fat guys do get married and go to proms and bar mitzvahs and confirmations and funerals and stuff, and they probably have to wear tuxes to all those things, even if they're fat.

I thought about that for a while and looked at myself a bit more, and finally I nodded to myself and went back to the dressing room and exchanged the silly dress for my faithful flannel shirt and jeans again. Then, imagining a trumpet fanfare in my mind, I strode out of the dressing room, words like "I'd like to see the tuxes, please" wanting to come out of my mouth in my deepest, most confident, and, okay, butchest voice, except I wasn't sure I could pull it off, and I also wasn't sure how Sara would feel about it—

And then I stopped.

There was my honey, standing in front of the same mirror Craig had stood in front of, in her own way looking every bit as gorgeous as Rachel, with her long golden hair flowing gently over the shoulders of a powder blue tuxedo jacket, under which was a crisply pleated white shirt with those same little studs, only these were also powder blue. Over the shirt was a pink vest and a matching pink tie.

My first thought was: *Shit!*

My second thought had to do with my wanting to go up to her and [CENSORED].

Sara twirled around like she was wearing a long, full skirt that would balloon out around her. Yeah, I know: how could anyone give that impression wearing pants? Damned if I know, but Sara sure did it.

Rachel was standing next to her smiling and holding Sara's books and purse and stuff, like the maid of honor at a wedding holds the bride's bouquet when the bride's doing her stuff.

"Whoa!" I think I said.

"Like it?" Sara asked me, her face all serious and anxious.

"Yeah," I told her. "Yeah, I do."

The very same saleswoman who'd been sort of snide to me was beaming at Sara like Sara was her daughter or something. "It's so sweet on you, dear," she was saying to Sara. "Perfect. And very feminine. Don't you agree?" she asked Rachel, who was standing next to her—wearing, I suddenly noticed, a sort of slinky turquoise strapless gown that made her look like a movie star. The guys—Max and Diver had come back—were standing in a little knot a few feet away with the cheerleaders, who were in various stages of trying on stuff. But they were all quiet for once, their eyes on Sara and Rachel.

"Oh, yes," Rachel said, but she had the decency to glance my way. "Yes, I do agree."

Her glance, I realized, was more defiant than, well, anxious.

There was a "harumph" sound from the gallery—you know, from the jock-knot.

"How about," Craig said, stepping forward and putting his hand on my shoulder, touching me for the first time since second grade, when he shoved me into a mud puddle on the playground. (I got up and shoved him back, by the way, and it took two teachers to separate us.) "How about you ditch the dress, Halloran?" (That's my last name; he always calls me that when he calls me anything.) "How about you ditch the dress and wear a tux, too? You know, a regular black and white penguin suit one?"

"Yeah," Joe and Max muttered together, at least it sounded like them, and a couple of female voices purred something that actually sounded like agreement.

I look at Sara, and Sara looks at me and I'm glad to see she wants me to least try it, too, so I nod, and a salesman with blond curly hair who's wearing the tightest, flashiest-but-tasteful sports jacket I've ever seen beckons to me and asks me embarrassing questions about my size and piles a bunch of clothes on me and shows me how to work the little studs. Then he shoves me into a dressing room—still an "F" one—and leaves me alone to put everything on except my tie, which I have to get him to tie for me; he comes through the curtain to do it.

When he's finished, he gives me this semibutch shove on the back, turning me toward a mirror. "You look terrific, buddy," he says and winks, and it hits me then that he's probably gay.

"Thanks," I say, and he escorts me the six feet or so to the mirror, like he's trying to keep everyone else from seeing me till I've seen myself.

You know what? I did look terrific! I didn't look like an overweight penguin at all, or a stuffed fish, or anything. I looked like me, and me looked okay, even with the extra pounds that make me look weird in most clothes. I don't know what it was about the tux—maybe the color—you know, the fact that it was black? Or maybe the way it was cut? But it looked so terrific I caught myself wishing I could wear it every day.

I wanted to say some of that to the salesman, but I couldn't think of how to do it, so I just said, "Thanks for everything." For understanding, I especially wanted to say, but I was too embarrassed. I did manage to add, "Thanks for tying the tie."

He handed me a piece of paper with diagrams on it. "Directions," he said. "For the tie. Hey, bud!" he called softly after me when I turned around to face my public, who I saw were all standing right outside the dressing room alcove, which wasn't big enough for all of them—turned around nervously because, even though I thought I looked good, I wasn't sure about the others, especially the jocks.

"Knock 'em dead!" George E. Salesman calls—and as soon as I take a couple of steps toward her, Sara, her eyes shining, comes up to me, still in the blue tux, and links her arm in mine, and Rachel and the jocks and the cheerleaders all clap and whistle, and, jeez, when I think of it now I can't believe I did it, but I grabbed Sara and turned her to me and kissed her right there in front of everyone.

And they all went right on clapping!

2000–

THE DECADE SO FAR . . .

THE GLBT HISTORY OF THE TWENTY-FIRST CENTURY WILL BE WRITTEN BY some of you who are reading this book. What will your world be like? It will be a world in which being GLBT is more widely accepted than ever before, but like today's world, it will probably still be one in which there's considerable tension between the advocates of change and those who would force us to turn back. Today there are still losses as well as gains, but the major issues and the major steps forward of the early twenty-first century show just how far we have already come.

More states, cities, businesses, schools, and colleges than ever before have passed laws and regulations protecting GLBT people, and even though some of those laws and regulations have been and are being challenged, more are still being passed.

Since the 1970s, when Elaine Noble and a few other brave GL people ran for public office and won, many more have followed, despite having to endure homophobic slurs during their campaigns. As of June 2005, there were 287 openly GL elected officeholders in the United States.

There is still no cure for AIDS, and medication is still so expensive that only a relatively small number of people can afford it. At least medical advances have made it possible for people with HIV to live AIDS-free for longer, and research is continuing. July 2006 saw a tremendous advance: the Food and Drug Administration's approval of a single pill that combines three pills that many people with HIV take every day. However, it's very expensive, doesn't guarantee survival or a cure, and has serious side effects; not everyone with HIV can take it.

It's an important breakthrough, but even more important are continuing efforts to prevent HIV-AIDS via education and research. Why? Well, for one thing, in the middle of this decade, the Centers for Disease Control and Prevention found that around 50 percent of those who contract HIV are under twenty-five years old.

There are still challenges to gay content in movies, on TV, and in books. For example, in 2005 after a Lexington, Massachusetts, kindergartner, like the others in his class, brought home a "diversity book bag" in which was a book called *Who's in a Family?* showing different kinds of families, including a same-sex one, his father complained that the child was being exposed to beliefs contrary to his family's religion. A bit over a year later, while the controversy continued, a different couple with a son in the second grade of the same school complained about another picture book. This book, *King & King* by Linda de Haan and Stern Nijland, is about a prince who decides to marry another prince instead of one of the princesses to whom his parents introduce him. The two Lexington couples filed a lawsuit in 2006 against school officials—and by then, interest in the controversy had spread to others, including a group fighting gay marriage in Massachusetts, and to one that seeks to ban homosexual-themed books from the state's schools.

Back in 2005 also, a number of Public Broadcasting System stations pulled an episode of the children's program *Postcards from Buster* because U.S. Education Secretary Margaret Spellings disapproved of the fact that a child in the episode had two lesbian mothers. Some PBS stations did air the episode, but the controversy itself was both long and bitter.

Despite these and other challenges, GLBTQ characters and stories have become almost commonplace in movies, in books, and on TV. Straight awareness and understanding of transgender people, long overdue, has been growing, thanks to antidiscrimination laws, trans organizations, and media exposure like that in the popular movie *Transamerica*, about a male-to-female transsexual and her teenage son, and the cable TV documentary *TransGeneration*, about trans college students.

The 1993 "don't ask, don't tell" policy still requires gays and lesbians in the military to remain closeted, and thousands have been discharged when their homosexuality has been revealed. But the cost of recruiting and training replacements for them—a whopping $200 million—has increased pressure on the military to abandon its official stand against homosexuality. Some members of Congress have expressed disagreement with that policy, and lawsuits urging its abandonment have been filed in federal courts, although all have been unsuccessful. In 2006, when the U.S. Supreme Court came out in support of a law that refuses federal funds to colleges that ban military recruiters because they're against "don't ask, don't tell," editorials urging abandonment appeared in *USA Today* and other newspapers. Also in 2006, gay groups increased pressure for discontinuing the ban, and Congressman Martin T. Meehan of Massachusetts gained the support of more than one hundred other lawmakers for a measure that would, if implemented, abandon "don't ask, don't tell" in favor of a policy forbidding discrimination because of sexual orientation. And the military itself, perhaps in part because of the need to keep the total number of active troops high to continue the Iraq war, has recently been allowing growing numbers of soldiers who are known to be gay to stay in the ranks.

Still, others continue to suffer under "don't ask, don't tell." For example, Major Margaret Witt, a much-decorated Air Force flight nurse, was outed anonymously by someone in 2004, and investigated. As a result, she was relieved of her duties and her pay in preparation for discharge hearings. In March 2006, she was "administratively discharged," and in April of that year, she sued via the American Civil Liberties Union, asking that she be reinstated and allowed to continue in her career. But in July 2006, U.S. District Judge Ronald B. Leighton dismissed her case, despite expressing sympathy for her and recognizing her fine

record and the fact that her homosexual conduct did not involve anyone in the military or take place on military property. Among his
reasons for the dismissal, he cited prior rulings and the military's
contention that homosexuals are bad for discipline and morale.

GLBT people have always risked physical attack simply because of
their homosexuality, and that's been no different in this new century.
For example, in 2002, a transgender youth, Gwen (born Eddie) Araujo,
was brutally beaten and murdered when her biological gender was discovered at a party. A docudrama of her story was aired on cable in
2006. Sakia Gunn, a fifteen-year-old lesbian, was murdered at a New
Jersey bus stop in 2003 when she and her friends told a stranger who
invited them to a party that they were gay. In New Mexico in 2005,
James Maestas, twenty-one, and Joshua Stockham, twenty-four, were
beaten by men who saw them kissing.

Nothing can bring back Gwen and Sakia and other GLBT people
who've been brutally murdered, and nothing can adequately compen-
sate those who've been beaten or whose property has been vandalized.
But at least there is now growing support for including sexual orientation and sometimes gender orientation as well in hate crime legislation. Where such laws exist, people who are clearly motivated by
anti-GLBT prejudice when they commit crimes can be punished more
severely than people who commit crimes without such motivation.

Sadly, GLBTQ kids and children of GL parents are still sometimes
subjected to homophobic slurs and bullying, and school boards sometimes argue or change their minds about including sexual orientation
in their antidiscrimination regulations. Schools and school districts in
some parts of the country still sometimes fight the formation of GSAs
or try to force the disbanding of those that are already established—for
example, in 2006, this was even attempted (unsuccessfully) in Utah,
where Kelli Peterson and her friends had fought so hard for their GSA
a decade earlier. And there are still parents who disown their GLBT
teens or try to have them "cured." But there is growing acceptance by
straight teens as well as by many straight adults, plus large numbers of

thriving GSAs, similar groups, and supportive hotlines (including the Trevor Helpline, toll-free at 866-488-7386, a national 24/7 hotline for GLBTQ kids, especially those considering suicide). All those plus other services for GLBTQ kids are doing a steadily effective job of counteracting negative moves.

So are GLBTQ kids themselves—and that's tremendously exciting! For example, back in 2001, when she was eighteen, Californian Eva Sweeney, who has cerebral palsy, began trying to find a group that would support disabled GLBT young people. She was unsuccessful, but instead of giving up, in 2004 she started one herself, called Queers on Wheels, which, in addition to a Web site (www.queersonwheels.com), offers workshops and a resource guide.

Joseph Amodeo, eighteen, who as a high school student in New York State suffered homophobia from teachers as well as students, founded a group called Schools Are For Everyone (SAFE) in 2005 to promote and support antiharassment policies as well as GSAs.

In the spring of 2006, thirty-three GLBT young people traveled by bus to nineteen colleges and universities—mostly conservative Christian ones. When they arrived to impart their message that Christianity and homosexuality can be compatible, they were sometimes arrested for trespass, and sometimes received graciously. Sponsored by Soulforce, Inc., which was founded by the Reverend Dr. Mel White and his partner, Gary Nixon, and codirected by Jake Reitan and Haven Herrin, both twenty-four, the Equality Riders modeled their mission on the black and white Freedom Riders of the sixties who traveled in the South urging an end to segregation. After disbanding, many of the Equality Riders planned to continue their work toward equality in various parts of the country.

Most religious groups continue to have conflicts, some bitter, over their positions on homosexuality, but the good news is that in most cases, serious discussions about new interpretations and possible changes in practice are continuing.

Like Jamie Nabozny in the nineties, some GLBTQ kids in the early twenty-first century have reacted with lawsuits when they've been mis-treated in school. In 2005, Nancy Wadington, eighteen, sued her New Jersey school district for neglecting to stop the bullying she'd faced as a high school freshman. Seventeen-year-old California student Charlene Nguon sued after being suspended for kissing and embracing her girl-friend on the property of their school, which didn't discipline straight students for similar displays of affection. And in 2006, two sixteen-year-old girls filed suit against their California school after they'd been expelled on suspicion—*suspicion!*—of having a lesbian relationship.

Help is even coming from unexpected quarters. For example, for many years, conservative Christian organizations have been in the forefront of efforts to resist antidiscrimination laws and regulations fa-vorable to GLBT people, to defeat GLBT candidates for office, to pre-vent same-sex marriage and gay adoption, and to keep GSAs, inclusive sex education, and books giving an accurate picture of GLBT people and life out of the nation's schools. But in March 2006, a group of con-servative Christian leaders and gay advocates drew up a set of promis-ing guidelines aimed at encouraging and helping schools to discuss these issues reasonably and respectfully, without demanding that either group change its beliefs. The hope is that such discussions may lead to a more secure climate for GLBTQ students.

And college scholarship funds, offered by some universities and by groups like PFLAG, the National Gay and Lesbian Task Force, the Point Foundation, Friends of Project 10, and other groups are helping to make sure more and more GLBTQ kids and straight kids who've worked for GLBT rights can go on to higher education, even if their families can't or won't support them.

Another exciting development came in May 2006, when the Cali-fornia Senate passed a very pro-gay bill introduced by State Senator Sheila Kuehl. That bill would have required public school textbooks used in California to identify the sexual orientation of GLBT people who have contributed "to the economic, political, and social develop-ment of California and the United States of America"—much as such books now identify the race, gender, and ethnic background of similarly important figures. If that bill had been adopted there's a good chance its provisions would have been followed nationwide, for, because of the way textbooks are bought in California and the huge number that state buys, publishers often tailor all books sold to public schools to California's requirements. Later in the summer, expecting Governor Schwarzenegger's veto, Kuehl weakened the bill so that it simply forbade activities and teaching that "reflects adversely" on GLBT people. But even that weakened bill was vetoed by Governor Schwarzenegger.

Even so, who would have dreamed even twenty years ago that of all the issues for which we've fought, perhaps the two most explosive—those involving gay parenting and gay marriage—would dominate the first decade of the twenty-first century as AIDS dominated the eighties and youth the nineties?

In earlier decades, a good many gays and lesbians who entered into heterosexual marriages had children. When their marriages collapsed, as many did, some divorced gay-straight couples worked out friendly custody arrangements. But others found themselves in bitter battles, with custody going to the straight partner and visitation rights denied to the gay one. As the eighties progressed and our community fought more openly for equal rights and found legal support in organizations like Lambda Legal and the Gay & Lesbian Advocates & Defenders (GLAD), many divorced GL parents went to court to keep their children—and that made the issue of gay parenting itself more visible.

In the nineties, increasing numbers of lesbian couples had children via artificial insemination, and gay couples had children via surrogate mothers. Many other couples, both gay and lesbian, adopted children, often from overseas orphanages. But most adoption laws prevented *both* members of a gay or lesbian couple from adopting. And it was usually not possible legally for one member of a GL couple to adopt his or her partner's biological child. For those reasons, most of the children being brought up by GL couples had only one really legal parent. Unfortunately, in many parts of the country, that's still true today.

Estimates of how many children are now growing up in GL homes vary widely, from 250,000, which I suspect may be too low, to 14 or more million, which I suspect may be too high. But one thing is certain: in the nineties, the "gayby" boom was in full swing among both ordinary people and celebrities like Melissa Etheridge and Julie Cypher, and Rosie O'Donnell and her partner, Kelli Carpenter O'Donnell. In 2002, when Rosie O'Donnell came out, she also came out as someone who supports adoption by gays and lesbians. Now she and Kelli are raising four children and running cruises for other GL families with children.

And now, in the twenty-first century, the gayby boom shows no sign of stopping.

However, that trend has brought with it growing controversy over whether gays and lesbians are fit parents and whether children need both a mother and a father in order to become healthy, well-adjusted adults. Studies about those questions are small and somewhat inconclusive, since there hasn't been time for large numbers of children with two moms or two dads to grow up. But by 2002, the American Academy of Pediatrics, the American Association of Child and Adolescent Psychiatrists, the American Association of Family Physicians, and the American Psychiatric Association had all come out in support of gay and lesbian adoption. And the American Psychiatric Association had also said that the emotional and mental health of children raised by same-sex couples is no different from the emotional and mental health of children raised by opposite-sex couples. Other studies have found the same thing, and in the summer of 2004, the American Psychological Association announced it had found that gay and straight couples are very much like each other as far as their effectiveness as parents is concerned.

As the nineties moved into 2000 and beyond, a few states began allowing both members of a gay or lesbian couple to adopt jointly (nine states, plus Washington, D.C., in the first few years of the current decade). More states, and some counties in other states, have permitted "second-parent adoptions," allowing one member of a gay or lesbian couple to adopt a child first, followed by the second member, or have allowed the second member of a couple to adopt the other member's biological child. But as of early 2006, there were growing efforts in a number of states to ban all adoptions by GL people, singly or in couples, even though back in 2005, anti-gay adoption bills had failed to become law in seven states. In Mississippi, although individual gays and lesbians can adopt, couples cannot. Utah prohibits unmarried couples from adopting, so of course gays and lesbians can't adopt there either. But only Florida, via a law passed way back in 1977, has a law specifically preventing *all* gays and lesbians from adopting. Ironically, though, in early 2006, it looked as if legislators there might vote on letting GL foster parents adopt their foster children. Other states have also been rethinking their prohibitions against GL foster parents. For example, in June 2006 the Arkansas Supreme Court ruled that the state can no longer exclude gays and lesbians from fostering just because they're gay. And in August 2006 the Supreme Court of Indiana decided to let stand an April ruling of that state's appeals court that permits unmarried couples, both gay and straight, to adopt jointly.

The Vatican in 2003 declared that adoption by gays and lesbians is "gravely immoral," despite the fact that for years many Catholic gay and lesbian couples had been serving as foster or adoptive parents to needy children—often children who, because of their age or special needs, were seen as "unadoptable." In early 2006, bishops in Massachusetts sought to exempt Catholic adoption agencies from a state law prohibiting discrimination in adoption on the basis of sexual orientation. That set off a bitter struggle, the outcome of which was that the Boston branch of Catholic Charities decided to discontinue its adoption services altogether. Governor Mitt Romney filed legislation, seen as unlikely to pass, that would exempt religious organizations, including adoption agencies and hospitals, from observing the antidiscrimination law. The San Francisco branch of Catholic Charities and other Catholic Charities branches elsewhere in the country that handle adoptions have found themselves in similar quandaries. San Fran-

cisco's Catholic Charities said in August 2006 that it would provide
staff and money to assist a statewide adoption agency in making place-
ments. Some children will therefore be placed with GL families, but
not directly by Catholic Charities.

Complications arise in those states where adoption laws differ
from county to county, and in the many states that lack any laws at all
that definitively either prevent or allow adoptions by GL couples. Each
individual case must therefore be decided separately by the appropriate
court. The resulting confusion, plus the variety of new, complex litiga-
tion in different states about gay adoption, gay foster parenting, and
the custody rights of gay couples who split up, makes life especially difficult for families who move; a child who's legally adopted in one state
or county may well not be considered adopted in the place to which his
or her parents move.

Some good news has come out of Oklahoma on this front, though.
In 2004, Oklahoma's legislature passed a law that prevented GL couples
from adopting, and also invalidated the adoptions of GL couples who
move to Oklahoma from states or foreign countries that allow such
couples to adopt jointly. But in May 2006, U.S. District Court Judge
Robin Cauthron ruled that the law is invalid, saying it goes against several important provisions of the U.S. Constitution. An appeal, and a
request for affirmation of Cauthron's ruling, will be argued after this
book goes to press.

Even so, by the time the twenty-first century's first decade was under way, so many GL couples already had or were having children that
child rearing almost seemed expected in some circles. In the past, the
number of dogs and cats "adopted" by GL couples prompted occasional chuckles about pets being child substitutes, especially when dogs
marched with their human families in Gay Pride parades. But by Pride
2004, in Boston at least, it looked to me as if there were far more GL
couples with babies and small children than with dogs!

The legal arguments for outlawing gay rights, including gay adoption and gay marriage, for many decades lay with the sodomy laws

(laws against nonreproductive sex). Those laws were among the oldest in the nation, and although they were rarely enforced in modern times, when they were, it was more often against gay people than against straight ones—despite the fact that nonreproductive sex acts are practiced by straights as well as gays. And despite the lack of enforcement, the mere existence of sodomy laws was used time and again to support the argument that homosexuality itself, not just homosexual acts, was illegal.

Back in the early sixties, there were sodomy laws on the books in all states. In 1962, Illinois adopted the Model Penal Code, which in effect struck down that state's sodomy law by permitting any kind of sex as long as it was in private and between consenting adults. No other states followed until the seventies, when around twenty others repealed their sodomy laws, but even so, many such laws still remained and some were made to apply only to gays. Then in 1986, in a case from Georgia called *Bowers v. Hardwick*, the U.S. Supreme Court ruled that police had been right to arrest a gay man in his own home for breaking his state's sodomy law; the ruling said that homosexual couples had no right to privacy. This was a bitter blow to those who had been working zealously for repeal! In early 2003, thirteen states still had sodomy laws, and in four of them, those laws applied only to gays and lesbians. And sodomy laws were still being widely used as the basis for ruling that gays and lesbians were by definition criminals unfit to raise children, hold responsible jobs, or enjoy other rights taken for granted by heterosexuals.

Then along came a case known as *Lawrence v. Texas*. Back in 1998, John Lawrence and Tyron Garner had been caught in bed when police stormed into Lawrence's apartment, having been told there was someone with a gun in the same building. The police took the two men off to jail and charged them with violating Texas's sodomy law. The case reached the U.S. Supreme Court in March of 2003, and that June the Court ruled against the Texas law, at last nullifying all remaining sodomy laws.

Things didn't get better overnight, however. Virginia's attorney general refused to nullify his state's sodomy law, and as late as 2005 that state was still attempting to keep its law on the books. It took Kansas until October 2005 to abandon a somewhat related law that provided harsher penalties for adults having sex with same-sex minors than for those having sex with opposite-sex ones—even though in an earlier Kansas case involving two boys, one eighteen and the other fourteen, the U.S. Supreme Court had told the lower court to reexamine its decision against the older boy with *Lawrence* in mind. Even as late as 2006, the Department of Social Services in Missouri tried to use its state's still-existing sodomy law to argue that a woman applying to be a foster parent wasn't of "reputable character" because as a lesbian, she was likely to break the sodomy law. But circuit court Judge Sandra C. Midkiff rejected that argument, saying, "No moral conclusions may be drawn from a constitutionally unenforceable statute."

In June 2006, when Missouri's governor signed a law repealing the state's anti-sodomy law, the state attorney general decided not to pursue an appeal to Midkiff's decision that had been filed by the state's Department of Social Services. And a month later, the department announced that although it wouldn't automatically allow gays and lesbians to become foster parents, it would now consider their applications.

As Judge Midkiff pointed out in the original Missouri case, since *Lawrence* it has no longer been possible for people to say truthfully that homosexual behavior is illegal and that homosexuals are by definition criminals. Gays and lesbians rejoiced over *Lawrence*, hailing it as a tremendous victory and hoping against hope that it would lead the way to many positive changes—including the establishment of legal gay marriage.

Of course, there have always been many arguments against gay marriage besides the legal ones, ranging from "Homosexuality is a sin . . . It's forbidden in the Bible . . . God made Adam and Eve, not Adam and Steve . . . Marriage is for procreation and gays can't have children" to "Gay marriage is bad for children . . . It will weaken traditional marriage . . . It will lead to polygamy or even marriage between humans and animals," and so on. At least they've progressed gradually to arguments about how the decision about gay marriage should be made: by the courts, in state legislatures, or by the people! All the arguments wax and wane; some weaken or go out of fashion only to be overshadowed or replaced by others, just as happened in the past with arguments against freeing the slaves or granting equal rights to Native Americans. Progress is notoriously slow when it comes to the rights of minorities, and the move to legalize gay marriage is no exception, as this decade is showing in many states and at the federal level as well. This has been true despite the earlier efforts of gay and lesbian couples to obtain marriage licenses, and despite the fact that there have always been gay and lesbian couples who have lived as if married, many for twenty, thirty, forty, or more years.

Have you ever seen a sign on a hospital patient's door saying something like NO VISITORS EXCEPT IMMEDIATE FAMILY? "Immediate family" usually means parents, adult children, siblings—and, especially, husbands and wives. The rule that sign expresses can be and has been used to prevent the partners of gays and lesbians from visiting their seriously ill or dying loved ones.

Under most circumstances, married couples automatically have the right to inherit all or some of each other's property when one of them dies, even if they don't have wills. Unmarried couples, including GL couples, need to create their own "right" of inheritance through wills and other legal documents. Not all do, however, and when they don't, inheritance passes automatically to the deceased partner's legal next of kin—"immediate family" again. But even when the couple has the appropriate legal documents in place, parents, children, siblings, and sometimes other relatives can and often do contest them. When they win, the surviving partner can be left homeless and destitute.

Hospital visitation and inheritance are only two of the many hundreds of rights (and responsibilities as well) that automatically come with marriage. Some come from a married couple's home state and others come from the federal government, but until very recently, none have come to GL couples, even if they've been together for many, many years.

In an attempt to rectify the inherent unfairness of denying gay and lesbian couples rights that are equal to those granted to straight couples, starting in the early nineties and continuing into the present decade, gay and lesbian employees of some cities, states, and businesses have been allowed to register themselves and their mates as *domestic partners*. These partnerships give GL couples (and, in some cases, unmarried heterosexual couples) rights similar to some of those enjoyed by married people—usually joint health insurance policies, for example, and death benefits. That's a good step forward. But the specific rights awarded vary depending on the city, state, or business granting the partnership, and in some cases, domestic partnerships have been or are being threatened with being discontinued long after they've been put into effect. Even when they remain, helpful as they certainly are, they fall far short of actual legal marriage.

Hawaii, Alaska, and Vermont led the way to legal marriage for same-sex couples.

In May 1993, the Hawaii Supreme Court ruled that a lower court should not have dismissed a lawsuit three same-sex couples had filed two and a half years earlier, when officials had not granted them marriage licenses. Allowing only heterosexual couples to have marriage licenses was probably unconstitutional, the court said; the state would have to prove there was a "compelling" reason for preventing gays and lesbians from marrying—a decision that was unimaginable back when my partner and I were growing up in the fifties! But almost immediately, the chairman of Hawaii's Republican Party promised to urge the passage of an amendment to the state constitution that would ban same-sex marriage. Soon similar battles raged in Alaska and Vermont.

In 1996, as the move toward same-sex marriage heated up, the federal government passed the Defense of Marriage Act (DOMA), which stipulates that the United States recognizes only opposite-sex marriage and that no state has to accept a gay marriage that's legal in another state. More than half the states passed their own DOMAs or similar laws in the nineties.

By late in 1998, voters in both Hawaii and Alaska had approved state constitutional amendments barring gay marriage. Hawaii's amendment provided for the legislature to rule that marriage is only for opposite-sex couples; the legislature passed a law that did just that. Those votes ended the pro-gay-marriage efforts in Hawaii and Alaska, at least for the time being.

In Vermont, however, in late 1999, the state supreme court said the state legislature must grant same-sex couples all the rights granted in Vermont to married opposite-sex couples—and this country's first law allowing statewide *civil unions* was born! Gays and lesbians flocked to Vermont from all over the United States to take advantage of that ruling, as, of course, did many gay and lesbian Vermonters. Within four years, nearly seven thousand GL couples had been joined in Vermont civil unions—and, although it seemed unlikely to progress quickly, in early 2006, Representative Mark Larson, a Vermont state legislator, began working toward a bill to legalize same-sex marriage.

Why do that, if a civil union can give a same-sex couple all the rights a state gives to a straight married couple?

For one thing, a civil union is usually recognized only by the state granting it, and the rights that go with it are limited to those granted only by that state, not by any other state, and not by the federal government. Besides, marriage is by no means solely a matter of rights. In addition to them, married couples, straight ones anyway, enjoy a unique position of respect and recognition worldwide. Those couples are widely considered to be joined by a special bond; everyone knows what marriage "means"—at least what it's supposed to mean: a permanent, intimate, loving relationship between two people who have the legal right to become parents as well as to have all the other rights and responsibilities of marriage. As far as respect and recognition are concerned, it's not clear what, if anything, a civil union means, both legally and in the eyes of the public, especially outside the state that granted it. And emotionally, civil unions, though they are more inclusive than most domestic partnerships, still fall so far short of marriage in the minds of many people, both gay and straight, that many of us have dubbed them "marriage lite."

In Massachusetts, the scenario began very like those in Hawaii, Alaska, and Vermont, with an effort on the part of gay marriage opponents to override a pro-gay-marriage ruling of the state's supreme court by adding an anti-gay-marriage amendment to the state constitution. But the outcome was very different.

In November 2003, the Massachusetts Supreme Judicial Court handed down a landmark ruling in a lawsuit (*Goodridge v. Department of Health*) brought by seven courageous and determined same-sex couples and argued by Mary Bonauto of the Gay & Lesbian Advocates & Defenders. That ruling said that not allowing gays and lesbians to marry is against the state's constitution. The court gave the state legislature 180 days to "take such action as it may deem appropriate" in reaction to it. That meant that if the legislature didn't find a way to prevent it, GL couples would legally be allowed to apply for and be granted marriage licenses starting on May 17, 2004.

The *Goodridge* decision was greeted with great excitement and tears of joy, not only among those of us in Massachusetts, but also among gays and lesbians nationwide. Encouraged by it, in early 2004, sympathetic officials in San Francisco, California; New Paltz, New York; Multnomah County, Oregon (which includes most of Portland); and Asbury Park, New Jersey, issued marriage licenses and/or performed same-sex marriages in defiance of their states' own existing laws and practices. Some officials, especially San Francisco Mayor Gavin Newsom and New Paltz Mayor Jason West, faced at best political heat and at worst criminal charges because of their courageous actions.

Lesbians all over the country cheered when on February 12, 2004, Phyllis Lyon and Del Martin, two of the founders of the Daughters of Bilitis, who had been together for more than fifty years and who were among the earliest and most influential lesbian activists in the country, were the first same-sex couple married in San Francisco. By a few weeks later, when the California Supreme Court ordered San Francisco to stop issuing marriage licenses, some four thousand other GL couples had already married there. The gay mayor of Nyack, New York, John Shields, with his partner and nine other same-sex couples, applied for marriage licenses in March and sued when the licenses were denied. At around the same time, couples in other towns also applied for licenses and were denied, and ultimately, all licenses granted during this period were declared invalid, including, as late as April 2005, some three thousand that had been issued to same-sex couples in Multnomah County, Oregon.

Back in Massachusetts in the spring of 2004, so many verbal battles peppered the hearings the legislature held during the 180 days the court had given it in which to react that it still was not certain whether the court's pro-gay-marriage decision would stand. Finally the legislature passed a preliminary constitutional amendment that would prevent gays and lesbians from marrying and instead would establish civil unions giving GL couples some or all of the same rights the state extends to married straight couples. Because amending the Massachusetts Constitution is a complicated process, involving a second favorable vote in the next legislative session and then a favorable vote by the citizenry, the earliest that amendment could have become law was 2006. In the meantime, though, since nothing had happened to prevent it, the court's decision still stood, and the state was ordered to issue marriage licenses to GL couples starting on May 17, 2004. Soon Governor Mitt Romney—and, when his effort seemed likely to fail, others—tried to force a delay in the issuing of licenses until the fate of the proposed constitutional amendment was decided. But by the time the move to delay had indeed failed, many gay and lesbian couples in Massachusetts (including Sandra Scott, my partner of thirty-five years, and I) were already legally married.

The fate of a number of couples from other states who had rushed to Massachusetts to get marriage licenses was uncertain and remained so into 2006, for when some out-of-state couples sought to marry in Massachusetts, Governor Romney invoked an unused nearly one-hundred-year-old state law that had been passed in 1913, when a majority of states (although not Massachusetts) prohibited interracial marriage. It says that a couple can't marry in Massachusetts if they can't marry in their home state. But five same-sex out-of-state couples who got married there and three who were refused licenses sued, saying that the law is discriminatory. At the end of March 2006, the Massachusetts Supreme Judicial Court ruled that the law must be followed, but that the couples from states that apparently don't explicitly ban gay marriage can apply to superior court to determine whether in fact that is the case. Of the eight couples who sued, two are from Rhode Island, which has no DOMA and no other law or constitutional amendment against gay marriage. On September 29, 2006, Judge Thomas E. Connolly, a superior court judge in Massachusetts, ruled that Rhode Island couples may indeed marry in Massachusetts. This doesn't mean, however, that those marriages will be recognized in Rhode Island, where it seems likely there will be action pro and/or con recognition of Massachusetts marriages and gay marriage in general in Rhode Island's courts and legislature.

Another couple is from New York, where there was no clear legal obstacle either at the time. State officials in New York nonetheless had refused earlier to give marriage licenses to a number of same-sex couples living in New York, and many of them filed lawsuits back in 2004. Four of those lawsuits, representing forty-four couples, were eventually combined and were heard by New York's highest court at the end of May 2006. On July 6 of that year, the court announced its decision, saying that New York's "constitution does not compel the recognition of marriages between members of the same sex," and in effect handing the question of gay marriage in New York over to the state legislature. The president of the New York State Bar Association, Mark H. Alcott, almost immediately announced that the association had urged the legislature "to provide one of the following remedies to same-sex couples: civil unions; domestic partnerships; or marriage."

It seems likely that the battle will continue in New York as well as in Rhode Island and will have an impact not only on GL couples in those states but also on couples from other states that don't clearly ban gay marriage.

The permanence of same-sex marriage in Massachusetts itself is also still uncertain. Those favoring a constitutional amendment banning gay marriage but allowing civil unions and having the public vote on that amendment in 2006 eventually adopted a new, initially successful strategy: a petition drive that asked for a new constitutional amendment that would outlaw both gay marriage and civil unions. This new amendment would prevent future same-sex marriages but would allow those already in place to remain valid. It would have to pass by one-fourth of the state's House and Senate in two consecutive legislative sessions to be put before Massachusetts voters in 2008. Right before this book went to press, the legislature met again in constitutional convention to consider the new amendment. First, though, the senators and representatives voted down a much earlier amendment banning gay marriage that would have forcibly divorced the more than eight thousand already married same-sex couples in Massachusetts. Then, before considering the new amendment, they voted to recess until the last day of the legislative session, January 2, 2007—whereupon the visitors' gallery erupted in applause and shouts of joy. That postponement was widely believed to have killed the new amendment's chance of passing, at least in terms of its appearance on the 2008 ballot, and to have made it far more likely that gay marriage *will* be permanent in Massachusetts.

Although Massachussetts same-sex marriages are not recognized —yet—in any state but Massachusetts, as I write this, New York's Westchester County and several New York State cities do recognize them: Buffalo, Rochester, Brighton, Ithaca, Nyack, and New York City itself.

As this book goes to press, the more than eight thousand GL couples who are legally married in Massachusetts are entitled to all the benefits and responsibilities granted by the state, but none of the many more rights and responsibilities granted by the federal government. For example, those of us who are married in Massachusetts may file joint state income tax returns, but we are required to file individual ones with the federal government, as if we were single. The same situation will exist in any other state that legalizes gay marriage.

Efforts to pass an anti-gay-marriage amendment to the U.S. Constitution failed in both the U.S. Senate and House in 2004 and therefore never went to the citizens for a vote (which amendments to the U.S. Constitution must do). But in February 2006, U.S. Senate Majority Leader Bill Frist announced plans to introduce a new anti-gay-marriage amendment in Congress that June. It was introduced, and it failed again, first in the Senate and then in the House. It seems likely, however, to come up again, and if that amendment or one like it is passed in Congress and then by voters throughout the United States, any gay marriages and, depending on the amendment's scope, perhaps civil unions and similar arrangements as well that are legal in specific states will almost certainly become invalid.

Without an anti-gay-marriage amendment to the U.S. Constitution, for gay marriage to become legal nationwide, the federal DOMA, plus all existing state DOMAs, similar anti-gay-marriage laws, and anti-gay-marriage state constitutional amendments would have to be repealed.

As of early spring 2006, forty-two states had DOMAs or other laws stipulating that marriage is legal only if it's between a man and a woman. Some of these laws also ban civil unions or legal relationships that amount to civil unions, and most forbid the recognition of same-sex marriages performed elsewhere. Even though DOMAs and similar arrangements make it look as if those who oppose gay marriage don't also need state constitutional amendments that accomplish the same thing, opponents of gay marriage see such amendments as a safeguard

against courts, like the one in Massachusetts, ruling in favor of allowing gay marriage. It's for that reason that by early spring 2006, seventeen states, most of them already with DOMAs, had amended their
constitutions to forbid gay marriage: Alaska, Arkansas, Georgia,
Kansas, Kentucky, Louisiana, Michigan, Mississippi, Missouri, Mon-
tana, Nevada, North Dakota, Ohio, Oklahoma, Oregon, Texas, and
Utah. (Hawaii, you may remember, never passed a constitutional
amendment banning gay marriage, but instead passed one empower-
ing its legislature to pass a law doing that. The legislature did, thereby
giving Hawaii a DOMA.)

The folks in Nebraska passed an anti-gay-marriage amendment
back in 2000. But in 2005, a federal judge ruled that it violated the U.S.
Constitution. That sounded promising, but in July 2006 a federal appeals court reversed his decision. Then, in late summer 2006, a request
to reconsider the appeals court's decision was denied, raising the total
number of constitutional bans to eighteen—although the state attorney general said opponents could try to get a pro-gay-marriage
amendment put on the ballot in an election.

Something similar happened in Georgia, which had passed a
DOMA in 1996. In May 2006, a Superior Court judge ruled that an
anti-gay-marriage amendment passed in that state back in 2004 was
invalid because it covered civil unions and other matters in addition to
gay marriage (as is the case in a number of other states' anti-gay-
marriage amendments). But the state attorney general quickly appealed to the Georgia Supreme Court, and the secretary of state and
others urged that the legislature be convened in order to reinstate the
marriage ban via a new amendment to be put on the ballot that fall. In
July 2006, the court itself reinstated the ban.

Starting back in 1997, a bill to *legalize* gay marriage has been introduced in Rhode Island's legislature almost every year. So far, no such
bill has passed, but supporters of gay marriage seem determined to
keep trying! In September 2005, California's legislature became the first
in the nation to actually *pass* a law allowing gay marriage. But Gover-

nor Arnold Schwarzenegger was quick to end the excitement that groundbreaking law generated; he vetoed it.

In June 2006, the voters in Alabama passed a constitutional amendment banning gay marriage in their state, and in November, Colorado, Idaho, South Carolina, South Dakota, Tennessee, Virginia, and Wisconsin followed suit, bringing the total number of states with constitutional amendments banning gay marriage to twenty-six. In many cases, any other marriage-like arrangements, such as civil unions and domestic partnerships, are constitutionally banned as well. The good news is that as this book went to press, voters in Arizona appeared to have been the first in the nation to defeat an anti-gay-marriage amendment in their state; the bad news is that more states will probably vote on similar amendments in 2008.

GL couples and their supporters in other states besides New York, including Maryland, Oklahoma, California, Iowa, Washington State, Connecticut, and New Jersey, have appealed to the courts to overturn DOMA laws and/or constitutional amendments against gay marriage, or have sought in other ways to grant GL couples marriage rights. There were high hopes in the summer of 2006 for successful outcomes in Washington State and New Jersey, as well as in New York. But in late July the Washington State Supreme Court ruled that the state's DOMA is not unconstitutional. Although the court stressed that it was not ruling on whether the law should or shouldn't allow gay marriage and said there's no barrier to changing the constitution via the election process, the decision was still a bitter blow to the gay community nationwide. A request for reconsideration was denied in the fall.

The Nebraska and Washington cases could conceivably be appealed to the U. S. Supreme Court. But that might be risky. If the Court decided that they did not violate the U. S. Constitution, all other efforts to legalize gay marriage would be seriously jeopardized. The current Court isn't seen as being very sympathetic to GLBT causes.

The New Jersey Supreme Court's decision was more encouraging. The justices ruled unanimously that it's against the state's constitution to prevent same-sex couples from being granted the same legal rights as straight ones, but they differed on whether to call their relationships marriage or something else. They gave the New Jersey legislature 180 days to decide what term to use.

Also unsuccessful so far have been efforts to overturn the Diné Marriage Act of 2005, which is the Navajo Nation's law against same-sex marriage, and to officially register the marriage certificate that Dawn McKinley and Kathy Reynolds, two Cherokee women, were granted by Cherokee Nation authorities in 2004.

Bad news? Yes, some of it is. But as a wise friend of mine once said, "Nothing is irrevocable." It helps that while the marriage battles raged back in the summer of 2004, the American Psychological Association came out in support of same-sex marriage—and that in July 2006 the American Academy of Pediatrics published a report saying that both children with same-sex parents and children with opposite-sex parents are better off in many ways when their parents are legally married or joined in a legal civil union. It's also encouraging that even despite opposition in some places, gay marriage is already legal in several other countries: Canada, Spain, Belgium, and the Netherlands—and that there have been strong movements, some successful, toward gay marriage, usually via civil unions, domestic partnerships, and similar arrangements, in many others, including South Africa, Ireland, the Czech Republic, Slovenia, the Scandinavian countries, the United Kingdom, Australia—and Mexico City, Mexico.

Here at home, efforts to challenge and change prohibitions against same-sex marriage and other rights for GLBT people show no sign of stopping; in fact, they are increasing. As the past fifty years have shown, as long as the struggle continues, there is hope, and progress as well. That's borne out by recent progress and victories in gay marriage—and by antidiscrimination victories, especially in the states of Maine and Washington. In 2005, after a struggle that had been going on in one way or another for around seven years, Maine's voters finally approved the addition of the words "sexual orientation" to a state law

outlawing discrimination in employment, housing, and public ac-
commodation. Washington passed a similar antidiscrimination law in
2006, one that had been in the works for even longer—twenty-nine
years! Maine's and Washington's votes brought the total of states with
such laws to seventeen—and seven of those laws specifically protect
transgender people as well as gays and lesbians.

There are continuing efforts, too, to establish statewide civil
unions, which can be seen as both good and bad. Connecticut passed a
civil union law like Vermont's in April 2005—the first such bill passed
by a legislature instead of being ordered by a court. That was exciting
and remains an important landmark, but nonetheless eight couples
sued on the grounds that civil unions are inferior to actual marriage.
They wanted marriage licenses instead of civil union licenses, and after
being denied them in July 2006 by a superior court judge, planned to
appeal to the Connecticut Supreme Court. Marriage opponents do
sometimes propose establishing civil unions in the hope that they'll
satisfy GL couples enough to stop same-sex-marriage efforts, but as the
Connecticut couples have demonstrated, that's probably unlikely to
work. Actually, it seems likely that the more people see that heterosexual marriage in Massachusetts hasn't come to grief because of same-
sex marriage, and that no harm has come from giving GL couples
some of the rights of married couples in civil unions in Vermont and
Connecticut, the easier it may be for people to accept the idea of same-
sex marriage.

Domestic partnership arrangements continue to be proposed and
passed also, although sometimes with difficulty. An especially poignant
case surfaced in New Jersey in 2006, after the passage of a bill to permit
local governments to give benefits, including death benefits, to GL
partners of state employees. Lieutenant Laurel Hester, an investigator
who'd worked for the Ocean County Prosecutor's Office for twenty-
three years, was dying of cancer and wanted to ensure that her death
benefit would go to her partner so her partner could stay in their

house. Hester's pleas moved so many people that Ocean County officials, who at first had refused, finally agreed to act on the state's partnership law. Only a few weeks later, Lieutenant Hester died.

Adoption and custody laws, including those that regulate custody
of children when parents divorce or dissolve a civil union, can have a
tremendous impact on the eventual acceptance or denial of same-sex
marriage. And those states that do not allow same-sex marriage but do
allow same-sex couples to adopt, or that recognize same-sex couples as
parents when they have children by some other means, are seen by
many as having taken an important step on the way to legalizing same-
sex marriage. For example, in August of 2005, rulings of the California
Supreme Court established that both members of a lesbian couple
who, as a couple, have children, must be considered parents equal to
heterosexual parents, even if they are not registered as domestic partners and even if they break up. And in 2006, the U.S. Supreme Court
refused to hear a case involving a lower court's ruling that a lesbian,
Sue Ellen Carvin, is the de facto (in practice) parent of her former
partner's biological child. They didn't comment either pro or con on
the case, but by refusing to hear it, they allowed the lower court's decision to stand. Not only is that a victory for families headed by same-sex
couples, but it also tends to validate the idea that same-sex couples are
or should be considered equal to straight couples.

What effect will all these developing legal decisions about the rights of
LGBT people and the new laws to which they lead have on your
twenty-first-century world? As African-Americans and members of
other minorities know well, even when laws protect minority rights,
prejudice still exists. But, conversely, when protective laws *do* exist, they
often help make it easier for minority and mainstream people to come
to understand one another better, and because of that understanding,
prejudice gradually tends to diminish. Like the struggle for equal rights

in general, the relatively new struggles for marriage and adoption rights are likely to continue for years to come. But as has been the case with our other struggles, we show no signs of abandoning them. It helps to keep in mind that interracial marriage was illegal in thirty states as late as the early fifties and wasn't made legal nationwide until 1967. Even so, South Carolina's state constitution continued to ban interracial marriage until 1998, and Alabama's banned it till 2000! It also helps to keep in mind that the children of both interracial marriage and interracial adoption are far more accepted today than they were even ten years ago.

It's hard to be patient when there are rights still to be won and attitudes still to be changed. But when I compare the world of the fifties with the world in the early twenty-first century, I see two very different places, one closed, the other open; one full of suspicion and fear, loneliness and shame; the other full of hope and promise, community and strength. If you're growing up gay, lesbian, bisexual, transgender, or questioning in the twenty-first century, not only do you have surer access to equal rights and fair treatment than at any previous time in U.S. history, but you also have far more access than ever before to books, magazines, entertainment, organizations both social and political, religious groups, and legal support that recognize and celebrate your right to live your life openly, safely, and happily. You can participate in Gay Pride Month and Gay History Month, cheer at the Gay Games, become a member of a GSA, go to a prom with your boyfriend or girlfriend, go to an LGBT summer camp, apply for a college scholarship specifically for LGBT students. You can read books with LGBTQ characters and news and magazine articles about real LGBT people who are not victims and who live happy, healthy, productive lives; you can visit Web sites and online chat rooms maintained for and often by LGBTQ youth. It's more likely than ever before that you can look forward to being out at work, to joining with your boyfriend or girlfriend in a commitment ceremony, domestic partnership, civil union, or legal marriage; you can look forward to going on a gay cruise for your honeymoon, becoming a parent—and even, when you're old and gray, spending your declining years in a gay retirement home!

Now, in the twenty-first century, "we are everywhere" as we've chanted at demonstrations and marches for many years; we at last can truly believe the familiar mantra "Two, four, six, eight; Gay is just as good as straight"; we are no longer invisible; we are strong, courageous—and, yes, even though many of us have wished and still wish for an end to labels, we can "Say it loud: Gay and proud!"

Author's Note

Many of the situations and cases described in this section are still in progress as *Hear Us Out!* goes into the final stages of production. Because of the lag time between the last opportunity to make changes and the date when the book will be available to readers, by the time you read it some cases and situations described here as being ongoing may be resolved, and some described as being resolved may have been reopened. Check local and national newspapers, the gay press (for example, *The Advocate*), and LGBT Web sites like the Human Rights Campaign (www.hrc.org), Lambda Legal (www.lambdalegal.org), and GLSEN (www.glsen.org) for updates!

LOVING MEGAN

"THERE SHE IS," I WHISPERED TO KAT, SLIDING MY LUNCH TRAY ALONG THE table so I'd be next to her. "There's Megan."

Katherine Emily Rogers, who'd been my best friend forever, looked up skeptically from her tuna salad. Then she looked again, her brown puppy dog eyes wide with what I could only interpret as heartfelt wonder.

"See?" I said. "See what I mean?"

Kat nodded silently. Then she murmured, "Yes, Penny, I do. Oh, yes!"

Megan, the object of my—and I thought *our*—admiration, was a senior, and we were freshmen. She was captain of the cross-country team and president of the drama club; I'd managed to find that much out in the first week of school. And she was gorgeous. Drop-dead, perfect, stunning, magnificent gorgeous.

Her corn-silk blond hair fell into a thick mane, held at the nape of her neck with either a scrunchie or a black velvet ribbon, depending, I decided, on whether she felt playful or sophisticated that day. We'd already noticed—I had, anyway—that she always wore the same long blue-and-yellow silk scarf, sometimes wrapped casually around her neck and draped over one shoulder, sometimes tied sashlike around her waist, and, rarely, wrapped around her head like a turban. She also wore lots of large silver rings, which I knew would make my mother sniff with disapproval and my sister, Alice, laugh. As a college sophomore, Alice thought she was a fashion expert. But I thought Megan's rings were kind of cool.

Kat left her lunch untouched. I ate mine, but I didn't really taste it.

"I'm in love with her," I announced to Kat.

Kat gulped her soda. "I noticed," she said, burping.

I looked at her severely. "Pistols or swords?"

"Huh?"

I shrugged. "If we're rivals," I told her, only half joking, "we'll have to have a duel." I know that sounds weird, but we'd read a lot of swash-buckling books as kids, and the guys in them were always having duels.

Kat gave me a funny look and stood up. "Penny," she said, picking up her tray, "we are not rivals."

"Why not?" I drew my imaginary sword and slashed at the air.

"Because . . ." Kat balanced her tray on one arm and matched me blow for blow with her own invisible weapon. "Oh, just because. See you at tryouts."

Cross-country tryouts were that afternoon. My grandmother had been a track runner when she was a kid, and she'd started me running when I was around eight; she even used to race me sometimes. I had plenty of experience both on the roads and in the woods, and I felt pretty confident I'd get on at least the junior varsity. Gramma, who was my biggest fan, said there was no reason why I shouldn't. "At least there isn't if those fancy coaches today know anything," she told me. Gramma had almost qualified for the Olympics back in the 1950s, and she had a lot of negative stuff to say about how things are done now. Mom sometimes called her a crusty old lady, mostly joking about it, but Gramma's occasional crustiness was okay with me. She was just about the most important person in my life along with my parents and Kat; Kat loved her, too.

Kat, by the way, had been running for precisely three months, eighteen days, and—she reminded me when we reported to the track for tryouts—fourteen hours.

"There she is," I whispered as Megan and the coach, Mrs. Lar-rimew, strode up to the bench where we were all huddled; they were in earnest conversation. Then Megan tossed her corn-silk hair and laughed, sending shivers down my spine. She'd braided the blue-and-yellow scarf into her hair where it was close to her head, and left it hanging free where her hair was against her back.

"What's the matter, Penny?" Kat asked. "You cold or something?" She gave my shoulders a rub.

I shook my head, pushed her hand away, and nodded toward where Megan was now standing in front of us with Coach Larrimew, eyeing us as if we were inferior cuts of meat at a deli counter.

"Oh," Kat said.

"Listen up, ladies." Coach Larrimew launched into a pretty standard beginning-of-the-year-type speech about sportsmanship and The Schedule and what we were going to do that afternoon.

What we were going to do was have a sort of mock race on the course we'd all walked the day before: through the woods in back of the school, across the football field, which the boys' coach had promised not to use till later that afternoon, and ending with two laps around the track. Megan and a couple of the other seniors on varsity would be running with us to check us out, and Coach Larrimew would time us.

Megan handed out numbers and actually pinned them on a couple of kids. I tried to ease over to where she was so I'd be one of them, but before I got very far, Kat grabbed a couple of numbers and pinned one on me.

"Thanks," I said sarcastically.

"What?" Kat looked surprised. She turned around and handed me her number.

Luckily Coach Larrimew blew her whistle and motioned us to line up, cutting off my nasty reply about Kat's not having the sensitivity to notice I'd wanted to get my number from Megan. Begrudgingly, I pinned Kat's on, crooked, and sprinted to the starting line, as close to Megan as I could get.

It wasn't long before I broke ahead of Kat; she'd been laboring from the first and I could see that she was having trouble navigating roots and rocks. "You go on," she panted, waving me ahead when we'd been in the woods for less than ten minutes. I gave her a wave back and picked up my pace. I could see Megan in front of us running with the leaders, but not so far away that I couldn't catch them, I was pretty sure.

I surged forward; the ground was pretty rough, with big roots crossing the path, and loose pebbles, not to mention wet pine needles and rocks. I had my eyes on Megan; there was no one close behind me, although I could hear kids coming.

And then, my eyes still on Megan, my foot slipped on the edge of a rock, and I went down, banging my knee on the way.

Tears stung my eyes, as much from embarrassment as from pain, but then a hand—a smooth, gracefully beringed hand—reached down to mine and pulled me up till my face was within inches of . . . Megan's!

"Keep your eyes open, Johnson, Jackson, whatever your name is," she said. "That'll cost you time."

I nodded, blinking the tears back and rubbing my knee. Then I realized I was still gripping her hand and she was trying to pull it loose.

I let go, reluctantly, but not before I'd noticed her clean, perfectly shaped nails and had seen that one of her silver rings had a tiny four-leaf clover dangling from it. "Th—thanks," I managed to say, but by then she was already gone.

Someone came up behind me, panting like she'd just run a marathon. Then Kat's hand was on my shoulder. "You okay?" she gasped.

"Yeah, I—I guess so," I said, still looking after Megan.

Kat gave me a little push from behind. "Then you'd better get going if you want to get on the team. Go on—scram."

I did qualify, but only just. I had the slowest time of those who did, which embarrassed me when I told Gramma. But when I told her about the fall, she said not to worry about my time but to worry about my eyes, meaning I should look where I was going instead of at whoever was ahead of or behind me. At least I was able to tell her I'd made up some of the time on the track at the end, even though my knee had begun to get puffy.

"Here," Megan had said in the locker room after tryouts, tossing something that looked like a limp soccer ball to Kat. "Make Johnson put this on her knee."

Kat, who hadn't qualified but was hanging around anyway, handed me the limp soccer ball, which turned out to be an ice bag.

"Thanks," I called. "It's Jackson, by the way. Penny Jackson."

Megan sort of smiled at me as she left. I think she also said "Whatever," but I might be wrong about that.

"How's your knee?" Kat asked.

"Okay," I lied. "Wasn't she great?"

"Who?"

I looked at her, astonished. "Megan, of course! Didn't you see her flying around the track at the end?"

"Nope." Kat gathered up her running clothes and stuffed them into her backpack. "You're the only one I saw flying around the track at the end."

"But Megan—"

"See you outside," Kat said. "At the late bus. If you hurry."

"Yeah, okay." But I iced my knee for a few more minutes, reveling in the fact that Megan had gotten the bag for me, and in the memory of her hair and her scarf streaming out behind her as she ran, with her white shorts and singlet shining in the early autumn sun.

I was sure Gramma'd be impressed with her, too, but she just gave me a look when I described Megan to her. "Handsome is as handsome does," she muttered crustily. "Watch her *technique*, Penny, if she's so good." Then she gave me a funny look—well, a penetrating look, maybe. "How come she doesn't know your name?"

"I'm only a freshman," I told her. "It's the beginning of the year."

"Humph!" Gramma grunted.

. . .

Kat and I had always done the same things together. I was better at some and she was better at others, but that was okay; the one who was better had always helped the one who wasn't so good. That fall, since Kat was determined to make the team next year, I coached her in cross-country, and she read the stuff I tried to write for the literary magazine.

Of course I wrote about Megan.

"She walks in beauty like the day" was how I began the poem I hoped would make it into the magazine.

"Derivative," Kat said promptly when I slid the first line onto her desk in homeroom.

"Huh?"

"Derivative. Like someone else's poem. Lord Byron's, for example. 'She walks in beauty, like the night.' "

I groaned and went back to my desk.

"Megan, Reagan, pagan . . . ," I scribbled, thinking maybe I'd better try for something that rhymed. "Beggin', Bacon . . ." (NO!) "Fagan, leggin' . . ." Well, I thought, I don't have to rhyme with her name, after all.

Finally I came up with this:

Your beauty is like the sun and the stars and the moon.
You walk with grace untold.
Your lips are two parentheses surrounding your mouth's pink cave,
Home to the whitest of teeth, the most silver of tongues.
Your voice is sweeter than birdsong,
And when you run,
Dust motes dance before you, carving your way through the air,
And the swiftness of birds is in your footsteps.

Kat studied my poem for a very long time without saying anything.

"No good, huh?" I asked anxiously, reading over her shoulder. "It's free verse, of course. But you got that, right?"

"Yes," Kat said. "I got that."

It did seem a little clumsy now that I was looking at it through Kat's eyes.

Kat licked her lips. "It's not *no* good," she said carefully. "It's got— it's got some good—er—some good bits in it. Like—"

I snatched my poem away. "It's okay," I said gruffly. "You don't have to sputter."

Kat grabbed my hand. "Oh, Penn, I'm sorry! It *does* have good bits in it. The last line, for instance, and—and 'sweeter than birdsong' and some other lines. Maybe you could work on it some more, but . . ." Her eyes were filled with all the sincerity and honesty and friendship and kindness that I'd always loved and admired in her. "Penn, it's pretty obvious it's a love poem to a girl," she said finally. "So it might not be such a great idea to send it to the magazine, especially since everyone kind of knows how you feel about Megan."

"Everyone?" I asked, feeling cold inside. "And what do you mean how *I* feel? We both feel that way, don't we? Hmmm? Don't we?"

"Well, to tell you the truth," Kat said, sounding like my mom's best friend, who said that all the time, "no. I—I like Megan, I think. I mean she's pretty and all, but—"

"Fine," I said, slamming my hand down on Kat's desk and turning away. "Fine. I'll write something bland that no one'll get."

"Try symbolism," Kat suggested softly.

So I did, once I'd cooled off. I wrote a sappy poem about strands of corn silk leading down to luscious yellow kernels, sweet and plump and juicy. Kat looked embarrassed when she read it, but the magazine accepted it, and when it was published, a junior came up to me and said, "That's the sexiest poem I've ever read in this magazine."

"I'll be writing porn next," I quipped, but inside I glowed.

· · ·

From then on it got easier. I wrote lots of flower poems and fruit poems, and once in a while I slipped a really good one into Megan's locker, unsigned. Okay, I guess it was stupid of me to think she wouldn't know who'd written those poems, but I couldn't help myself. Besides, Megan had really been smiling at me now and then in practice. Once she yelled, "Pick up your feet, Johnson, for God's sake, or you'll fall again!" which, despite the wrong name, I considered a valuable running tip.

One morning, Kat handed me this:

> My love knows my love not and is so blind
> She sees not my true heart nor aching mind.
> My love is swift; her grace is like the deer's,
> But swifter is her blindness to my tears.
> Her eyes turn elsewhere and she sees me not;
> With pain and sadness my poor heart is shot.
> So, shadow-like, I wait and watch and pray
> In dismal hope my words will find a way
> To melt her heart. Oh, bring her gaze around,
> And show her that in me, true love is found!

"Well, what do you think?" she asked. Her face was very pink, and her eyes were anxious.

"I think it's pistols or swords again," I told her after a couple of minutes in which I realized (1) that it was much better than anything I could ever write, and (2) that I was jealous and mad.

"Huh?"

"You heard me," I said. "We're rivals again."

"We're *what*? Oh my God!" Kat clapped her hand to her head. "It's not about Megan, you dork! It's—" Her pink face turned bright red, and she stormed down the hall.

Later, at lunch, I asked Kat who the poem was about and if she was going to send it to the literary magazine.

"I don't think so," she answered, toying with her food and avoiding, now that I think of it, the first part of my question. "It still needs work, for one thing. And I'd have to change the pronouns."

I grinned. "Or your name. How about Anonymous?"

"Yeah." Kat snapped a celery stalk in two as if she were trying to execute it. "That fits me perfectly. Anonymous. A. Nonny Mouse."

Her voice sounded weird—bitter, really—and she looked as if she was going to cry, so I brushed her hand with mine. "What's wrong, Katty?"

She just shook her head bravely and changed the subject to the fall dance that was going to be held at the end of the month.

I dreaded that dance. I mean, I can't dance worth beans anyway, and I knew enough about myself at that point to know I didn't want to go with a boy. Heck, I didn't even want to *dance* with a boy; I wanted to dance with Megan. I didn't want to put a label on how I felt, even though I was pretty sure I knew what label would fit—especially when Kat pointed out a poster in the hall announcing the first meeting of the school's gay-straight alliance.

"So what?" I said, wishing my stomach hadn't suddenly started to do gymnastics exercises.

"Well, I thought I might go. Would you come with me?"

I shrugged.

"You don't have to be gay to go," she said quickly, running her finger along the place where the poster said ALL WELCOME—GAY, BI, STRAIGHT, QUESTIONING.

"I can read," I said.

Okay, that was mean, but the poster and Kat's wanting both of us to go to the meeting annoyed me in a way I didn't want to think about.

"Well, I might go anyway," Kat said.

We left it at that.

.   .   .

I did go to the dance, though; my mom made me, and Gramma kept saying it couldn't hurt even if I did have to dance with a boy. "Boys don't bite, Penny," she said. "At least not most of them. Some of them are even nice. Like your grandfather, after all, and your daddy."

I had to admit she was right about Grandpa and Dad, but even so, that didn't make me eager to go. Mom kept telling me what fun my sister, Alice, always had at dances, but, hey, I'm not Alice, you know?

Mom drove me there, with Kat. We didn't have dates, thank God. I figured we'd sit in a corner and watch everyone else having a wonderful time.

Ha! Sure.

Only moments after Mom had left us at the door and chirped "Have a lovely time, girls! See you at eleven," Megan arrived.

And naturally she wasn't dropped off by her mom. No, no, Megan came floating in on the arm of Chris Pollack, who even I knew was the school's star football player. Chris had on skintight black pants and a red shirt I could die for, open almost to his huge brass belt buckle, and Megan had on a sleeveless, slinky, green minidress, the bottom of which was cut in sort of scallops, only instead of being rounded they were pointed, making her look like a mermaid dressed in strips of that long green seaweed—kelp, I think it's called. The scarf clung to the front of her neck so its two ends hung down her back, her corn-silk hair floated over her shoulders, and huge trashy gold earrings dangled on either side of her face. Gold and green and black bangles encircled both her arms almost to the elbows.

I couldn't take my eyes off her, and I hated Chris with every fiber of my being.

That was when I realized I probably *should* plan to go to that gay-straight alliance meeting. I lay awake all night after the dance, imagining myself making out with Megan the way I'd seen Chris doing in his car when Kat and I were waiting for Mom to pick us up. It embarrasses me to say it, but I touched myself the way I knew Chris had probably been touching Megan. I liked the way that made me feel, but even so, it was frustrating and lonely with only me doing it.

Afterward I had a weird dream, but all I remember is that Megan and Kat were both in it, and that when I woke up, I was all sweaty.

We had our first cross-country meet not long after that. I managed to stay in the lead pack with Megan almost the whole way, even though now that I'd seen her with Chris, I knew that she was probably never going to notice me the way I now knew I wanted to be noticed. Still, it was great emerging from the woods with Megan and the other leaders, hearing Kat's voice and Gramma's screaming, "Go, Penny, go!" and feeling Megan's hand slap my back when we'd both crossed the finish line. "Good going, kid," Megan said, turning her head toward me; we were both bent over, hands on knees, getting our breath back.

"Thanks," I said, glowing.

That night Gramma told me she agreed with me that Megan was pretty. "Handsome does fine in her case, Penny," she said, "as far as running goes, anyway. Her form is as gorgeous as the rest of her, and she runs like a dream. So do you, by the way. You've come a long way."

That made me tingle with happiness, but it was as much what Gramma said about Megan that pleased me as it was what she said about me.

Gramma gave me one of her funny looks. "You like her a lot, don't you?"

I nodded, and Gramma nodded, too, thoughtfully, as if she understood.

Later, in my room, instead of going to sleep, I wrote a poem about a palomino mare outrunning a thoroughbred stallion, and I put it in Megan's locker the next day.

That afternoon at dismissal, when I went to my own locker to get my books before practice, I saw Megan standing at hers with Chris; she was showing him a piece of paper and giggling.

Ignoring Chris, I said, "Hi, Megan, going to practice?"

Megan looked up, grinned at Chris, and said, "*Um*," loudly, to him, not to me.

Chris laughed and called, "Hey, baby butch! You're the stallion, right?"

Megan laughed then, the same laugh as before. It sent chills down my spine again, but this time they were bad chills, and I realized what the paper must be. Without thinking, I snatched it out of Megan's hand and ran past my own locker, past Kat, who had just come into the hall, past the door to the gym locker rooms, and outside, where I ran home faster than I'd ever run in practice.

Then I threw myself on my bed and cried till Gramma came into my room and held me while I told her everything. "Oh baby," she said, all her crustiness gone. "It's not the end of the world. Just"—here she tipped my face up and smiled into my eyes—"just be careful who you love."

I moaned something about no one loving me back, and Gramma shook her head. The crustiness returned a little, or firmness anyway, when she said, "Uh-uh, Penny, don't waste your time in self-pity. You lose a race, you lose a love, you pick yourself up and go on. There are more races and more loves waiting around the corner." She patted my shoulder. "That Megan may be a good runner, but maybe that's all she is."

"Megan was just trying to impress Chris," I said stubbornly to Kat on the phone that night when I'd calmed down enough to talk about it. "Maybe she wants him to write poems to her and he won't, and maybe she'll realize that I can, and maybe . . ." I couldn't think of what that might lead to, though, so I stopped.

"Penny." Kat's voice was so soft and gentle I barely heard it. "Penny, she's straight. She—"

"I know." I cut her off, too upset to even pretend to argue against the implication that I was probably gay. "I know. But maybe she isn't *really* straight. And she likes me, Kat, I know that. She thinks I'm a good runner. She—she . . ."

I could hear Kat sighing on the other end of the phone. "I know," she said. "She gave you a running tip, and she smiles at you sometimes. But—"

I cut her off again. "I'm pretty sure Megan and I could be—friends, at least," I said. "It's just going to take time, that's all. Time and patience."

"Okay, Penn." Kat's voice sounded sad, somehow. "If that's what you want."

I didn't put any more poems in Megan's locker after that, but I wrote plenty. Sometimes I showed them to Kat, but most of the time I didn't. I started going for long runs after practice till Mom complained that it was getting too dark for that to be safe. But I got so my time was almost as good as Megan's, and our team began to get a reputation as being the best in our district. We won meet after meet, and Megan started including me in her strategy talks with the other leaders. Sometimes she even sat next to me on the bus going to or from races. Okay, so when she wasn't talking strategy, she usually slept or sang along with everyone else, so it wasn't as if we had any intimate moments. But I liked sitting beside her, especially feeling her slightly damp body next to mine after a race. Kat had become assistant manager, so she was usually with us. But I didn't always make a big effort to sit with her if I saw Megan coming my way.

One Friday night when my parents and Gramma and I were having supper—codfish cakes and baked beans, not exactly my favorite—

Gramma suddenly put her hand up to her head and said, "Sorry—I think I'd better be excused. I've got a terrible headache." She stood up, sort of swaying. Mom looked at Dad and said, "I'll get you some aspirin, Momma. You just stay put."

"No," Gramma said, "don't trouble . . ."

And then, before Mom could reach her, Gramma melted into a heap on the floor.

The emergency room doctor said Gramma had had a stroke and was unconscious. They were going to admit her, but they had to do some tests or wait for an empty bed or something first, so Mom and Dad and I all sat there holding hands in the waiting room, worrying and trying not to cry.

Finally I asked, "Can I call Kat?" Mom said, "Of course," and Kat and her mom were there in about twenty minutes. Mrs. Rogers talked to Mom and Dad, and Kat and I went outside.

Kat held both my hands so tight I thought they'd break while I told her what had happened. But I didn't mind; it was as if the strength of her grip was making me stronger.

She and her mom stayed with us till long after the hospital had admitted Gramma into intensive care. Finally Mrs. Rogers and Kat drove me home so I could get my pj's, and then took me to their house, where I spent the night sitting on the window seat in Kat's room, staring out at the stars and talking about Gramma while Kat sat next to me and rubbed my back.

The next couple of days are pretty much a blur in my mind. Mom's sister—my aunt Judy—and her husband, Uncle Larry, flew across the country from New Mexico, where they live, and Alice came home from college, and we all spent most of our time at the hospital. Mrs. Rogers dropped Kat off there both Saturday and Sunday morning, and Kat and I took lots of long, sad walks around the hospital's neighborhood. I remember seeing an old lady raking leaves outside one of the houses, and I hated her because she was so well and Gramma was so sick.

On Sunday night they let me see her. She had her mouth open and her eyes shut, and she was breathing very slowly, and she had tubes in her and cords like electric wires going from her to machines. At first I couldn't take my eyes off them. But then I thought, No, that stuff's got nothing to do with Gramma, and when Mom left me alone with her, I sat there holding Gramma's hand and telling her what a good person she was and what a good runner and what an inspiration she was to me and how much I loved her. And I told her that I'd run every race for her and that I'd try to remember what she'd said about losing races and there being other ones around the corner. Then I remembered she'd said that about losing loves, too.

After a while a nurse came in and told me I had to leave, so I gave Gramma a kiss and told her again that I loved her, and then I smoothed her soft, almost-white hair back off her forehead and left.

Later that same night, Gramma died.

The next day I couldn't go to school; I mostly slept and then went with Mom and Dad and Alice and Aunt Judy and Uncle Larry to the funeral home. I waited till after everyone else had gone up to Gramma's casket, and then I slipped in a couple of the ribbons she'd won and had given to me. I kept one for myself, but somehow I felt she ought to have the others with her wherever she was going.

The day after that Mom made me go to school, but I don't remember anything about my classes except that Kat sat next to me in most of them and poked me when we had to do something like open a book or write.

After school I ran to the funeral home to have a few minutes with Gramma before practice; I figured there'd be time. But I guess I stayed longer than I should have, because when I got back, the team had finished stretching and was already on one of the woods paths we used sometimes. I caught up with them pretty quickly and was just about to say "Sorry I'm late" to Megan when she turned around and gave me a really black look. Then she surged ahead as if she didn't want to have anything to do with me.

In the locker room after practice, Megan came up to where I was changing my shoes; Kat, who'd come in to walk home with me, was sitting next to me on the bench. Megan's corn-silk hair was out of its scrunchie and tangled around her shoulders, and she looked really mad. "Johnson," she said quietly, like she was forcing herself not to yell, "you've turned into a good runner. But we don't need prima donnas on our team. We need people to come to practice every day—on time. Got that? This is a warning."

I felt tears fill my eyes, but I was too numb to do anything except look up at her stupidly.

Kat wasn't numb. She stood up, facing Megan, and she said, "For the hundredth time, Megan, her name is Jackson, not Johnson. And she missed practice yesterday and was late today because her grandmother died. You'd be a better captain if you tried to get to know people before you yelled at them."

Megan looked startled. But then she recovered and snapped, "Well, *JACK*son, that's a bummer. But life has to go on. So does this team. We're all part of it, even you. And if you can't be here, you'd better call. Those are the rules. Follow them."

She wheeled and stalked away.

I lost it then. I completely lost it. I hadn't cried since we were all at the hospital that first night, and now it was as if three days' worth of tears brimmed up inside me and spewed out.

Kat shooed everyone else out of the locker room and put her arms around me. "Shhh," she said. "It's okay, Penny, it's okay. Let it out, go ahead and cry. Shh, Penny, shh, my love, my dearest love, it's okay . . ."

I clung to her, sobbing so hard it took a long time for her words to reach me.

But when they finally did, what Gramma had said about new races and new loves came back to me, and it finally hit me that I'd been too stupidly starry-eyed over Megan to see that there was an old love waiting for me much closer than around the corner.

I looked at Kat and saw those gentle puppy dog eyes of hers looking softly into mine.

"What?" I whispered. "What did you call me?"

"Love," she whispered back, and I could see tears in her eyes, too. "I called you love." Very slowly, Kat moved her head closer to mine, and before I was really aware of what was happening, I was kissing her and she was kissing me. The knowledge that I'd almost thrown Kat away swept over me like an immense tidal wave.

"It's us," I said, "isn't it?"

Kat moved back a little and smiled at me. "Yes, Penny," she said. "It always has been. You just didn't figure it out till now."

"Katherine Emily Rogers," I said, "I love you." And Gramma, I added silently, you were so right. Handsome is as handsome does.

"I love you too, Penny," Kat said, pulling out a tissue and using it to wipe my eyes and then hers.

And I knew that from then on, always, it would be Kat.

PRIDE

AT ELEVEN O'CLOCK ON THIS BRIGHT JUNE MORNING, THE OLD CHURCH'S brownstone walls form a backdrop for the people congregated on its steps and along the adjacent sidewalk. Few cars pass along the street, which is gradually filling with more people, smiling, laughing, chatting, all apparently heading toward the park a few blocks away. Some carry banners and posters. Couples—men with men and women with women—walk hand in hand or push strollers carrying babies and toddlers, some of whom are of different races than their parents. Although it is not yet hot, it is sunny, and the weatherpeople have promised high eighties; many of the revelers—for surely this is a celebration—are wearing shorts and tank tops or shorts alone. One man in tight-fitting leather pants and, instead of a shirt, a vest bedecked with chains, skillfully weaves his unicycle in and out of the growing crowd; applause follows him. Six or seven teenagers, their hair sprayed green, violet, or blue, rainbow rings on chains around their necks, silver studs and rings along the edges of their ears, pass a multicolored beach ball back and forth as they hurry by. A smiling but already sweating T-shirted vendor twists fantasy shapes out of balloons—dogs with pink bodies, yellow heads, and blue tails; purple cats with green ears; fireman's hats of red and gold. With a flourish, he hands a cat to a grinning, towheaded toddler in a Mickey Mouse stroller while the toddler's two moms, one of whom wears a white T-shirt whose front shows a huge pink triangle and the word PRIDE and the date, look proudly on. A pair of African-American men, hands clasped, smile at the toddler; as the men pass, one of the toddler's moms points to the backs of their shirts, both of which read NEWLYWEDS in large lavender letters, and she shouts "Congratulations!" The men turn back, wave, and hurry on.

Huddled at the edge of the church's steps but not on them, a small, thin, and grimy girl of around thirteen or fourteen squats, apparently uninterested in or perhaps even unaware of the excitement around her. A closer look, however, reveals that her almost-black eyes are darting from steps to street to church, and her narrow chest is heaving with rapid, shallow breaths; in fact, it appears that she is almost panting.

The church bell, jubilant in the rapidly warming air, strikes eleven; the massive doors open and are held, one by a young man and the other by a woman, both in lavender and white PRIDE T-shirts. They beckon to the crowd on the steps, and as the people surge inside, the greeters hand each one a common pin and a two-inch scrap of rainbow-striped ribbon. People smile and pin the ribbons to their clothes.

The girl stands up uncertainly, and watches.

When the steps are empty (but the crowd is growing fast), the woman greeter walks down them and bends close to the girl. "Coming in?" she asks.

The girl looks alarmed and shakes her head, but although one would expect her to dart away, she does not.

"It's just a quick service," the woman explains, "before the march." When there's no response, she adds, "It's the gay pride march; did you know that?"

Surprisingly, solemnly, the girl nods. She is a runaway; of course she knows; in fact, she has come for the march, having read about it in a discarded newspaper the day before, camped out under a bridge with three other girls, all of whom are straight and none of whom know that she, Lisanne, is gay and that that is the reason she has left school and home and almost the world itself—not, as she told them, because she'd been raped and had a miscarriage and was thrown out by her unfeeling mother. Only the part about her unfeeling mother's throwing her out is true.

"Come in then." The woman extends a hand.

As if moving against her own will, Lisanne climbs the steps to the doors; she refuses the woman's hand but accepts the ribbon, which she thrusts into the pocket of her stained jeans.

"Sit anywhere," the woman whispers kindly, and Lisanne, after glancing timidly around at the crowded pews, chooses one well in the back and slides like a shadow into it, dropping down on the aisle seat as lightly as an autumn leaf.

She has chosen a pew in which there are both men and women—two women and two men. The men, both white, have a brown-skinned baby; Lisanne's seat is next to them. They smile at her, but she shivers and looks forward, toward the front of the church and the pulpit, from which a lavender-robed woman is making a welcoming speech.

Lisanne hears very little of it. For one thing, she is hungry. For another, she is overwhelmed; surely all these people can't be gay—not the gray-haired ones older than her own parents, not the same-sex couples with their children, two or three of whom have wandered into the aisles. Surely neither the woman in the pulpit is gay nor the man standing beside her, who is now leading the congregation in song!

And surely, Lisanne thinks, this can't be a real church, despite the altar and the pews and the stained-glass windows, for the church in her tiny rural town would never have such a service!

Now the singing has stopped and the congregation is laughing, for the woman is asking people to raise their hands in answer to silly questions: "Lesbians here who don't have cats? Gay men who don't go to the gym?" When the laughter subsides, she asks "How many people are here for the first time—the first time at any gay pride celebration?" Lisanne trembles; she wants to raise her hand. She is astonished to see that a number of hands do go up, a few even belonging to kids around her own age: a black-shirted boy with brilliant blond hair and many rainbow rings; a girl in a long, flowered dress, a whole group of teenagers of various races in jeans and PRIDE shirts with a sign they briefly hold up saying PATTERSON HIGH GSA—but by the time she summons the will to lift her hand, the question has changed to "How about people for whom this is the second one?" and the questions go on till at "thirtieth or more" they finally stop, but Lisanne sees with awe that a dozen or more hands go up even for that one!

The men next to her, she noticed, raised their hands, clasped together, when the fifth time was called.

Five times, she thinks. Five years together? She wants to ask, but instead she gives the baby, who is staring at her, a timid wave. He grins and ducks his head behind the arm of the dad on whose lap he sits, and plays peekaboo with Lisanne.

"As is our custom," the woman in the front says, "we will now honor those of our number who have passed away but are with us in spirit." Quietly, lovingly, voices offer names. No one interrupts, no one hurries, and Lisanne remembers a television documentary she once saw very late at night after her parents were in bed. It was about a gay boy who, years earlier, had been beaten, tied to a fence, and left to die; Lisanne whispers, "Matthew Shepard."

Then there is a song about "gentle angry people," and the christening of two babies, and prayers and readings, and another song, and finally the two greeters from before pass out brightly colored crepe paper streamers. The people in the pews hold them above their heads until the congregation is roofed with rainbows.

A few moments later the rainbow roof lowers and disappears and people turn to one another across pews and hug, saying "Happy Pride," and Lisanne timidly accepts a hug from the man next to her, who holds her gently, as if he knows her pain and her confusion. "It'll be okay, sweetie," he whispers to her. "Whatever it is, it'll be okay. Look at all of us; we've all been through it; we know."

One of the women next to the two daddies leans across them and, smiling at Lisanne, points over to the group of kids with the GSA banner, and Lisanne sees that they are beckoning to her. "March with us?" one of them calls.

Lisanne swallows hard against the mingled joy and fear that is rising from her chest to her throat; she wants to say yes, but automatically she shakes her head. Of course they're okay, she tells herself, not like the kids at her school—but by the time she has begun to change her mind, the GSA group has been swept away with the crowd and she herself has been moved out of her pew along with the two couples and the baby and, outside, she finds herself with them between a float holding a gigantic wedding cake flanked by two women in wedding gowns and two men in tuxedos and a small army composed of lawyers in jeans or shorts and T-shirts bearing the name of their firm. Lisanne sees TV cameras outside and crowds of spectators lining the sidewalk, and suddenly she is terrified: what if someone from her school sees her face on TV, what if her parents do? She ducks her head and is glad she hasn't told anyone her name.

"In the old days," says one of the women—Lisanne is between the two couples, and she sees that the women are both considerably older than the men—"we used to wear sunglasses when we marched, as a disguise."

"Not at Pride, though," the other woman says, leaning across her partner toward Lisanne. "That was before Pride, when we marched for, oh, legal things. Ages ago." She sticks out a hand. "I'm Gail," she says, "and this is Louise, my partner, and these three doofuses"—she indicates the men—"are Bill and Donald and their son, Kyle. Kyle's from Cambodia, aren't you, Kylie?" She tickles the baby gently under his chin, and he giggles.

There are no longer any cameras; by now the small group has progressed past the park and is turning with the other marchers down a street lined with tall office buildings.

"And you are . . . ?" Gail asks.

"Um . . ." Lisanne clears her throat.

"It's okay," one of the men—Bill, she thinks—says quickly, "if you don't want to tell us."

But suddenly that seems absurd. The parade has stopped now, momentarily stalled, and ahead Lisanne sees a smiling, waving drag queen dressed in spangles and gauze, and the kids with the GSA banner, and a slender, beautiful person of indeterminate gender. Along the sidewalk to her left and to her right are more kids her age and a woman with a sign saying I'M PROUD OF MY GAY DAUGHTER, and there are dogs wearing lavender scarves, and more babies in strollers and toddlers on shoulders, and a clown on a skateboard, everyone cheering and smiling and laughing except for a few police officers—*police officers!*—who look bored. Not angry. Just tired, perhaps; uncomfortable, and bored.

Then one of the officers smiles at something a marcher says to him.

"It's okay," Louise says, patting Lisanne's shoulder. "It can be scary at first. My first march years ago? I was terrified. People weren't so nice, then. People watching used to hold their noses and carry mean signs and say nasty things. But look at them now!" She raises her hand, saluting a group of cheering, waving spectators.

Lisanne clears her throat again. She is about to speak when someone way ahead of them in the parade starts a chant, and soon the words drift down to Lisanne and everyone joins in: "Say it loud: gay and proud!" and "Two, four, six, eight, gay is just as good as straight!" It is deafening and joyous and defiant all rolled into one.

And Lisanne looks up at the blue sky and at the clown and the dogs and the children and the balloons and at her new friends, and she says softly, "My name is Lisanne."

Suddenly it is as if a heavy black cloak has slipped off her shoulders and from around her, freeing her from its crippling grasp.

"My name is Lisanne," she says again, loudly this time. "My name is Lisanne Bartlet."

And as she joins the chant, her new friends take her hands, one couple on each side of her, and one of the women says something to one of the men. He gives her a business card; the woman reads it, nods, and passes it to Lisanne, and Lisanne sees that it bears the name of a gay organization and shelter for kids. And as they continue the march together in front of the lawyers and behind the drag queen and the kids with the GSA banner, Lisanne thinks about maybe dropping in there instead of going back to the bridge and the three other girls and the lie about the rape and the miscarriage.

FURTHER READING

Bass, Ellen, and Kate Kaufman. *Free Your Mind: The Book for Gay, Lesbian, and Bisexual Youth—and Their Allies*. New York: HarperPerennial, 1996.

Cain, Paul D. *Leading the Parade: Conversations with America's Most Influential Lesbians and Gay Men*. Lanham, Md.: Scarecrow Press, 2002.

Carter, David. *Stonewall: The Riots That Sparked the Gay Revolution*. New York: St. Martin's Press, 2004.

Duberman, Martin; Martha Vicinus; and George Chauncey, Jr., eds. *Hidden from History: Reclaiming the Gay and Lesbian Past*. New York: NAL Books, 1989.

Duberman, Martin B. *Stonewall*. New York: Dutton, 1993.

Due, Linnea. *Joining the Tribe: Growing Up Gay and Lesbian in the '90s*. New York: Anchor Books, 1995.

Faderman, Lillian. *Odd Girls and Twilight Lovers: A History of Lesbian Life in Twentieth-Century America*. New York: Columbia University Press, 1991.

Ford, Michael Thomas. *The World Out There: Becoming Part of the Lesbian and Gay Community*. New York: New Press, 1996.

Fricke, Aaron. *Reflections of a Rock Lobster: A Story About Growing Up Gay*. Boston: Alyson Publications, 1981.

Huegel, Kelly. *GLBTQ (Gay, Lesbian, Bisexual, Transgender, Questioning): The Survival Guide for Queer and Questioning Teens*. Minneapolis: Free Spirit Publishing, 2003.

Jennings, Kevin, ed. *Becoming Visible: A Reader in Gay and Lesbian History for High School and College Students.* Boston: Alyson Publications, 1994.

McGarry, Molly, and Fred Wasserman. *Becoming Visible: An Illustrated History of Lesbian and Gay Life in Twentieth-Century America.* New York: New York Public Library / Penguin Studio, 1998.

Marcus, Eric. *Making History: The Struggle for Gay and Lesbian Equal Rights, 1945–1990: An Oral History.* New York: HarperCollins Publishers, 1992. (Marcus published a revised and updated edition in 2002 [Perennial/HarperCollins] called *Making Gay History: The Half-Century Fight for Lesbian and Gay Equal Rights.*)

Martin, Del, and Phyllis Lyon. *Lesbian/Woman.* New York: Bantam Books, 1972.

Shilts, Randy. *And the Band Played On: Politics, People, and the AIDS Epidemic.* New York: St. Martin's Press, 1987.

Shilts, Randy. *Conduct Unbecoming: Lesbians and Gays in the U.S. Military: Vietnam to the Persian Gulf.* New York: St. Martin's Press, 1993.

Teal, Donn. *The Gay Militants.* New York: Stein and Day, 1971.

Woog, Dan. *School's Out: The Impact of Gay and Lesbian Issues on America's Schools.* Boston: Alyson Publications, 1995.

Web sites include: www.advocate.com / www.glsen.org / www.hrc.org / www.lambdalegal.org / www.pflag.org

Periodicals include: *The Advocate; The Boston Globe; Newsweek; The New York Times; San Francisco Chronicle*